exposure

smart, and could be surprisingly sensitive and thoughtful. Perceptive, too. And loyal as bloodhound.

Before The Game, anyway. Before he betrayed us.

"Why is Ben following?" I whispered. "Wando is the other direction."

"Be cool," Shelton replied. "He'll want to see this, too."

My eyes narrowed. "See what?"

"Hold your horses." Hi was still grinning like an ape. It made me nervous.

Ben finally reached the group. He'd slipped on dark Ray-Ban sunglasses, hiding his eyes. Freed from the Bolton Prep dress code, he wore his typical black tee and jeans.

"Well?" Ben demanded.

"Well what?" I said defensively.

"Not you." Ben was looking at Hiram. "What'd you snag?"

Hi dug a folded sheet of paper from his pocket.

"I should be a secret agent." Hi blew on his fingernails, then buffed them on his lapel. "Or a magician. Maybe both. Someone write that down."

"Give me some warning next time!" Shelton snatched the page from Hi's fingers. "You know I'm terrible at improvising."

"*Check their lockers!*" Ben mocked. "You sounded crazy."

"*Somebody* had to distract the *police officers,*" Shelton griped. "Stolowitski's not as smooth as he thinks. I could hear him rifling Harris's desk clear across the room."

I spun to face Hi. "You *stole* something? Seriously?"

The scene replayed in my head. Shelton awkwardly drawing attention to himself. Hi puttering around the office. Things suddenly made sense.

Except, of course, why Hi had risked swiping something in the first place.

"Just look." Hi tapped the sheet Shelton had unfolded. "You're welcome."

The page was a color photocopy of a single object.

"Ah."

I flashed Hi a thumbs-up. He winked.

The image was some kind of old-fashioned playing card. An odd figure adorned its face: an elderly bearded man, dressed in what appeared to be a toga, wrestling a giant snake that coiled around his body. Above the figure was a lone symbol: Φ

"This *must* be the clue from Lucy's room!" I squawked. "Hi, you're a genius."

"Of course I am," Hi replied. "I spotted the pic while you were talking, and knew you'd obsess over it. Now we don't have to break in at three a.m. to get a look."

"How about we don't steal or rob at all?" Shelton suggested, eyes scanning the cross streets for hidden eavesdroppers. "I was looking forward to a felony-free semester. Been a while. And won't Harris know you stole this? That cop said it's the only evidence they have."

"The folder had four copies," Hi said. "If we're lucky, she won't even notice."

I tapped the symbol above the figure's head. "This is Greek. The letter phi."

"Duh," said Hi. "But who is Captain Snake Wrangler?"

"No idea." My voice firmed. "But we're going to find out."

"See what you did?" Shelton glanced heavenward. "Now Tory won't *ever* let this go."

"Wise up, kid." Hi tapped his temple. "She wasn't letting this go, period. Not after hearing there's a freaking clue."

All three looked at me.

I shrugged. "Hi's right. I'm hooked."

There was something unnerving about the image. The man with the snake gave off a cold, sinister vibe. Dead eyes. Unsmiling lips. His stern visage sent a chill along my spine.

The card itself looked old, maybe even ancient. Though hard to be sure from a copy, the figure appeared hand-painted. My gut said the card was rare, and probably valuable. I hadn't the faintest idea where you'd find something like it.

I didn't know Lucy well, but this didn't strike me as something she'd purchase.

My sixth sense shivered in warning.

"The twins might need our help," I said. "Maybe we should dig a little."

"Need us how?" Shelton took off his glasses and wiped them on his tie. "The police are already on the case. What can we offer that they can't?"

"You really have to ask?" Ben scoffed.

Shelton looked at him blankly.

"We have superpowers, dummy." Ben smirked as he scuffed a shoe against the sidewalk. "I doubt those CPD clowns can match that."

Ben's flippant attitude infuriated me. "Shouldn't you be heading the other direction?"

"I'm taking a personal day." Ben stretched his arms, locked his hands behind his head. "Wando can get by without me until tomorrow. Plus, I parked around the next corner."

After moving to Mount Pleasant, Ben had taken his share of our stash and purchased a beat-up blue Ford Explorer. The mid-nineties clunker looked ready to die at any moment, but Ben now had wheels to complement his Boston Whaler runabout.

The rest of us didn't have so much as a motorized scooter.

"I'm not suggesting we put ourselves at risk." I spoke carefully, addressing all three boys rather than just Ben. "Or go on some wild flaring binge. In case you've forgotten, we have plenty of abilities besides the ones we inherited from Coop."

Ben snorted. I could sense his eyes rolling behind his shades.

"In fact," I continued, disturbed by his dismissive manner, "I think we should be more careful about our powers in general. At least until we access Karsten's flash drive."

"How are we gonna do that?" Hi nodded toward Shelton. "Hack-Master General here says he can't crack the code."

"That's *commercial*-grade encryption we're talking about," Shelton replied testily. "Top-of-the-line security software. I'm good, but not *that* good."

"Then we need an expert," I mused. "Someone who'll do the job, but also keep their mouth shut."

"Good luck," Shelton grumbled. "I doubt Anonymous could hack that drive."

Ben crossed his arms. "What do you expect to learn, anyway?"

He'd addressed me directly. I was forced to respond.

"We need to know *exactly* what Karsten was doing with Parvovirus XPB-19." I ticked off fingers. "How he constructed the supervirus, what happened during testing, and how the microbe might mutate in the future."

"The future?" Shelton reached for an earlobe. "Why so concerned? Is this because of that . . . feeling . . . you get?"

"Partly." I took a deep breath. "I won't lie. I'm worried about the stability of our flare powers in general. Things have gotten weird lately. We need to be careful."

Shelton's eyes dropped. Hi shuffled his feet.

They didn't like talking about it. Wanted to avoid the issue altogether.

But I wouldn't budge. "We need to know if our condition will continue to evolve. And, if so, whether there's a possible vaccine. Some kind of cure."

"A cure?" Ben hooted. "Insane. Why in the world would we *want* a cure?"

I opened my mouth, hot words at the ready. Then closed it.

Was Ben right?

We had a unique gift—special abilities unknown to the rest of our species. Was that something we should consider giving up? Something we *could* give up?

I shrugged off the question. Ben was being a jerk.

Watching him now, he didn't seem like the same friend I'd known for so long. I couldn't put my finger on it, exactly. The arrogant set to his shoulders? The bitter sarcasm dripping from every word?

Ben had always had a temper, but this seemed worse.

I worried the media coverage had affected him. As the centerpiece of the prosecution's case against the Gamemaster, Ben had been alternatively cast as victim and villain, depending on the source. Either way, he'd been at the eye of the storm.

At first Ben had seemed spooked, almost paralyzed by the spotlight. Though I'd kept my distance, Hi and Shelton had reported his skulking, disappearing aboard *Sewee* for hours, always trying to avoid being seen.

Then, abruptly, he'd seemed to accept the notoriety. Maybe even relish it a little. According to Hi and Shelton, in the last few weeks Ben had been out and about, wearing his dark designer shades, apparently unfazed by the gossip and the stares.

The sudden change concerned me. It felt like a front.

I was sure something was wrong. That Ben was bottling his issues deep inside.

But I wasn't ready to talk. Still couldn't bring myself to forgive.

As we lingered on the sidewalk, I examined Ben from the corner of my eye. He seemed relaxed, almost languid. Carefree. An unnatural response to the morning's events.

Then Ben yawned like a jungle cat uncurling from a nap. His movements snared my attention. Scratching his nose, Ben's fingers moved just a little too fast.

Pieces suddenly clicked together.

Dark shades. Quick hands.

Alarm bells began clanging in my head.

Ben!

My hand shot for the Ray-Bans, but Ben caught my fingers mid-flight.

"It's not nice to grab," he said calmly.

"You're *flaring,*" I hissed. "Right now!"

Ben chuckled. "So? No one can tell."

"Oh, man!" Shelton whirled to scan the block. "Bad idea, Blue. *Spectacularly* bad."

"Why are you flaring in public?" I whisper-shouted. "For no reason!"

"You have some kinda death wish?" Hi snapped. "You wanna end up dancing for quarters in a government zoo? Because that's what you're risking, and you have terrible rhythm."

"Relax." Ben's voice had an edge. "I'm wearing sunglasses. Being careful."

"You are burning our secret superpowers, in broad daylight, in the middle of downtown Charleston!" My eyes flicked to a couple rounding a nearby corner, and heading our way. "Here come some tourists, Benjamin. Wanna show them your special skills?"

"I should," Ben snickered, waggling his shades. "It'd make their visit memorable."

I was about to straight flip the frick out when Ben's shoulders quivered, sweat beading at his temples. Then he sighed, sucked in two deep breaths.

Ben slipped off his shades to reveal normal brown irises. "Happy, grandma?"

He tossed a mocking wave at the tourists as they strolled past.

"No," I said, once the couple was out of earshot. "I'm pretty damn far from happy." Then, with a monumental effort, I moderated my tone. "You're playing with fire, Ben. And if you screw up, we *all* get burned."

"I'm not a child, Victoria." Replacing his Ray-Bans, Ben strode away up the block.

"Well, *that* wasn't great," Hi said dryly. "But at least you two are talking now, right?"

"I can't handle all this tension," Shelton moaned. "Too much fighting."

Hi nodded, watching as Ben disappeared down a side street. "We need to work on our conflict management. Maybe attend a seminar."

"Ben's going all flare crazy," Shelton muttered. "Hi's burglarizing the DA's office. Nobody's *talking* about anything. Things are getting out of hand."

My palms came up. "What can we do? Ben's impossible."

Shelton surprised me by jabbing a finger in my face. "You do nothing but look daggers at him, when you bother to acknowledge his presence at all. How's he supposed to act? When are you gonna get over this, so we can move on?"

"When Ben creates a time machine," I shot back. "And undoes what he did!"

Dumb words, but I didn't care. I was seething.

"Ben's been flaring a lot lately," Hi said quietly. "Every day, I think. I wonder if he's just chasing the rush."

Those alarm bells became blaring sirens.

Ben seemed totally different. I'd assumed it was stress from the trial, but now I worried it was something else. A more disturbing possibility.

I knew our powers were becoming unsteady. I'd felt the tremors myself.

But had they also become addictive? Or destructive?

Ben was flaring often, even in public. Could *that* be changing his personality?

Or could Ben's overindulgence be causing the problems in the first place?

What have we gotten ourselves into?

Shelton checked his watch. "We'd better move. The headmaster wants us back by lunch, and we're cutting it close."

"Fine." What more was there to say?

I walked the last few blocks in a fog, my mind sifting unpleasant possibilities. Considering dire scenarios. The chronic problem of our viral transformation suddenly seemed urgent. We'd put off seeking answers for too long.

We *had* to learn more about the experiment that changed us.

Which meant, we *had* to get into Karsten's flash drive. But how?

Thoughts wandering, it took me several moments to notice a feeling I'd been ignoring.

The odd sensation had returned. That itch I couldn't scratch.

Two days in a row. It's happening more often.

As soon as I recognized the vibe, it began to dissipate.

Concentrating, I struggled to capture its essence. Felt a *closeness* I'd not noticed before. As though my mind were trying to connect with something outside my body.

But how? I'm not flaring.

Then, like a sigh escaping, the moment passed. I nearly ground my teeth in frustration. Another opportunity to learn something—*anything*—had slipped through my fingers.

With my mind a thousand miles away, I didn't see the land mine right in front of me.

Hi grabbed my arm. I glanced up, startled to see Bolton's wrought-iron gates.

And more surprised to see Chance Claybourne standing between them.

My stomach backflipped.

Some reactions are purely involuntary.

Chance was exiting the grounds, a dog-eared folder tucked under one arm. He wore a hand-tailored black suit, crisp white shirt, silver tie, red argyle socks, and black patent-leather shoes. The outfit oozed casual expense.

He paused mid-stride, chiseled face unreadable.

Chance seemed carved from shadows, with dusky skin and deep, dark eyes. He had a swimmer's build—tall and slender, yet wiry strong, with lustrous black hair framing a perfect chin. His every move was graceful.

Chance was, hands down, the best-looking person I'd ever met in real life.

"What are you doing here?" I blurted.

"Manners, Victoria." Chance *tut-tut*ted. "And here I thought we were old friends."

I cleared my throat, buying time to pull my thoughts together. Finally, "I didn't expect to see you at Bolton. After you graduated, I mean."

"I didn't expect to be here again," he replied airily. "But apparently my employer needs a transcript for my file."

An eyebrow rose. "Your employer?"

"Candela Pharmaceuticals. I've been named to the board." Chance casually plucked a fallen leaf from his sleeve. "Not all that surprising, since I *do* own most of the company."

I stiffened. Candela triggered bad memories.

"They put *you* in charge?" Hi snorted. "Remind me to sell my stock."

"Thanks for the vote of confidence, Hiram."

"How can an eighteen-year-old run a major corporation?" Shelton said. "You were still in high school, like, five minutes ago."

"It's not a one-man show," Chance said dryly. "I've been tasked with running a small division focusing on special projects. The rest of Candela's leadership stays the same."

"Special projects," I repeated. Felt a chill.

"Research and development, mainly." Chance stepped onto the tree-lined sidewalk. "I'll get to play around a little. Crack a few eggs, so to speak."

My voice raised an octave. "What does that mean?"

Chance's face was unreadable. "It *means*, I'll be able to work on whatever I want. Get some answers I've been seeking."

"How dramatic." Hi tapped his head. "You wanna make a difference? Create a deodorant that doesn't suck. The brand I use leaves pit stains on all my undershirts."

"I'll pass." Chance's hair dancing rakishly in the light ocean breeze. "My interests are a touch more exotic."

His eyes found mine. I looked away.

Chance's past accusations flashed through my mind.

"I have to go," he said abruptly. "Maybe I'll see you soon."

He walked past without another word.

I watched his form recede down the block. Chance never glanced back.

"That guy ain't right," Shelton whispered. "But at least he's out of our hair now."

"Yeah."

But I had a sinking feeling.

Special projects.

Cracking eggs.

Answers.

For some reason, I felt like Chance had threatened me.

CHAPTER 7

Chance dropped the battered file on his desk.

He'd studied its contents a hundred times. The hundred-and-first reading had revealed nothing new.

Bong. Bong.

A grandfather clock chimed 2:00 p.m. Chance could barely make out the stately timepiece, tucked as it was in the far corner of his father's private study.

My study, rather.

He still hadn't gotten use to that.

Long shadows crisscrossed the wood-paneled walls and expensive Persian rugs. He meant to install more lights, but never got around to it.

Chance spun his chair to face giant floor-to-ceiling windows overlooking the estate's inner yard. Below, a landscaper was carefully sculpting a wall of the hedge maze. Chance didn't know the man's name. Claybourne Manor had dozens of gardeners.

Once more, Tory Brennan crashed his thoughts.

Maddening.

He was no closer now than on the day he'd first discovered the information.

No closer, but out of ideas.

And time, perhaps.

Frustrated, Chance swiveled back to his desk. Lifted the folder once more. Eyed the red block lettering stamped on its face:

CANDELA PHARMACEUTICALS
DR. MARCUS KARSTEN—RESEARCH NOTES
TOP SECRET. PROPRIETARY R&D

He'd found five more folders identical to this one. A hidden cache, locked away in his father's private cabinet. Another secret among the many Hollis Claybourne had kept.

His father never mentioned this project. Not once.

Chance grinned sourly.

The Old Man hadn't shared much before getting hauled off to prison.

Chance opened a desk drawer. Placed the file inside with the others.

He was obsessed. And knew it. But recognition made no difference. He could more easily hold back the tides than abandon this endeavor.

Tory Brennan.

So many emotions, derived from a single name.

The girl was nothing. A transplant science geek from the barrier-island sticks. Still a sophomore in high school. She didn't come from wealth, or have an influential family name. It was borderline miraculous that he was aware of her existence at all.

But he was. In fact, he noticed *everything* about her.

Chance leaned back and closed his eyes.

Inevitably, his mind began picking at the memories he'd been counseled not to trust.

Tory and her Morris Island friends, in the darkness of his basement. Moving way too fast, eyes glowing unnaturally bright.

Those same four, darting like arrows across a pitch-black beach. Same unnatural speed. Same blazing irises.

He'd thought himself crazy. His doctors had agreed. Together they'd painstakingly constructed a new reality—a *rational* one—where Chance hadn't seen those things at all.

Then it happened *again*.

The debutante ball.

He hadn't witnessed the last event firsthand—Tory had seen to that—but those outcasts had accomplished the unthinkable. A feat of strength beyond anything remotely reasonable.

It. Was. Not. Possible.

Third time's a charm.

His tortured laugh echoed in the cavernous chamber.

Chance's gaze dropped to the drawer. He tapped the handle with an index finger.

These folders hold the key.

He didn't know how. Didn't understand why. But Chance was certain.

Karsten's records would solve the riddle of Tory Brennan and her sidekicks. The answers he sought lurked somewhere inside those reports.

Chance yanked the drawer open again. Slapped a new file onto his desk.

He paused a moment, shaking his head at the part of the story he knew.

A hidden lab. Secret tests. Corporate espionage. Payoffs and payouts.

His father had ordered an illegal medical experiment, off the books, bankrolled by an untraceable shell corporation using Candela funds. The harebrained scheme violated dozens of laws and regulations. It was both a criminal and fireable offense.

The arrogance of it boggled Chance's mind.

Thankfully, his father had been careful. Chance had checked for records thoroughly, spending hours sifting through boxes at Candela's file storage warehouse, and even more time combing the database. He was satisfied no other documents existed.

No one would learn of Karsten's work.

No one but me.

It'd taken Chance months just to comprehend what he was reading.

At first, the connections were hidden. Even with a mole at LIRI feeding him intel, Chance had learned little of use. Dr. Mike Iglehart was a major disappointment. The secret link to Loggerhead Island hadn't borne much fruit.

But then he'd found it.

Chance flipped to back of the file. Selected a computer printout.

The bridge had been there all along. He just hadn't seen it.

Page sixty-four. Third paragraph. Second line. Twenty-five words.

Subject A for Parvovirus XPB–19 is a wild canine hybrid captured on Loggerhead Island, the offspring of a female gray wolf and male German shepherd.

In other words, a wolfdog.

So simple. Yet he'd missed it repeatedly.

"Cooper," Chance whispered. Tory's too-smart mongrel was the key.

Though, admittedly, Chance *still* hadn't put it together at that point.

Karsten had used Coop as a parvovirus test subject. So what? The dog had clearly recovered and survived. Perhaps Tory had adopted him afterward. What difference did it make?

But Chance had held tenaciously to his theory. And his diligence paid off.

He'd simply needed to find the other pieces.

Chance removed a third file from the drawer and placed it beside the other.

Paging to the middle, he found the crucial line. He'd only apprehended its significance that morning.

Bottom margin. Handwritten. So easily overlooked.

The highest caution must be employed. Due to its radical structure, Parvovirus strain XPB-19 may be infectious to humans.

There.

There there there.

A connection. One that might explain *everything*.

What he'd seen. What he'd experienced with those Morris Island weirdoes.

What, exactly, had Cooper carried?

What happened after Tory took him home?

Chance didn't know. But he was going to find out.

At that moment, a startling thought occurred to him. Something that, shockingly, he'd never considered before. The implications shot ice through his veins.

Chance quickly dug out and opened his MacBook. Fingers flying, he accessed his secure database and scanned the research protocols for Brimstone, the first project he'd commissioned at Candela. His anxiety level rose.

Dear God.

He'd green-lit the secret venture immediately upon discovering Karsten's files, content to improvise, learning as he went. Hoping hard science would give him answers, even without knowing the exact questions.

But had he taken the proper precautions?

Switching to an outside server, Chance reviewed several encrypted files with an entirely new set of concerns. What he discovered sent his heart hammering.

Chance's hands found his forehead.

Was it dangerous?

I don't know.

Popping from his seat, Chance strode for the door. He hurried down two flights of stairs and into the grand entrance hall.

At the massive front doors, he paused.

Squeezed his eyes shut.

Drawing a deep breath, Chance straightened his tie and smoothed his hair.

Then he stepped outside and called for his driver, desperately hoping he hadn't made a colossal mistake.

CHAPTER 8

All hail MegaDock!"

Hi led us across the marina parking lot, heading for the southernmost section known as Pier Group Z. There we'd meet *Hugo* for our trip home.

The afternoon sun had ramped up the heat. I stopped a moment to shed my jacket. Shelton shuffled along beside Hi, loosening his navy-blue-striped Bolton tie.

The Charleston City Marina is a behemoth, with over nineteen thousand feet of dock space covering forty acres of water. Located in a sheltered zone where the Ashley River flows into the harbor, the sprawling facility is packed with amenities, including restaurants, stores, bars, and a floating boathouse.

And MegaDock, of course.

At a whopping 1,530 feet, MegaDock is the longest freestanding, floating fuel dock in the Southeast. Equipped with state-of-the-art power uplinks, boat-side assistance, and twenty-four-hour security, plus every other nautical perk you can imagine, its length is always crammed with massive yachts and expensive pleasure boats.

We trooped through the marina twice every school day. I barely noticed the opulent crafts any more, though at first I'd gawked like a tourist.

I trailed the boys, stuck in a funk.

Chance was in my head. I couldn't shake a feeling of impending doom.

Was it coincidence we'd run into each other? Or had Chance been waiting? And what was up with his new job?

I'd assumed that, after graduation, Chance would relax into a life of playboy luxury. Work on his polo game. Collect oil paintings, or Italian sports cars. Date Victoria's Secret models. After all, he didn't have to work. Didn't *have* to do anything but spend his money.

So why take on a dreary job at Candela? It made no sense.

We passed a small outbuilding crammed with yacht sales offices, then swept by the Variety Store Restaurant. As we approached the pier walkways, I heard a TV newscast floating from inside Salty Mike's Deck Bar.

The faint audio caught my attention.

"Hi! Shelton!" I pointed, then ducked through the open door.

Salty Mike's interior was rough but clean, with neon beer signs adorning a large central tiki bar. A pair of gnarly dartboards flanked a flat-screen TV on the right-hand wall.

I raced over, tried to figure out the volume. Heard feet behind me.

"What is it?" Hi asked. "I thought you were anti-booze. Plus, it's three o'clock."

"Shh!" I jabbed a button, then hissed in frustration as snow filled the screen. The bartender shot me an irritated look.

"Here, let me." Shelton somehow corrected the feed and jacked up the sound.

A tinny voice filled the room. "Repeating our top story this morning, police sources have told Channel Five News that two Charleston teens have officially been designated missing persons . . ."

Smiling pictures of Lucy and Peter Gable flashed onscreen. Each wore a Bolton uniform.

"Holy crap," Shelton breathed. "Guess the cat's out of the bag."

Hi snorted. "Color me *shocked* that those ace cops couldn't maintain radio silence."

"Quiet!" I barked. "There's more."

The image shifted to a live shot of Bolton's front gates, where a breathless female reporter took up the story. "The Gable siblings are both juniors at Bolton Preparatory Academy, the same prestigious private high school that recently made headlines for its connection to the sensational Gamemaster trial."

The three of us groaned in unison.

"Headmaster Declan Paugh declined to be interviewed for our broadcast—" they cut to a clip of Paugh, red-faced, waving the camera away, "—but stated that the school will cooperate fully with the police investigation. Currently, there are no leads regarding the twins' disappearance."

Shelton covered his mouth. "Oh, man, he looks upset."

The program jumped to a noticeably annoyed Commissioner Riggins, standing on the steps outside police headquarters. "At this time we have no evidence of foul play, or even that a crime has been committed. We ask the media to refrain from creating undo panic and let us do our jobs."

The scene shifted to a large waterfront house with several police cruisers parked outside. A deep male voice began narrating. "Rex Gable, father of the missing teens, is a prominent local businessman who serves on the Charleston University Board of Trustees, and is an alderman at Saint Michael's Church. Channel Five has learned that police investigators searched the family's Daniel Island home early this morning."

The coverage shifted to a flashy news studio, where a silver-foxed anchorman addressed the camera. "The Gable family has temporarily relocated to assist with the investigation."

"Maybe we'll get lucky," Hi offered. "This should bump the Gamemaster's trial from page one."

Shelton slapped Hi's shoulder. "C'mon, man. Not cool. We know those guys."

The anchor continued. "If you know the whereabouts of Lucy or Peter Gable, please contact the Charleston Police Department. A reward is being offered for information leading to their safe return."

The broadcast switched to an empty-headed weatherman predicting partly cloudy skies. Shelton turned the volume back down and we stepped outside.

Absently, I began walking toward our slip, where *Hugo* would arrive any minute. The boys followed. But my feet slowed as we approached the long wooden walkway to Pier Group Z. Halfway across, I stopped altogether.

The boys halted behind me, uncertain, matching puzzled expressions on their faces.

For a long moment, I stared out over the harbor in silence.

A feeling was hardening inside me. A resolve.

"We *have* to do something," I said finally. Forcefully. "We *have* to get involved."

Shelton scratched the back of his head. "Okay. Fine. But what?"

"We've got that voodoo card," Hi suggested. "Let's find out what it means."

"More," I urged. "We need to fully investigate the twins' disappearance."

"I distinctly remember being told this was a police matter," Shelton grumbled. "More than once, yo."

"But we can help." I spun to face them. "What *are* we doing these days, anyway?"

Hi's face scrunched. "What do you mean?"

"I mean, what's our purpose? We have these—" I stepped closer and lowered my voice, "—*abilities,* but no direction. No goal. We should be doing more."

"We're keeping our heads down," Shelton countered. "Avoiding the spotlight while we figure out what happened to us. Jeez, Tor. Isn't that enough? I thought that's what you wanted?"

"No. Not anymore. I was wrong."

Both boys gave me confused looks. I couldn't blame them.

I tried to express what I was feeling. "We need to *do* things. Accomplish something. Make a difference with . . . whatever it is these powers are."

Hi spread his arms wide. "With great power comes great responsibility. Ask Spider-Man."

"So now you two wanna fight crime?" Shelton shook his head, incredulous. "Where is this coming from? Should we make costumes?"

Hi's face lit up. "I've *definitely* got some ideas in that area, if—"

"Of course we don't need costumes!" I paused, took a breath. "Look, I'm not even sure what I want. And, yes, I realize this is coming straight out of nowhere. I was the one who said we shouldn't be flaring at all."

I glanced at the door to Salty Mike's. "Maybe it was seeing Lucy's and Peter's pictures onscreen. Like mug shots. It just hit me—we *have* these powers, why not *apply* them to something worthwhile? Solve problems normal people can't."

Shelton's eyes narrowed. "You sound like a guidance counselor."

I ignored him. The more I thought about it, the more I believed in what I was saying.

We *did* need a purpose. Could this be it?

"Hey, why not?" Hi shrugged. "We know the twins, and they seem all right. And it's only a missing persons' case anyway. What are you afraid of, Devers?"

"The unknown," Shelton snapped. "Jail. Being dissected by Navy Seals."

He petulantly kicked a rock. I crossed my arms, waiting.

Shelton removed his glasses and ran a hand across his face. Finally, he sighed. "I guess we could help out a little. Can't see the harm in that."

"So what's the plan?" Hi cracked his knuckles. "Head into North Charleston and shake down some perps? Buy hand grenades? I've mapped out the first couple verses of a Virals theme song, so—"

"The Gable house," I said. "The report said the family relocated, probably so the cops can tear it part. No one should be there. Let's snoop around a little."

"*Arrgh.*" Shelton pressed both fists to his skull. "More midnight black ops. We've done so much B and E this last year, we should apply for college credit. I think my black sweat pants are dirty, and I don't—"

"No, doofus. Let's go right now. If the Gable family isn't staying there, the house should be deserted. Hi, can you—"

"On it." Hi began tapping his iPhone. A moment, then, "Daniel Island. Nice digs, too, not that I'm surprised. The lot borders the Wando River."

"Waterfront," Shelton said quietly. "They probably have a dock."

"Easiest way to avoid detection," Hi added in a singsong voice.

Both boys looked at me.

There was no way around it. We needed Ben. He had the damn boat.

"Fine." I practically growled. "Text him."

Shelton punched in the message. His iPhone buzzed back in moments.

"Ben's in." Shelton rolled his eyes. "Snarky as hell, but he'll pick us up at the Morris dock."

"Getting the band back together!" Hi tossed Shelton a high five, then aimed one my way. "Look out, world!"

I raised my palm in reluctant acceptance.

Look on the bright side. We'll do this at full pack strength.

If only I knew how to feel about that.

CHAPTER 9

Sewee's nose kissed the Gables' private dock.

Ben killed the engine and running lights. Shouldering my pack, I vaulted the port rail and tied off the bowline while Shelton and Hi tightened the stern ropes. Vessel secured, Ben and Coop leaped to join us and we hurried down the planks.

The sun was setting in a fiery tangerine ball, giving a hint of cover. I prayed the neighbors wouldn't notice our boat, but it was a risk we had to take. Thankfully, the Gable property was tucked into a tree-lined cove that blocked an easy view by passing watercraft.

An hour earlier I'd managed to beg off dinner. Kit and Whitney had accepted my study group explanation without too much fuss. After all, I'd promised to be home by eight. What trouble could I possibly get into?

Daniel Island is all the way across Charleston Harbor from Morris. An affluent four-thousand-acre planned community situated between the Cooper and Wando Rivers, the pricey real estate had only recently been developed. In addition to residential neighborhoods, the islet boasts a swanky golf club, its own schools, churches, and parks, and a vibrant little downtown featuring boutiques, restaurants, and high-end office space.

Fresh, conspicuously green, and close to downtown, Daniel Island had quickly become a coveted address. It's where I'd live, if given the choice. With my friends close by, of course.

We halted in the shadow of a boat shed at the end of the dock.

"You guys ready?" I whispered.

A round of nods. Coop sat back on his hind legs with an expectant look.

"We shouldn't have brought the freaking wolfdog," Shelton griped. "We can't take him inside the house. What if he barks? Decides to chase rabbits?"

"Coop will stand guard," I assured him. "Plus, he amplifies our flare powers. That might come in handy, don't cha think?"

Assuming they work properly. Or at all.

I brushed the unpleasant thought aside. To pull off this home invasion, we *had* to use our powers. There was no way around it. Lucy and Peter needed our help.

We'd just have to be vigilant to any . . . irregularities.

"Enough talk." Ben's eyes already gleamed. "We need to be quick. If anyone spots *Sewee* before we get back, we're cooked."

I ignored Ben. My current strategy was to pretend he wasn't there.

Closing my eyes, I tripped the mental breaker.

SNAP.

Fire. Ice. The opposing forces sent waves thrumming through my body.

Raw energy balled within my chest, compressing and compounding until I felt ready to explode. The power *raged*. Primal. Bestial. Something ancient, yet newborn at the same time. The intensity was unlike anything I'd felt before.

Shelton dropped to a knee, bathed in sweat. "What . . . what . . ?"

Hiram shook, his lips moving soundlessly.

"Amazing." Ben staggered sideways, steadying himself against the shed.

I didn't move. Couldn't. Every muscle in my body had seized.

The maelstrom peaked, then shattered like a dropped vase. Darts of adrenaline circumnavigated my nervous system.

My canine DNA rose from its hiding place. Stretched it paws.

Every sense hummed. The world around me sharpened to a laser-like precision unlike anything my species was built to experience.

My eyes cut like diamonds. I scanned the cove, searching for signs of movement. Detected none. My ears picked out a ticking clock inside a neighboring house, fifty yards away. Distant car horns blared inside my head.

I flexed my fingers, reveling in their sudden dexterity. My arms and legs throbbed with energy. Lifting my nose, I sniffed, read the panic sweat dripping from the other Virals.

Except Ben.

He reeked of something else entirely. A sweet, musky scent. My mind made connections, though I didn't understand how, or why.

Was it . . . hunger? Joy? Triumph? I couldn't be sure.

"That was . . . intense." Hi's voice cracked on the last word.

"We haven't flared all together in a while." Shelton pocketed his spectacles. "Tory's right. The powers are getting . . . wilder. Almost rabid."

Sister-Friend.

I glanced down. Coop was at my side, tail wagging. I rubbed his snout.

Hello, Coop.

The boys jumped. Six golden eyes shot to me.

I grinned. Shut my eyes once more.

Stilling my thoughts, I delved deep into my subconscious. Visualized the hidden connections between our minds.

I *knew* they were there. Had learned that much about our powers.

Wherever we went, whatever we did, telepathic bonds linked us. Viral to Viral. Those bonds were the essence of what made us a pack.

A web sprang to life—flaming cords, stretching between us in a fiery grid, dancing and humming with vitality.

So much easier than before.

Guided by instinct, I . . . *reached* somehow, gripping the gleaming ropes with my consciousness, overlaying my thoughts in a manner I can't fully explain. My spirit soared as I imbedded myself into our shared thought matrix.

I sent a message.

Hello to you guys, too.

"Oh, man." Shelton grabbed his head. "I'm *never* going to get used to that."

"Is it like before?" Hi asked, wide-eyed. "Can you see through our eyes? Read our thoughts?"

"She better not." Ben took a step back down the dock.

"Relax." Cradled inside this magnificent *oneness,* I felt totally at ease. *Just like before.*

I tried to untether my mind from my body. At the same time, I willed the flaming cords to grow and expand. Transform into conduits through which my thoughts could pass.

No good. Something blocked the flow.

I couldn't create the tunnels. My mind wouldn't travel.

I don't understand.

The links were discernible. My pack was assembled. Everything felt in place.

But I couldn't force the union. The pack refused to coalesce.

The bonds connecting us thrummed wildly, like guitar strings wound too tight.

Frustrated, I concentrated on the wolfdog, knowing he focused our power.

Coop's ears perked. His gaze locked on to mine.

One last time, I tried to *force* the mind-meld, picturing the Virals as an extension of Coop. The effort failed. I couldn't untie the pack.

"Tory?"

My lids opened. Hi was waving a hand in front of my face.

"I can't connect our thoughts. I don't understand it. I can't even hear yours."

"Sounds perfect." Ben jabbed a thumb at the house. "Can we get on with it?"

I nodded. He was right. We had a task to complete.

But this isn't over.

Kneeling beside Coop, I ruffled his fur. A surge of love flowed along our bond.

"Stay here, boy." Holding my palm before his nose. "Keep watch for anyone approaching the house."

I felt a flash of annoyance from Coop. He snorted, then pawed the wooden planks.

"No back talk."

Taking his head in my hands, I forced the wolfdog to meet my gaze. *Stay. Watch. Please.*

I released him. Coop whined softly, but circled three times and sat. *Watch. Guard.*

Impressions more than words.

"Good boy. See you in a few."

A small backyard stretched to the rear of the Gables' white stucco house. We crossed it quickly, then waited for Shelton to pick the back-door lock.

"Come on, maestro." Hi was bouncing on the balls of his feet. "Work your magic."

Click.

"Gotcha." Shelton took a breath. "Here goes. Be ready to haul ass if an alarm goes off."

Cringing, he turned the knob, then slowly eased the door open.

Nothing. No wailing sirens. No flashing lights. The system was deactivated.

"Move!" I hurried everyone inside, leaving the door cracked for a quick getaway.

Unleashing my flare senses, I searched for any sign of occupancy.

Just because a house is *supposed* to be empty, doesn't mean it is.

Flaring, I heard a ticking clock. Purring AC. Tiny feet scritch-scratching inside the stucco walls. Sand mice. They're everywhere on the islands.

The Gables need an exterminator.

"Nobody's here," Shelton said at last. "At least, nobody that's breathing."

I exhaled. If Shelton's ears gave the all-clear, then I was satisfied.

We stood inside a large kitchen with a central island. A breakfast nook hooked off to the right. Beyond it, a narrow back staircase rose to the second floor. To the left of the island, a pair of doorways accessed the rest of the ground floor.

"Let's split up," Ben suggested. "Shelton and I will look down here."

"Hiram and I will check upstairs." I spoke as though the two-pronged approach was my idea. Technically, I still wasn't speaking to Ben.

I led Hi up to the second level. A long hallway ran the length of the house, ending at a closed door. Two additional doors spaced each side. In the center of the corridor, a wide staircase descended to the foyer and front door.

"I'll take this side." Pointing left. "You sweep the other."

Hi nodded. I moved to the first room and slipped inside.

The square chamber was small, with a single window. Desk. Computer. Bookshelf. File Cabinet. Clearly a home office. The room's most notable feature was how immaculate it was. Clear desktop. Empty trash can. Not a displaced pen or paper clip. The carpet still had vacuum lines. I wondered if anyone ever went in there.

Forgoing the lights in case of any watchful neighbors, I prowled in the growing gloom, trusting my flare vision to pierce the shadows. Senses on high alert, I poked around—opening drawers, jiggling handles, checking the closet—but quickly moved on. I'd seen nothing relating to either twin.

Back in the hallway, I bumped into Hi.

"Office," I said.

"Guest bedroom," he replied. "These people sure like Pottery Barn."

My next door accessed a much larger chamber, with bay windows overlooking the water. A king-sized bed occupied stage center, heaped with lacy throw pillows. A Katy Perry CD was resting on the bedside table.

Sensing I'd found Lucy's domain, I closed the drapes and flipped a wall switch.

The card had been found in there. Her room required a thorough examination.

The first thing I noticed was pink. Everywhere. Walls, sheets, bed-spread, even a lighter shade for the plush wall-to-wall carpeting. *Blech.*

The furniture was elegant and tasteful. Simple wooden pieces, painted white—bed, side tables, dresser, bureau, bookcase, desk. A pri-vate bathroom split the far wall, next to a large walk-in closet. Framed prints adorned the walls. Monet. Dalí. Van Gogh. Classics, all, but highly impersonal. An easel and violin stood in the corner. A day bench curved beneath each window.

I crossed to the dresser, where a handful of framed pictures were aligned in a row. Lucy and Peter playing violin. Lucy smiling as she received an award. A Gable family portrait. Lucy's yearbook photograph.

As I looked around, two things bothered me.

First, Lucy's room was as spotless as the office. Either these people were neat freaks, or they had one hell of a maid.

Second, The room lacked . . . character. It was cold, and impersonal, like a hotel suite. Beyond the violin, I saw nothing that made me think of Lucy Gable, the person.

Get to work, I chided myself. *Not everyone is Hiram.*

Harnessing my flare senses, I inspected the bedroom from top to bottom. I rifled the dresser, checked inside the desk and bureau, crawled under the bed, and even snooped behind the bookcase and headboard. Everywhere a personal item could be stashed.

But what I was hunting?

More weird cards? A note? Signs of foul play?

I didn't know, and so far my probe had turned up diddly-squat.

Opening the closet, I received my first surprise—a giant Ryan Gosling poster taped to the back of the door.

"That's more like it." I took a moment to admire the artwork.

Finally, a little spark. Some evidence that Lucy had a normal human personality.

But why was it hidden in there?

World's Sexiest Man aside, the remainder of the closet disappointed—nothing but pricey clothes, Bolton Prep unis, and more shoes than four girls could wear. No box full of love letters, no trashed Google Maps printouts, no secret diary filled with shocking revelations, stashed inside a winter coat pocket.

My spirits sank. I began to worry I'd forced us here for no reason.

A quick search of Lucy's bathroom drew a similar blank. Sighing, I slapped off the light and stepped back into the hall. Hi was exiting the door at the end of the corridor.

"Media room." His golden eyes gleamed in the darkness. "A total snoozer. Although somebody bought *The Last Airbender* on Blu-ray, which might be the worst purchase ever."

"Is that the last door?"

Hi nodded. "I already checked Peter's room. Other than being the lamest sleeping chamber ever conceived, there's nothing suspicious. Not that I know what I'm doing. Because I don't, FYI."

I suppressed a sigh. "I trust your instincts. I got the same vibe from Lucy's room. It's a little weird. Other than a few framed pictures, the place felt like a high-end corporate rental or something."

"We may need to face the fact that the Gable twins are the two most boring people on earth." Hi paused. "Though Peter did have a pretty killer CD collection. White Stripes. Nine Inch Nails. Death Cab. He keeps it under his bed, though, which is kinda bizarre."

"Huh."

Under his bed? And Lucy hung her poster in the closet. What was that all about?

"Did you find anything like Señor Snake Scarf?" Hi asked.

I shook my head. "Based on her room, I can't believe that card belongs to Lucy."

"Let's check with Shelton and Ben," Hi suggested. "Maybe they found something downstairs." But he didn't sound optimistic.

I'd taken one step down the main staircase when an image arrowed into my head.

Cooper. *Inside.* Scratching at a thick wooden door.

I stumbled, nearly fell. Hi grabbed my arm to prevent a header down the stairs.

"Tory?"

"I'm . . . okay." The image faded, but I knew what it meant. "Hurry. Coop's inside the house. He wants to show me something."

"Your dog just spoke to you, inside your head?" Hi shivered. "Crazy sauce."

"Just come on!"

I felt an electric charge in my nerves.

Coop *had* sent me a message. The image was only part of it.

The wolfdog's nose had caught something we'd missed.

A harsh, coppery scent.

One I had no trouble identifying.

Cooper was on the trail of blood.

CHAPTER 10

Shelton and Ben were waiting at the foot of the stairs.

"We found zilch," Shelton grumbled. "What are we even doing here?"

Ben jabbed a thumb over his shoulder. "That way is the living room, den, and dining room. Everything's completely normal. We were about to recheck the kitchen, since we don't know what else to do."

"There's a second passage off the kitchen," I said. "Coop's there."

"Coop?" Shelton's hands flew up. "What's he doing in the house?"

Ben frowned, golden light smoldering from his dark brown eyes. "How do you know he's there?"

"He told me. I think he found something."

Shelton's arms dropped. "Told you?"

"Yes. Now follow me."

We hurried back to the kitchen. I spotted Coop standing, legs splayed, halfway down the back corridor.

Coop looked at me, a low growl rolling from his throat.

"What do you mean, Coop told you?" Shelton was tugging his earlobe double time. "You mean, like . . . like, he spoke to you? Mind to mind? I didn't hear anything. How come you and the mutt can connect, but we can't?"

"No idea." I reached down to scratch Coop's ears. His body was rigid, head to tail. He pawed the oak door in front of his snout.

"It was more like an impression, and it only lasted for a second." I said. "Coop caught an odor. In here."

With my flare still burning, I felt the tiniest of tickles along my skin.

I placed my hand near the crack, where the wood met the jamb.

Air flow. This wasn't a broom closet—there was open space behind the door.

The knob turned easily in my hand. The door swung open, revealing a narrow set of carpeted stairs descending into darkness.

Coop fired down the steps.

"Cooper! Stop." But the wolfdog was gone.

"A lower level?" Hi's brow furrowed. "The Zillow listing for this address didn't mention a finished basement. Those are pretty rare for Charleston. The Gables must've completed this recently. They're *supposed* to update their total heated square footage, but I bet they're trying to avoid a higher property tax assessment."

We stared at Hi.

He shrugged. "What?"

"Total heated square footage?" Shelton asked.

"Property tax assessment?" Ben added.

"My uncle's a real estate agent," Hi said defensively.

"Enough." I flipped a switch, illuminating both the staircase and the room below. Waving for the others to follow, I started down after Coop.

The area below was spacious, spanning half the house. The single room was divided into nooks, with a small bathroom to one side. The black-and-white tile floor held a pool table, an elliptical machine, a wet bar, and a small movie theater with four recliners. On the far wall, two skinny rectangular windows flanked a thick steel door, which allowed access to a courtyard beside the house. Two more windows dotted the near wall, allowing a ground-level view of the Gables' backyard and dock.

"Being rich seems nice," Hi commented. "Remind me to get on that."

I was already moving to where Coop was snuffling beside the steel door.

"Heel, boy." I didn't want him destroying evidence.

The wolfdog trotted a few steps away, turned, then crouched on his paws, watching me.

"How'd he get inside?" Ben scratched his cheek in annoyance.

"We left the door cracked, and he smelled something." I pointed to the floor space that had drawn Coop's attention. "Over there, I assume."

"That's our big lead?" Shelton gave the wolfdog a hard look. "This mutt could be tracking a bologna sandwich."

I shook my head. "Coop sent me his perception—it wasn't lunch meat. Coop thinks he smelled blood."

"Do what now?" Shelton took a step backward. "Did you say *blood*?"

"Yikes." Hi ran a hand through his hair. "This just got serious."

"Agreed." I slipped my pack from my shoulders, thankful I'd thought to bring my evidence kit. "First, we turn this room upside down."

As I knelt to lay out supplies, Ben began a careful circuit of the basement, golden irises blazing. After a moment's hesitation, Shelton joined him.

I tried to hide my nerves, but was scared of what we might find.

Cooper's nose had been sure.

Still nothing to worry about, Detective Hawfield?

"Whatcha thinking?" Hi squatted down beside me, wearing an eager look. He loved experiments more than anyone, and had guessed my intentions.

"I'm gonna spray this area with Luminol."

"Luminol? How'd you get that? Sounds expensive."

"Not if you make your own."

"Make your own?" Hi shifted to get a look at my face. "Victoria Grace, have you been holding out on me?"

"Sorry." I shoved aside my fingerprint kit, sticky tape, digital camera, and box of plastic baggies. The brown cylinder of homemade Luminol was nestled in the bottom of my bag.

"Well, at least tell me how you did it," Hi insisted.

"You cut up vinyl gloves and boil the pieces with rubbing alcohol." I pulled out an empty spray bottle and poured in the cylinder's contents. "That process extracts a compound called diethylhexyl phthalate. Filter that solution, then boil it again with water and some drain cleaner. After a few more filtration hoops, you have pure phthalic anhydride."

Hi seemed to be memorizing my words. "And that's Luminol?"

I shook my head. "After that it gets . . . complicated. I'll forward you the link from ChemHacker. Promise."

"Yes, you will. I can't believe you did this without me."

"Sorry." I tested the spray bottle. "The chemical process has some dangerous byproducts, and the whole thing was pretty hard to pull off, even working at LIRI. My first attempt bombed."

"Kit lets you synthesize chemicals in his labs?"

"What my father doesn't know won't kill him."

Hi snorted, but let the matter drop. "So we spray this science project on the floor to detect . . . what, exactly?"

I cleared my throat. "Blood."

"Ugh." Hi paled. "That's what I thought."

"You think there's blood on the floor?" Shelton had spoken close to my ear, causing me to jump. "I don't see any."

Ben stood beside him. "Circuit complete. Nothing unusual." Pointing to the base of the doorframe. "That's where Coop was poking around. Did he find something?"

"I don't know yet." Curt. "I'm going to spray and see."

"See what?" Ben appeared unfazed by my frosty tone.

"Luminol exhibits chemiluminescence." *Grrr. I'm not talking to you!*

Shelton frowned. "Chemi-what-now?"

"Chemiluminescence." I inched closer to the door. "In other words, it glows when mixed with an oxidizing agent. Blood contains hemoglobin, which, in turn, contains trace amounts of iron. That's what causes the Luminol to react."

"Just watch where Tory sprays." Hi popped up and slapped the wall switch. The only remaining light beamed from ten glowing eyes. "If you see a blue glow, that's means blood."

"Thanks, Hi." Adjusting my weight, I leaned forward. "I'm going to saturate this whole area evenly. Any blood, and the glow should last about thirty seconds. Shelton, can you snap a few pics with my Nikon? Use a long-exposure setting."

"One sec." Shelton lifted the camera and popped off the lens cap. A few more fidgets, then, "All set."

Deep breath. "Here goes nothing."

I pumped the nozzle, applying the chemical evenly as I moved my arm in a slow arc.

The reaction stunned even me.

A strong glow sprang immediately to life—a thick blue patch that covered the door's bottom quarter and a three-foot semicircle on tiles beneath it.

I moved robotically, expanding the circle by pumping more spray. The only sound was the rapid-fire click of the Nikon. Shelton, frozen in place, simply held down the button.

So much blood.

Cool radiance oozed from the floor. As I continued spraying the perimeter, tiny arrows of illumination fired outward from the solid disk centered on the doorway.

When I'd finished, I stared at a glimmering blue sun, edged by broken streaks.

My mind practically gibbered in horror.

No one moved. The glow crested, then slowly faded from existence.

"So much blood," Hi whispered. The golden light vanished from his eyes.

Inside my head, a string abruptly severed.

SNUP.

Waves of dizziness crashed over me. I braced myself on the floor with both hands, waiting for the world to stop spinning. Slowly, it did.

Shelton began coughing so hard, I feared he'd vomit. Ben wrapped an arm around his shoulder and pounded Shelton's back. Both of their flares were gone.

"My flare shut down on its own again." Hi shivered as if spiders were crawling his back. "*Poof.* Gone." Shelton looked up, but could only nod. Ben glanced away.

"Same here." I pounded my leg in frustration. "What in the hell is going on?"

"Hit the lights," Ben ordered.

Hi scampered over and turned them on.

"My God," Shelton wheezed, eyes glued to the doorframe. "Nobody can lose that much blood and live!"

It was true. The blue circle had been massive, and dense throughout.

I tried not to imagine that much blood spilling across the floor. Could think of nothing else.

Lucy. Peter.

Sweet Jesus, what happened down here?

The analytical portion of my brain rebooted, came back on line. Made a connection.

Of course.

"Wait!" I hissed. "That's not blood!"

"Oh please please *please* tell me that's true!" Shelton was maniacally shirt-cleaning his glasses. "'Cause otherwise . . ."

"It *can't* be." I shoved my nose within an inch of the tiles. "There's no visible bloodstain here. That's impossible for such a huge reaction to Luminol."

"True." Hi cupped his chin. "And the edge of that circle seemed pretty regular, now that I think about."

I rifled through every fact I knew about Luminol.

An answer popped out at me.

"Bleach."

Hi looked at me sideways. "Huh?"

"Bleach reacts to Luminol just like blood." The pieces started falling into place. "Someone scrubbed this area with a bleach solution."

"So someone was cleaning up," Ben said. "But why bleach? And why use so much?"

"What were they cleaning?" Hi asked grimly.

I remembered the streaks at the perimeter of the glowing circle.

My eyes found Coop. I recalled the tangy, metallic odor he'd sent my way.

He'd been certain. Now I was, too.

My heart sank.

"I think something terrible *did* happen down here."

Ben grunted. "Explain."

"Remember the spatter along the rim of the circle? Those streaks reacted to the Luminol, too. And based on their form and shape, I doubt they were part of the cleaning process. I think the Luminol picked up two different substances."

"So there *was* blood," Hi said. "And bleach was used to clean it up?"

I nodded. "Someone spent a *lot* of time and energy cleaning that area. My guess is, they were concealing evidence."

"Of a violent crime," Shelton finished. "Oh Lord."

Hi gulped. "The Gable twins didn't run off, did they?"

I shook my head. "I think somebody snatched them. Or . . . worse."

I didn't want to finish that thought.

"What should we do?" Ben asked.

I considered our options. "We already took pictures. Now we treat this entire room like a crime scene. I'll dust the door for prints, while—"

A loud bang broke the stillness.

My head whipped to the windows facing the backyard.

I saw a dark form kneeling in the grass outside.

Watching.

"Whaaaa!" Shelton wailed.

Cooper lunged across the room, baying at the apparition.

Hi dove behind a couch. Ben pulled Shelton under the pool table.

I froze, staring at the shadowy figure.

The basement lights reflected off the glass, blurring the scene outside. Our observer was kneeling, stone still, ignoring Coop as he growled below the sill.

As I watched, the figure rose and vanished, a moment before Ben slapped off the lights.

Hiram's head popped from behind the couch. "Tory, what should we do?"

"That wasn't a cop!" Shelton shrieked. "Believe that!"

"Relax!" Ben moved to the bottom of the staircase and peered up. "It's probably a neighbor. They likely saw *Sewee* and came to—"

An ear-shattered wail sounded from upstairs. All five of us jumped.

"The alarm!" I shouted.

"Someone must've set it off!" Ben yelled. "From inside the kitchen, too!"

My eyes shot to the door so recently cleaned with meticulous care. "Out this way!"

I jammed everything into my bag and bolted for the door. Frazzled moments passed as I scrambled to throw the deadbolt. Finally, the way swung open.

Cool air flowed around me as I paused on the threshold, scanning the darkness for any sign we weren't alone. The blaring alarm rattled my concentration.

"Go left." Hi was crouching beside. "We have to get to the boat."

"Through the backyard?" Shelton hissed. "That's where the dude was!"

"Move!" Ben ordered from behind us. "I think someone's coming down the stairs!"

That clinched it. Time for a sprint.

But, turning to go, I noticed Coop stalking back toward the steps. Ears flat. Tail rigid.

I felt a rush of panic. "Coop, no! Here!"

Coop growled, his entire posture expressing reluctance.

I slapped my side. "Heel, boy! Now!"

With a last snarl at the staircase, Coop spun and bounded to my side.

"Go, go, go!" I pushed the boys ahead of me, one by one, then grabbed Coop's collar just to be safe. Together we raced into the night.

A dozen strides brought me to the corner of the house. The boys were halfway across the yard, sprinting toward the dock.

Porch lights flicked at houses adjoining the Gable property. Neighbors. Alerted by the commotion.

Coop needed no further prodding. Side by side, we pounded after the other Virals, shooting across the yard, down the dock, and aboard *Sewee*.

Hi and Shelton frantically untied the lines, then piled aboard.

Ben gunned the engine and threw it into reverse.

Sewee lurched from the pier, spun a tight 180, and then fired into the river, leaving behind nothing but choppy wake and a lightly rocking dock.

PART TWO

JINXED

CHAPTER 11

Wednesday

I rose early the next morning.

The moment my eyelids opened, there was no going back.

Last night's scare had soured my dreams.

So I sat on my bed, half asleep, examining the photocopied Man with Snake. I turned the page this way and that, hoping a change in orientation might trigger some insight. *Nada.*

On a whim I grabbed my laptop and tried a few Googles, but quickly gave it up.

Searching "Old Man + Snake + Toga" is not an exercise I recommend.

A glance at my clock. 6:07 a.m.

Gonna be a looong day.

My mind began to wander. For the umpteenth time, I wondered who'd seen us inside the Gable home. A concerned neighbor? A cop? For some reason, I didn't think it was either.

Why had the person crouched outside the basement window? Why set off the alarm?

The more I thought about it, the more uneasy I became.

How long had that stranger crouched there, in the dark, spying on us? I broke out in goose bumps, remembering the feel of those hidden eyes.

Once spotted, our watcher hadn't run. Hadn't immediately charged inside. Hadn't raised a shout. The figure had remained frozen in place, observing us for a few moments more. As if committing our faces to memory. I shivered at *that* thought.

We'd high-tailed it back to Morris Island, watching *Sewee*'s wake for any sign of pursuit. None had appeared. Back home, Coop and I had scurried into the townhouse. I'd spent the rest of evening pretending nothing was amiss.

But I couldn't stop thinking about the Gables' basement. The glowing circle of blue.

Blood on steel and tile, carefully and methodically cleaned.

We have *to do something.*

Lost in thought, I glanced at the page in my hands. Was startled by its clarity.

I could make out tiny wrinkles on the paper's surface. Microscopic creases, creating subtle variations in color and grain. The black ink practically leaped off the page, refining into a hundred variations of gray and assuming almost three-dimensional properties. Its acrid smell infested my nostrils.

A loud clicking made me jump. My eyes darted to the clock, where every shift of the second hand now reverberated like a snare drum.

I became aware of a raft of scents surrounding me. Shampoos and soaps wafting from my bathroom. Frying bacon drifting from downstairs. A half-gnawed bone Coop had deposited underneath my bed.

I sprang to my feet, unsure what was happening.

Too quick—I toppled over backward in a heap. Lay there panting.

"What the hell!?!"

Moving more carefully, I hurried to my bathroom. Knew what I'd find.

The mirror revealed a frazzled-looking redhead in light blue paja-mas, a distressed expression crimping her face. Impossibly, her eyes glowed with golden fire.

"Whoa whoa whoa!" I backed away, stunned.

I was flaring. But I hadn't reached for my powers. Hadn't invited the wolf to come out.

There'd been no *snap.* No grueling transition. No spikes of pleasure or pain.

My powers had simply switched themselves on.

I sat back down on my bed, mind racing. What did this mean? Had I lost control? The thought of my powers randomly coming and going, without warning, was beyond terrifying. I wouldn't avoid detection for a single day!

The flare came so easily this time.

The realization stopped me cold.

Usually, the transition all but floored me, testing my strength and endurance. And lately, that struggle had become more pronounced. I'd begun to worry my powers were getting too wild to trust. That remov-ing the leash was growing too dangerous to justify the benefits.

Yet *this* flare had bloomed without the slightest ripple of difficulty, unfolding so gently I'd fail to notice anything was happening. I had no idea what to make of that.

Was there a better way to flare? Had my unconscious mind found a solution?

Have I been doing it wrong, all along?

A prickling sensation crashed my train of thought.

I wasn't alone.

Close by, someone *else* was flaring, too.

I squeezed my eyes shut.

The flaming cords sprang to life—fiery ropes that connected my mind to those of my packmates. The lines thrummed wildly, illuminating then fading as they skittered across the black field of my unconscious mind. I could barely follow their frenetic movements. Had never seen them react like this.

One line in particular danced and twirled, glimmering with twice the radiance.

I sensed Coop, snoozing in his doggie bed downstairs. Calm. Unperturbed. But the wolfdog always seemed linked to our pack's shared head space. His presence was never fleeting, like that of a flaring Viral. Coop wasn't who I'd detected.

Concentrating, I *shifted* my perspective, attempting to impose my will on the links in the manner I'd tried the night before.

This time, the cords became tunnels with ease.

I didn't hesitate, firing my consciousness down the gleaming conduit.

A shock of cold. A blast of heat.

Suddenly, I was in another bedroom, staring at a computer through thick-lensed glasses. Dark-skinned fingers pounded a keyboard faster than I could follow.

Shelton?

My vision lurched as the typist shot to his feet, head swinging wildly.

"Who's there? Tory? Is that you? This ain't funny!"

I felt an unpleasant tearing sensation as my awareness slammed backward. *Outward.* Like a pilot's ejector seat. Untethered, my thoughts tumbled in a black haze.

I could hear Shelton shouting. Then, oddly, I sensed Hi's presence. Both boys seemed to be trying to communicate something, but my mind was wrapped in cobwebs. I floated farther and farther away.

An image appeared, small at first, but rapidly growing in size.

Cooper.

My pet. Charging toward me. Teeth bared. Tail low.

Not rest. Bad place.

Hey, Coop. Good boy.

The wolfdog drew close.

Drifting, listless, I reached out a hand.

Coop's teeth sank into my flesh.

An electric shock sizzled through my brain. My mind recoiled like a rubber band.

SNUP.

I awoke from the trance. Heard Coop whining and scratching at my bedroom door. I stumbled over and unlocked it. Coop bowled me to the floor, then planted his front paws on my chest and licked my face.

"Thanks, boy."

○   ○   ○

Sixty seconds later, I was bounding up Shelton's front steps.

He opened the door before I could knock, eyes wide behind his clunky black specs. Shelton slipped outside and followed me down to the common.

We huddled on the dew-covered grass, me in girly pastel PJs, him in yellow basketball shorts and a Green Lantern tee. The sun was just breaking the horizon, sending out tentacles of soft yellow-orange light.

"What's going on, Brennan?" Shelton grimaced like he'd eaten something rotten. "I just emptied my stomach into the porcelain god. Do I have you to thank?"

"I don't know. Probably." In a rush, I told him how my flare had sprung to life on its own, and about the harrowing out-of-body experience that followed. "I think something is seriously wrong with our powers," I finished.

Shelton looked everywhere but at me.

"The transition came easily." I tilted my head, trying to catch his eye. "I could reach you with no trouble. Which means *you* must've been flaring, too. Right?"

Shelton bobbed a guilty nod. "I was feeling run-down this morning. Tired. Bad headache. But lately, if I flare for a few minutes, whatever's bothering me seems to fade away."

I was about to scold him—couldn't Shelton understand how *dangerous* that sounded?—but managed to hold my tongue. At that moment, I was in no position to criticize.

But using our powers as some kind of magical cure-all? A way to sidestep the daily grind? My instincts screamed in warning. Nothing is ever free.

Every shortcut has a price. Every action, a consequence.

I was about to say as much when a door opened a few units down from where we stood.

Hi emerged, spotted us, and hurried over. He also wore sleeping attire—black pajamas adorned with the crest of House Stark. *Where does he get this stuff?*

"Where'd you get those?" Shelton asked, but in a reverent tone.

"The Internet." Hi popped his shirt, then made hand explosions. "Serious business, Devers. They've got House Lannister, too, if you prefer reppin' the baddies."

"Why are *you* up?" I asked.

"Good morning to you, too," Hi answered primly. "I saw you guys from my window, thought I'd mosey on out, and inquire into what just happened to my brain."

"What do you mean?" Though I knew the answer.

"Well, I was minding my own business, enjoying some pre-breakfast toilet time, when I felt eyes on my back." Hi frowned. "No, not my back. More like, *inside my skull.* Not a great feeling while manning the throne, I assure you. Then you and that mutt hijacked my thoughts and started dancing Gangnam Style on my cerebral cortex. Next thing I know, Shelton's inside my head, yelling, Coop's howling like a rabid monkey, and then something red-hot came and scrambled my brain completely. When I snapped out of it, I was lying facedown on my bathroom floor, which isn't nearly as cool as Taylor Swift would have you believe. Oh, and I was suddenly flaring, FYI."

"Oh, man." Shelton reached for his earlobe. "That's not good."

Hi snorted. "No, Shelton, it isn't. So, would either of you mentalists care to shed some light on these events?"

Glumly, Shelton and I filled Hi in.

Color drained from Hi's face. "If we can't control when our powers come and go, we're screwed with a capital S. Hell, in *all* caps."

My eyes strayed to the last unit in the row. It occurred to me that I hadn't felt anything from Ben during the flare incident.

"Is Ben here?" I asked quietly.

"No," Shelton answered. "I texted him last night. He's at his mom's this week."

"We need to know if he felt what happened." My tone made it clear that *I* wasn't going to ask. "Are his flares getting screwy at all? Have any sparked uncalled? Find out."

"Yeah." Hi's gaze flicked to Shelton.

"Um." Shelton looked at his shoes. "About that."

"What?" I knew I wouldn't like what was coming.

Hi cleared his throat, then looked me square in the eye. "We told you Ben's been flaring a lot, but it's worse than that. He's like a bonfire, all the livelong day."

"Almost every time I see him," Shelton confirmed.

Worse than I thought.

"Tell me everything."

"You're not gonna be happy," Hi warned. "Don't kill the messenger."

"Or his good-looking buddy," Shelton added.

I motioned impatiently for Hi to continue.

"Last week, Ben and I went to Captain's Comics over in West Ashley. So there I am, browsing back issues of *The Walking Dead,* having a grand old time. I look up, and *boom*. Ben's rockin' his stupid shades inside the store, burning like a Roman candle. My skin got tingly ten feet away. When I discreetly flipped out on him, he just chuckled, and kept strolling around. There must've been a dozen other people there."

Stunned, I turned to Shelton.

"Pretty much the same." He took a deep breath. "On Saturday Ben and I drove to Johns Island to see *Skyfall*."

"You did?" Hi said sharply. "Thanks for the invite, jerks."

Shelton raised his palms. "You were at temple. We're supposed to just wait around? Plus, you've seen that movie like five times."

"You still could've *asked*," Hi grumbled. "I don't—"

"Guys!" I clapped my hands once. "The story, please."

"An hour in, I go for a popcorn refill." Shelton shuddered. "When I get back, Ben's sitting in the dark, flaring away, and he's not even wearing his sunglasses! I almost wet myself. He said he wanted to watch the movie in Viral HD. Man, I don't remember a single minute from the rest of the film."

"In a theater!?" My temper exploded. "That stupid mother—"

"Hiram!"

Our heads whipped. Ruth Stolowitski was standing on her front stoop.

"Get back in here this instant! You're not dressed."

Ruth wore a fuzzy pink bathrobe, her free hand vising the garment closed. Her eyes darted, as if worried that cagey perverts were surveilling our remote island, waiting for just this opportunity to get an eyeful.

Hi covered his face. "Kill me now."

"We'll talk more later," I whispered. "But no flaring until we figure things out."

Hi nodded, already hurrying back to his stoop.

Shelton hesitated, watching me nervously. "What are you going to do?"

I inhaled deeply. Exhaled. Tried to keep my anger in check.

"Our top priority is hacking Karsten's flash drive," I said. "We have to access those files somehow. But we can't forget about the Gable twins either. Not after what we found. Seems like our only move *there* is to identify the playing card. Let's give that a shot before going to the police."

Shelton looked at me funny. "I meant, what are you going to do about *Ben*."

My mouth formed a hard line. "I plan on having a chat with him. Soon."

Shelton massaged his forehead. "That oughta go well."

I nodded, ignoring his sarcasm. For an instant, I let my fury boil.

I'm gonna rip you a new one, Blue. Count on that.

CHAPTER 12

Five hours later, the bell rang for lunch.

"Thank God." Shoving textbooks into my bag, I trudged for the classroom door.

Shelton and Hi waited in the hallway.

"Need to hit your locker?" Hi asked, straightening his inside-out blazer.

I peered down the hall. Saw Jason Taylor lingering.

Pivoting, I herded the boys in the opposite direction. "I think I'll buy my lunch today."

Running on fumes, I was too brain-dead for banter. Couldn't handle a flirty chat to nowhere. *No offense, Jase.*

"*O-kay.*" Shelton hitched his pack onto his shoulders. "The long way it is."

"So many gentleman admirers," Hi mused. "Must be tough, being a heartbreaker."

"Zip it. Unless you wanna see a leg-breaker, too."

Hi shook his head. "And such violent thoughts. I blame Bravo."

We worked our way around the building, eventually reached the cafeteria's side entrance. Lunch-less, I grabbed a tray and joined the line. Sloppy joe day. Hooray.

Someone poked me between the shoulder blades.

"Sellout!"

I spun, slightly panicked. Ella was standing behind me, a sly grin on her face.

"I thought you were above common cafeteria grub." Twirling, Ella flashed a dimpled smile at the two boys in line behind me. "Okay if I cut? I need to catch up with my friend."

Both stammered their permission. Ella nodded thanks, snagging a tray.

I wish I could do that. Wait, do I?

"So?" Ella asked. "Was it a sloppy joe that called to you, or the microwave pizza?"

"My delicious chicken caesar wrap is currently trapped inside my locker." A slight hesitation, then I leaned closer. "Jason was practically standing guard, and I didn't want to deal."

Ella's mouth puckered. "You're dumb, Brennan. Jason Taylor is hot, cool, and totes into you. Stop being a diva."

I gave a very un-diva-like snort. "Yeah, that's me. A Real Housewife of Charleston."

"I'm serious, missy. Ask me, you could use a little Taylor-touching time." Ella winked one gorgeous green eye. "Might ease the tension in your shoulders."

My ears burned, but I forced a laugh. Ella was only teasing.

And the truth was, I *loved* gabbing like this. Ella was the first real girlfriend I'd had in ... ages? Ever? I hadn't realized how much I wanted one until she came along.

Don't get me wrong, the Virals were great. Nothing meant more to me than my pack.

But the boys were always . . . well . . . *boys*. There were only so many *Battlestar Galactica* episode debates one girl could take. I'd seen *Varsity Blues* like twelve times.

Reaching the buffet, I surveyed a grim array of greasy offerings. Elected for an all-vegetable plate. The meaty-armed cafeteria lady who served me seemed to take personal offense at my choice. Oh well.

"See you in class!" Ella called as I headed for the register line.

I took another step, then stopped. "Come eat with me."

Ella adopted a mock-serious tone. "Will your bodyguards consent?"

I giggled. "If Shelton and Hi are my muscle, I don't like my chances. And yes."

Ella received her bacon cheeseburger—because, of course, she could eat anything—and the two of us paid. Then we crossed to the Virals table in the back corner of the cafeteria.

Shelton's eyes widened as we approached.

"So I'm not using anything but two-ply from now on," Hi was saying. "Otherwise, the stuff just shreds—"

Noting Shelton's expression, he abruptly cut off. Turned. Went beet red.

"Hey." Sitting down as if nothing was unusual. "You know Ella. Okay if she joins us?"

"Okay if she joins us?" Shelton repeated. "I mean, yes. Join us. Okay."

"I was talking about art supplies," Hi blurted. "I'm into papier-mâché."

"Thanks, guys," Ella said as she sat. "I be *starving*." She dove into her cheeseburger.

Shelton stared, as if he'd never seen someone eat before. Hi nervously fixed his tie.

I suppressed a snicker, but filed away several choice quips for the next time we were alone. I didn't want to embarrass them now. I understood Ella's effect on the opposite gender.

But later. Whoa boy, there'll be some fun later.

"When are you coming back to practice?" Ella asked between massive bites of her burger. "Coach Lynch understands, but he's getting frustrated at not having his starters together."

"Hopefully next week," I replied, munching a baby carrot.

Honestly, I had no idea. Recent events had pushed my burgeoning athletic career from the back burner to somewhere off the stove completely. But I didn't want to tell Ella that.

"Sports are good," Hi said. "To play, I mean."

Ella paused, mid-bite.

"How's the season going for you?" Hi followed up quickly. "Winning things?"

I winced. *Stop talking, Hi.*

"We haven't started playing games yet," Ella answered patiently. "I think we have enough talent to make the playoffs, if no one gets hurt." She aimed a finger at me. "And if our best players show up."

"I see." Hi nodded sagely. "Make the playoffs. Is that, like, a process?"

Ella eyed him strangely. "Yes, Hiram. Whether we make the playoffs is determined by our number of wins and losses."

"Ah." Another nod. "That seems fair. Good stuff." Hi abruptly busied himself with his sandwich.

Ella flashed me a confused look. Rolling my eyes, I waved off her question.

I'd long since given up trying to explain Hiram Stolowitski.

"You plan on avoiding Jason forever?" Ella spoke through another mouthful of burger. "That doesn't seem like a workable solution."

"No." Idly twirling my fork. "But I don't know how to let him down easy. This isn't an area of personal expertise."

"Direct is always better," Ella said confidently. "Like pulling a Band-Aid. Otherwise feelings get hurt. Then, suddenly, you're not even friends."

"I know you're right. I'm just a wuss. I'm not used to being pursued."

"Please. You could have your pick of these silly little boys. Heck, take two."

Shelton coughed into his fist, eyes glued to his hoagie. I didn't have to be psychic to sense how uncomfortable the girl-talk made him.

Get over it. I listened to you two doofuses handicap a wresting match between Kate Upton and Maria Sharapova. For once, lunch conversation will be my choice.

Ella and I chatted for the next few minutes. I cleaned my plate, surprised by the tastiness of the veggies. Score one for Mrs. Meaty Arms.

The boys ate in silence, though I knew they were listening to every word.

Ella finished her burger and dug into a side of fries. Hi watched, enraptured.

She couldn't help but notice. "Would you like one?"

"What? Sure." Hi smiled, made no move.

After a moment, Ella nudged the bowl his way. "Careful, they're still hot."

"Oh, no problem." Hi fumbled for a fry. "I like food that's hot."

I caught Shelton slowly shaking his head.

"Oh, shoot!" Ella winced. "I forgot to stop by the office. My mother had to drop off my shin guards." She slid her fries over to Hi. "Enjoy. They're hot, which you apparently like."

"Got that right. Hot hot hot!" Hi awkwardly shoved another fry into his mouth.

"Okay, wow." Ella gathered her things, then brushed my cheek with a kiss. "Later, Tor." Shouldering her bag, she hurried from the cafeteria.

A loud thunk drew my attention back to the table.

Hi's forehead was resting on his tray. "Tell me that wasn't as bad as I think."

"Worse," Shelton said. "So, so much worse."

The head rose, then thunked back down. "I don't remember parts. I think I lost time."

I patted his shoulder. "That's probably for the best."

"Such." *Thunk.* "A." *Thunk.* "Dumbass." *Thunk.*

Shelton laughed nervously. "See? That's why I don't talk."

Hi's face shot up. "Tell her I have brain seizures. A serious medical condition. Or that I have an evil twin who sometimes takes my place, but can't talk for crap."

"Got it," I promised. His head dropped once more.

Shelton changed the subject. "So what's our next move?"

I thought a moment. *So many balls in the air.*

Chance. Karsten. Ben. But I had no ideas for any of them.

Those people aren't in danger. The twins surely are.

"We check out Old Man Serpent," I said. "Let's find out who he is, and why his card was on Lucy Gable's bed."

Hi lifted his head halfway. Squinted at me. Nodded.

"Okay." Shelton stroked his chin in thought. "How?"

"A quick fact-finding trip." I downed the last of my Diet Coke.

"And I *think* I know just the place."

CHAPTER 13

I skidded to a stop beside a weathered purple rowhouse.

The boys were a few seconds behind, Hi on his skinny Schwinn ten-speed and Shelton pedaling a mud-covered black BMX. Dismounting, I walked my Trek across the gravel lot to a rusty rack at the side of the building.

Bike secured, I checked the rainbow-colored sign hanging out over Center Street.

Fairy Dust Bookstore and Gifts. This was the place.

Folly Beach is the closest population center to Morris Island. The only community on Folly Island, the sleepy little hamlet has a two-street downtown made up of surf shops, boutiques, restaurants, and bars. Monopoly-like houses line the remainder of the island, a haven for laid-back vacationers seeking cheap vacation rentals and peace and quiet. The atmosphere is very chill—nobody moves too fast in Folly Beach.

The Morris bridge connects to Folly, whose police department has nominal jurisdiction over our remote neighborhood. Not that those bozos ever cross to our side. They prefer we look after ourselves.

But we Morris Islanders venture over quite a bit. Folly Beach has the closest grocery store, post office, and takeout pizza. But in all my trips, I'd never stepped inside Fairy Dust.

I'd persuaded Shelton and Hi that a visit there might do some good. Truthfully, I didn't really know. Returning home, we'd ditched our uniforms and biked over, the ride taking less than twenty minutes.

The store's front door was painted red and had a tarnished brass knob. The posted hours were Monday–Thursday, from noon to four, which gave me an idea about the owner. Not exactly a breakneck schedule.

Hi scanned white lettering stenciled on the shop window. "Tarot readings? Belly dancing instruction? Why Tory, it's not even my birthday!"

"Paganism 101." Shelton was frowning at a list of classes taped to the door. "Chakra Balancing. Reiki. Spiritual Counseling. What the hell kinda bookstore is this?"

"New Age." I pulled out my iPhone and read the store's online description. "Fairy Dust is a metaphysical ritual supply store for both pagans and non-pagans alike."

"Pagans?" Shelton tugged his earlobe. "You're talking about witch-craft. Do not like."

"Relax," Hi said. "These are the granola kind of witches. The ones that make herbal tea, and smoke clove cigarettes. I bet we find some killer crystals in there."

"It's a Wicca store," I said, "but the website claims they also have an astrology section. Those are my best guesses for ID-ing our toga-wearing pal. You got a better idea?"

Shelton shook his head. "Spells, though? Dancing in the woods at midnight? Creepy."

"Quit whining, wuss." Hi pointed. "This place *can't* be dangerous. They take Visa."

"Only one way to find out." I pulled open the door and stepped inside.

The tinkle of wind chimes announced our entry. The shop was long and narrow, with wooden shelves lining both walls. Every inch was packed with mysterious items. Books filled the left side of the store, grouped by subject matter—moon phases, dream studies, botany and horticulture, Druidism, the Sacred Wheel. Some designations, like Gaelic Polytheistic Tribalism, I couldn't even follow.

The opposite wall was like a hippie version of Bath and Body Works. Candles. Oils. Incense. Spiritual washes and cleansing waters. Even bags of feathers. Deeper into the store was an eclectic selection of items. An assortment of small cauldrons. Mortar-and-pestle sets. Hundreds of different crystals. Dried herbs. Crushed minerals. Tarot cards. Ouija boards. Rune stones. Hundreds of other things I couldn't peg. The place was certainly interesting.

Astrological items were in back, beside a circular wooden table covered in red felt and flanked by matching chairs. Beyond, a black curtain blocked off the rear of the building.

"This place is a tourist trap," Hi said. "You can get most of this stuff at an Indian casino."

"It still gives me the willies." Shelton tapped a cloth package hanging from an iron hook. "I've never heard of Bat's Heart Root, but I don't want it near me."

I was admiring a crushed-velvet star chart when the curtain parted. A young, brown-haired woman emerged. She had gray eyes, a small mouth, and wore an old-fashioned green dress that fell past her knees. She considered us a moment before approaching.

"You three looking for something specific?" Her voice was surprisingly melodious.

"Any sacrificial knives?" Hi raised an index finger. "Nothing too fancy, and I'll need a solid, no-slip grip. Me and the coven have some goats lined up for Saturday's bonfire."

I could've kicked him. I think I tried. Fortunately, the woman laughed.

"A comedian, eh?" she said dryly. "I *do* have some new knife-ware, actually, but for chopping herbs, not blood sacrifice. That's one of the many myths about witches that simply isn't truth. Wiccans respect the sanctity of *all* life. Animals are part of the same natural cycle as humans. I won't even eat one. My name is Clara. How about telling me what it is you're looking for?"

I slipped the photocopy from my pocket and handed it over. "We'd like to learn about this symbol."

Clara glanced at the page. Her eyes widened slightly. Then she looked up, subjecting the three of us to an entirely new level of scrutiny.

"You recognize the figure." I didn't phrase it as a question.

"Of course." Clara's free hand rose, fluttered aimlessly, as if she was unsure what to say next. For some reason, I thought she might ask us to leave.

I broke out my "earnest" face. "Any guidance you could provide would be greatly appreciated."

"Yes. Certainly." Clara gave her head a slight shake. "Please, sit. I'll grab more chairs."

She slipped behind the curtain and was gone.

"She got weird," Hi whispered. "But looking at this shop, that's not much of a shocker."

I nodded. Something about Snake Man had set Clara on edge.

"Of course she's being crazy—she's a witch, man!" Shelton face was pinched. "We need to get *gone,* before she comes back with her broom."

Fabric swished. Clara emerged carrying a pair of folding chairs.

"May I ask your names?"

We each took a seat as Clara placed the photocopy on the felt.

"Tory Brennan. These two are Hi and Shelton."

Clara nodded with each name. "This isn't a tarot reading, or a fortune-telling session, but I think that, under the circumstances, the same rates will apply. Forty dollars, please."

"*Forty doll—*"

I kicked Hi under the table. "No problem."

I nodded to Shelton. Grumbling, he dug out his wallet and forked over two twenties. Virals funds. We let Shelton be the bank.

"Excellent." The bills disappeared into the folds of Clara's dress. "So. What would you like to know?"

My finger tapped the paper. "Who is this guy?"

"That is Ophiuchus, thirteenth symbol of the zodiac."

"Hold up, lady." Hi gave her a sideways look. "As a proud Aries, I know there are only twelve zodiac signs."

"Incorrect," Clara replied, with some amusement. "And, FYI, you're likely *not* an Aries, though it's understandable how you've gotten it wrong your whole life. Most people have."

Hi sat up straight. "Excuse me?"

Clara adopted a lecturing tone. "Ophiuchus is one of thirteen con-stellations that cross the ecliptic at the celestial equator and, therefore, has been called the thirteenth sign of the zodiac." She cocked her head slightly. "That's not *quite* right, as it confuses signs with constellations, but it's basically accurate."

I scratched the back of my head. "I'm not following."

"Let's start with the basics," Clara said. "The *ecliptic* is an imaginary line that marks the path of our sun through the sky. It's mathematically predictable, in relation to the earth's orbit."

"Okay." I understood that.

"Now, imagine every star in the heavens as part of a great dome sur-rounding our planet. That's known as the celestial sphere. As the sun travels through our sky, astrologers pay attention to where it is in rela-tion to the sphere. Specifically, they mark which constellations the sun passes directly through."

"You lost me," Shelton admitted.

Clara thought a moment. "Close your eyes. All of you."

After a few skeptical looks, we complied.

"Imagine you're riding a carousel. On horses, you swing in circles around the ride's central pillar. Watch the pillar a moment, then look *past* it, focusing on what appears behind it as you spin. A roller coaster. A ticket booth. A cotton candy stand. As you rotate, the scene changes until you complete the circuit and begin again. Now, replace the horses with planet Earth, the pillar with our sun, and the amusement park with the stars."

"I *think* I get it." Hi opened his eyes. "Because our planet is always spinning around the sun, the stars we see behind it change, depending on where we are in the Earth's orbit."

"Perfectly said." Clara spread her hands. "And that's how the zodiac constellations were determined."

"How did they pick?" Shelton asked. "Aren't there lots of constellations?"

"But only a handful through which the sun *directly* passes," she explained. "Twelve were selected as the tropical zodiac, which is the version most people are familiar with."

"You said people confuse signs with constellations," I stated. "What did you mean?"

"The current zodiac *signs* are a mathematically equal, twelve-way division of the ecliptic, aligned with the seasons. The dates for each have been set in stone. The *constellations*, however, are unequal in size, and based on the actual positions of the stars. They generally don't coincide with their signs anymore. For example, the constellation of Aquarius now largely corresponds to the sign of Pisces. This is because the time of year when the sun passes through Aquarius has slowly changed over the centuries, from when the ancient Greeks and Babylonians originally developed the zodiac. But the *sign* Aquarius has remained fixed to certain dates."

Shelton glanced at me askance. I didn't get it either.

Clara smiled. "Simply put, the dates for zodiac signs are no longer properly aligned with their constellations. The *whole* system is off-kilter."

Hi was wide-eyed. "Lady, you just blew my mind. You're saying I might *not* be an Aries? What? My birthday is this weekend! I've got all this ram crap at my house. My planet is Mars. My element is fire. It all fits!"

"Sorry, kid." Her eyes flicked to a giant star chart on the wall. "Next week, you said? Turns out you're really a Pisces."

"Pisces!?" Hiram's hands flew up. "A damn fish? No freaking way!"

"Tell me about the snake man." I wanted to get the meeting back on track.

"Ophiuchus is a sad story," Clara replied. "He was omitted from the tropical zodiac centuries ago, but remains in the heavens, and continues to hold sway. He occupies most of the days currently assigned to Sagittarius."

"Hold up." Shelton stared at Clara over the rim of his glasses. "*I'm* a Sagittarius."

"Birthdate?"

"November thirtieth."

Clara chuckled. "My dear boy, *you* are an Ophiuchan!"

"Am *not*," Shelton shot back, hugging his sides. "I *hate* snakes. Ask anyone."

"Sorry, dear. But the sun rises in Ophiuchus from November twenty-ninth to December seventeenth."

"That's one opinion." Shelton snatched off his glasses and wiped them on his shirt. "I'm gonna need a discount double-check on this stuff."

I waved for Clara's attention. "Ophiuchus?"

She turned to me. "The classical form of Ophiuchus is described by Manilius in his poem *Astronomica*: 'He holds apart the serpent, which with its mighty spirals and twisted body encircles his own, so that he may untie its knots and back that winds in loops. But, bending its supple neck, the serpent looks back and returns: and the other's hands slide over the loosened coils.' Their struggle will last forever, since man and serpent have equal power."

"Wait." Hi finger-jabbed the table. "Just stop. Before I accept that my entire life has been a lie, explain to me *exactly* how I'm not a freaking Aries."

Clara folded her hands on the table. "Slight changes in the Earth's wobbly orbit, over millennia, mean that our planet is no longer aligned to the stars in the same position as when the zodiac table was first conceived. In some cases the dates are nearly a month off, and that's not including those poor souls like Shelton, whose sign is rightly Ophiuchus, the thirteen symbol."

"Allegedly," Shelton snapped.

"Does Obama know about this?" Hi demanded, hands gripping his head. "How could this be true and *everyone* not know it? Am I speaking with a crazy woman?"

"This isn't groundbreaking," Clara replied. "It's two-thousand-year-old information to astronomers, and one of the reasons they mock astrology. But the ancient tropical zodiac has never been changed. People have grown attached to their incorrect signs."

"Not incorrect!" Hi insisted. "I'm an Aries. Everything about me *screams* Aries. I like diamonds. I live for the thrill of the moment. I'm adventurous, active, and outgoing. *It all fits.*"

"No need to get worked up." Clara reached under the table, retrieved a handout, and slid it over to Hi. "Take this, if you'd like to learn more. The zodiac's configuration has always been *somewhat* arbitrary. Constellations have shifted many times over the centuries, as has the sun's path through them, allowing for a wider range of signs than just twelve, or even thirteen. Ophiuchus was only excluded to begin with because the ancient Babylonians liked the symmetry of twelve astrological signs."

Hi looked to me, then Shelton. "I do *not* like this. My sign is *my sign.* It's not variable!"

"You're not the one stuck with the snake dude," Shelton groaned.

"Tell us more about Ophiuchus himself," I asked. "Specifically."

Clara glanced at the ceiling in thought. "The 'Serpent Bearer' appears in forms of sidereal astrology, which calculates the zodiac by using fixed stars instead of the celestial equator, showing the sun's true position against the constellations. This is very popular in Japan, where Ophiuchus is known as Hebitsukai-Za."

"Oh, snap!" Shelton sat forward. "I've heard of this dude. He's in Final Fantasy Legend!"

Blank stares from me and Clara.

"A video game series," Shelton explained. "From Japan. Hi knows. It's big."

Hi waved away Shelton's comment. "This whole meeting is under protest."

"However," Clara continued, "even mainstream sidereal astrology—which includes Hindu and sun-sign astrology—still use the traditional twelve-sign zodiac. Correctly realigned, of course, but dividing the heavens into twelve equal parts, rather than using constellational boundaries. Therefore, even those systems do not regard Ophiuchus as a true sign. But the sun rises in him every winter. That's a fact."

"If Ophiuchus *was* a thirteenth sign," I asked, "what would the associated characteristics be? What would it mean to have him as your zodiac symbol?"

Shelton huffed loudly, but I could tell he was paying attention.

"That's harder to answer. The Serpent Bearer has been excluded for millennia, and isn't regularly interpreted." She tapped her lip in thought. "Also known as Serpentarius, Ophiuchus has an affinity with snakes, obviously, and is said to offer protection from poisons. He's been associated with doctors and healers, likely because of the similarity between poison and medicine."

"Don't like snakes," Shelton grumbled. "Though Serpentarius sounds kind of awesome."

Clara flared a brow. "An Ophiuchan seeks wisdom and knowledge, has a flamboyant fashion sense, and usually doesn't reject authority. Twelve is the lucky number. They make great architects, have large families, and leave home at an early age. That's about all I can tell you."

I thought about everything Clara had said.

Interesting, all of it, but not helpful.

The info told me nothing about the Gables' disappearance.

"What type of person would be drawn to Ophiuchus?" I asked. "Who would the Serpent Bearer appeal to?"

"A poisoner, obviously." Clara stood, face troubled. "Beyond that, I can't say. And your time is now up. Please excuse me."

And like that, she spun and dipped through the black curtain.

"Um, bye." I was stunned by the woman's hasty retreat. "Thank you!"

"Stranger and stranger." Shelton popped from his seat. "That's all for me, folks. I'm out."

"I don't wanna be a stupid fish," Hi whined, trudging to the door behind Shelton.

I followed the boys outside, trying to digest what we'd learned.

A lost astrological sign? Snakes? A poisoner? How did any of it fit?

Maybe the zodiac has nothing to do with the twins at all.

But why had Clara reacted so strangely? Twice. I felt sure there were pieces missing here.

My thoughts were interrupted by the screech of tires on gravel.

I whirled. Ben's beat-up Explorer was idling ten feet behind me.

He leaned out the window. "You clowns need a lift?"

"No." I turned furious eyes on Shelton and Hi.

Shelton cracked first. "I told him. He's still a part of this, too, right?"

Before I could answer, Ben cut me off.

"Don't flip out, Victoria." He wore a satisfied smile. "I have news."

My hands found my hips. "Well?"

"Still wanna hack into Karsten's flash drive?" Ben asked innocently.

"Of course."

"Good. Because I can make it happen."

CHAPTER 14

Clara Gordon watched the kids load bicycles into an SUV.

They drove off. She exhaled, stepping away from the window.

Who'd have thought? *Exactly* as described. And so soon!

Clara rubbed her arms to quiet a rash of goose bumps. The whole business had her on edge.

A reading. Before I do anything.

Clara strode to a mahogany cabinet. Closing her eyes, she mumbled an incantation under her breath. Then she unlocked the door, removed a cloth-wrapped bundle, and returned to the table where she'd spoken to her vistors.

I shouldn't have done that. I may have said too much.

Clara unwound the sky-blue velvet, revealing a worn set of tarot cards. Hand-painted. French. Seventeenth century. A gift from her mentor only days before passing, Clara considered them her most precious possession in the world.

Clara shuffled the cards slowly, emptying her mind of distraction.

It'd been weeks since she'd done a personal reading.

Why? She carefully cut the deck, then placed the stacked cards on the red felt surface. *Am I hiding something from myself?*

Deep breath. Deep breath. Give thanks.

She allowed a question to crystalize in her mind. Clear. Concise. Simple.

Then, grounded and centered, she fanned out the cards. Flipped one at random.

The Tower.

Clara felt a chill travel her spine. A card of the Major Arcana, the Tower meant disaster. Upheaval. The destruction of peace and harmony.

Easy, now. Not always.

The symbol could also represent sudden change. Or revelation. The Tower energy was both a destructive *and* creative force.

Old attitudes and beliefs, perhaps? Something that must be let go, liked or not?

Troubled, Clara flipped a second card.

Justice. Reversed.

Clara's alarm grew. A second card of the Major Arcana. A rare occurrence.

This reading spoke of more than a mere day-to-day experience. That much was clear.

The cards foretold a life-changing event, with long-term influences.

Focus. The lesson here is important.

The inversion altered the card's meaning. Upside down, Justice stood for unfairness. Dishonesty. Lack of accountability. *To myself, or others?*

Clara thought furiously. Had she'd failed to scrutinize her own actions? Was she trying to dodge a bullet, or blame another for her mistake?

The key is to take responsibility. But how?

She thought of the two cards in conjunction. The Tower. Justice, reversed.

Disaster and Dishonesty. Upheaval and Unfairness.

The answer she'd sought abruptly smacked her in the face.

Those kids. The charge. Of course.

Clara nearly ended the reading right there, but some instinct compelled her to continue. Hands shaking, she flipped the last card in the deck.

And flinched. The chill on her spine morphed to an electric shock.

A *third* card of the Major Arcana. In ten years of readings, that had never happened.

The image grinned up at her. An armored skeleton, mounted on a white horse.

Death.

Clara moaned softly, though she knew the card wasn't literal. Death merely indicated that a significant transformation awaited. Change. Transition.

The end of something. But what will replace it?

Clara stared at the three cards. Tower. Justice. Death. She'd not flip a fourth.

Something profound was happening. Something that could go terribly wrong.

Disaster. Deceit. Change.

The message is clear. Do as instructed.

Clara gathered the cards and returned them to the cabinet. Grabbing her keys, she locked the shop and hurried to her car.

Do as instructed.

Three cards. All Major Arcana. Each fraught with danger.

She fired the engine, then spun from the parking lot, heading north.

Clara Gordon raced downtown like a bat out of hell.

CHAPTER 15

"Tory, you're a Capricorn now, so you'll have to accept an affinity for goats."

"Thanks, Hi. I think I'll be fine."

In the rearview, I saw Hi shake his head. "You're just being stubborn, like the Aquarius you *used* to be. But your days as a water bearer are over. It's time to accept and move on."

"I can't believe you follow that garbage." Ben turned onto the James Island Expressway. From there we'd link up with 17 North, cross the peninsula, and then traverse the massive Arthur Ravenel Jr. Bridge to Mount Pleasant.

"This affects you, too, pal." Hi snapped his fingers. "Like that, you've jumped from Capricorn to Sagittarius. Which suits you well, since you're both cocky *and* reckless. Plus, you look like a centaur."

"See this?" Ben glanced at the mirror and pointed to his chin. "This is my 'couldn't care less' face."

"Philistine." Hi turned to Shelton, with whom he shared the back-seat. "Tell me you've debunked this outrage by now."

"Unfortunately, the witch is right." Shelton glowered at his iPhone.

"About all of it, even Sir Snake Sleeves. But nobody seems to care. The first article I found is from 2010."

"No one cares because it's *astrology*." Ben rolled his eyes. "The whole concept is dumb, so who cares if it's accurate?"

"All *we* should care about," I cut in, "is whether Ophiuchus has anything to do with the Gable twins' disappearance. Whether that card is a clue, or not."

Shelton scratched his cheek. "I'm not saying I know her well, but radical astrology? Doesn't seem like something Lucy Gable would be into. Or Peter."

"Agreed." Still shunning Ben, I aimed my words at Hi and Shelton. "So the question becomes, did someone intentionally leave that card in Lucy's room? And if so, why?"

No one had an answer. We drove the next few miles in silence.

Hi broke it as we entered Mount Pleasant. "What's this guy's name again?"

"Eddie Chang," Ben replied. "I heard about him at Wando. He used to go there, and apparently he now makes fake IDs, rips movies and music, that kind of stuff. This dude I know says Chang is a serious hacker, too. Maybe even a member of Anonymous."

"So we don't really know anything about him," I said. To the windshield.

Ben's expression hardened. "You said we needed to hack the drive. I found a hacker."

I didn't respond, but mentally conceded the point. It's not like I had a better plan.

Ben turned into the parking lot of a run-down apartment building, one of a handful in the otherwise wealthy community. The brick-and-concrete box rose ten depressing stories, bristling with rusty metal balconies.

I knew Ben's mother rented an apartment somewhere close by. Was it like this building? Suddenly, I couldn't believe I'd never seen the place where Ben spent half the life.

"This is it." Ben killed the engine.

"You been here before?" Shelton asked, nervously eyeing the complex.

Ben shook his head. "My friend Ronnie has. He bought a killer fake from Chang."

He got out and slammed his door. Without other options, we hurried after him, across the cracked and crumbling blacktop to a glass-enclosed entry a dozen yards away.

We slipped through a pair of blurry glass doors into a small foyer. A second Plexiglas-and-steel barrier barred further access. A dingy call box was bolted to the wall beside it. Above the box, a metal-encased security camera glared down at us.

"Jeez," Hi muttered. "This feels like a gas station in Compton."

Ben pulled a scrap of paper from his pocket, read, then punched a four-digit code into the call box. It began to ring. At the same time, a red light appeared on the side of the camera.

A click. Static.

"Yeah?"

Ben cleared his throat. "I'm here to see Eddie Chang."

"Wrong number." There was a second click as the line disconnected.

Shelton shifted his weight. "Um, okay."

Ben glanced at the paper, then winced. "Damn. Hold on."

He jabbed the keys again. This time, no one picked up for several rings.

CLICK.

"Yes?" Irritated.

"I'm here to see . . . Variance. About a model airplane."

Dead air.

Buzz. The interior door swung open.

Ben waved us into a gloomy lobby. Spotting a decrepit-looking elevator, he mashed the up button.

I had a thousand questions, but held my tongue.

I will not *speak to you, Ben Blue.*

We rode to the ninth floor, where Ben led us down a drab floral-papered hallway to the last unit on the right.

The reinforced door had steel plates screwed into the wood. A newer, more expensive-looking video camera was mounted above its frame. It swiveled as we approached, tracking our progress down the corridor.

"Who is this guy?" Shelton whispered. "Are we in the Matrix?"

"I'm not taking any blue pills," Hi warned. "Zion sucked."

"Just be cool." Ben was about to knock when static poured from a speaker on the camera.

"Who are you?" a voice demanded.

"My name is Ben. My friend Ronnie said you can . . . provide certain services."

The lens panned left, then right, scanning the group. "Who are they? Why'd you bring them here?"

Ben shrugged. "Our project involves all of us. We have money."

The camera froze for a moment, then swung back toward the elevator bank.

A full minute passed.

"*Welp.*" Hi stretched. "This was fun. Anyone want to hit that Arby's on the—"

A series of bangs. The jangle of a large chain. Then the armored door swung inward.

I peered into the apartment. Saw no one.

"This is buggin' me out," Shelton whispered. "Let's bail."

"C'mon." Ben strode inside, forcing the rest of us to follow.

The unit was small. Beside the front door was a phone-booth-sized bathroom. Ahead was a modest living room crammed with computer equipment.

And I mean *crammed*. Racks of hardware lined the walls and covered every square inch of the baseboards. The sheer quantity of it put our modest bunker setup to shame. In the far corner, a narrow hallway led to the rear of the apartment, which presumably contained a kitchen and bedroom.

The living room's only furniture was a sprawling circular workstation, the kind used by fancy corporate receptionists. It held an array of monitors, laptops, modems, and drives, along with other devices and gizmos I couldn't identify.

Sitting in the center was an Asian man with spiky black hair and blue eyes. I guessed his age at maybe twenty. Chang wore a gray sweatshirt, cargo shorts, and diamond studs in both ears. Mandarin characters tattooed both his forearms.

"You're Ben?" Chang's voice was soft.

"I am. You're Eddie Chang?"

Chang smiled. "For this request, I'm known as Variance. Did you bring the flash drive?"

Ben nodded, then snapped his fingers in my direction.

"You told him?" I hissed, furious. The snap hadn't helped. "Just like that?"

Ben gave me an exasperated look. "How else was I supposed to explain the job?"

"Relax," Chang said smoothly. "You're Tory, I presume?"

He knows my name. Damn it, Ben.

"I am." Icy. "I take it Ben has already explained what we want?"

"Yes. And don't worry, I'm a pro. Cracking files is what I do, and I know how to keep my mouth shut." Chang leaned forward. "A trait I expect *your* party to emulate. Clear?"

"Clear," I said.

"No problem at all." Hi stared at our host with something close to awe. "And if you need, like, an assistant on weekends, or something, I'm your man. I know how to brew coffee."

"True that." Shelton was eyeballing Chang's equipment, his prior reservations forgotten. "This is the coolest place I've ever seen in my life."

Chang winked. "Thanks, guys, but I work alone. It's a hacker thing. Now let's get down to business, shall we?"

Ben nodded my direction. "She has the drive."

"We'll get to that. You said you have the money?"

"Five hundred," Ben replied. "As agreed."

"Excellent. Now would be a perfect time to hand it over."

Ben looked to Shelton, who scrambled for his wallet. He handed Chang a thick wad of twenties we'd withdrawn before leaving Folly Beach.

"Cash is going fast these days," Shelton muttered. "Better be worth it."

"Thank you, sir." Then Chang gave me an expectant look.

I hesitated. The contents of Karsten's flash drive could potentially devastate our lives.

"We have to show it to someone," Ben said quietly.

Ben was right. Sighing, I dug the drive from my pocket and extended it to the hacker.

Pulled it back just as his fingers drew near.

"One condition."

Chang smiled wryly. "Of course."

"You don't read the decrypted files. Ever. If you *can* access them, that is."

"Fine." He shrugged. "Honestly, I'm not all that interested."

I dropped the drive into his open palm.

"Much obliged." Chang popped the data stick into a USB drive and began tapping keys.

"The files are encrypted," Shelton said. "Commercial grade."

"I imagine so," Chang quipped, "or you wouldn't need me. First step is to determine how tightly the windows are nailed shut."

Minutes passed as Chang typed, studied the screen, typed, then studied more. Then he swiveled his chair, his fingers hammering a second keyboard. A stream of characters filled the monitor to his right.

Finally, Chang rubbed his chin. "Well, this isn't the kiddie stuff I expected."

"Can you explain what you're doing?" I asked.

Chang spun back to face us. "What do you know about file encryption?"

"Almost nothing," I admitted. "That's Shelton's department."

I felt Shelton swell beside me, but he didn't speak. A trainee does not interrupt a master explaining his craft.

"Encryption is the process of encoding information so that only a person with the proper key can read it." Chang tapped the monitor filled with letters and numbers. "Computer encryption is based on traditional cryptology, which has been around forever. Microchips just give it more juice."

"So it's just fancy codes," I said. "And the ciphers needed to unlock them."

We had some experience on those counts.

"Exactly. Online, ciphers are called algorithms. They allow a user to craft a message and give a certain range of possible combinations. A key, on the other hand, helps the user figure out the one correct answer on any given occasion."

I followed so far. "So what's on this flash drive?"

Chang pointed to a monitor on the opposite side of the workstation. "These files are protected by a simple symmetric-key encryption. To open them, we have to match the key used by the originating system."

"So you need to crack the code."

"Of course. But there's a problem."

Chang leaned back in his chair. "The strength of any key is determined by the length of its code, which is measured in bits. I can crack any 56-bit DES system with brute force, and that's working through seventy quadrillion possible combinations."

Hi whistled. "I take it you don't type them in, one at a time."

"Not on your life. But that's not what we're facing here. These files are protected by an AES key system. A real nasty one, too, with 128-bit keys. That's more combinations. A *lot* more."

"How many?" Shelton asked.

Chang grinned. "A brute force attack—trying all possible combinations one at a time—would have to cycle through 3.4×10 to the 38th power number of keys. The human mind can't grasp a number that big."

I blinked. "That sounds impossible."

"It *is* impossible. That's the point. Even with a supercomputer, it'd take a billion billion years to run all those combinations. Exponentially longer than the universe has existed."

I gave him a flat look. "So how are you going to beat the encryption?"

Chang thumb-tapped the desktop. "I could look for a cheat algorithm, to give me some portion of the key, but even that wouldn't help much against 128-bit encryption. I'll have to use a backdoor instead."

My arms crossed. "Backdoor?"

"Some encryption programs have a weakness," Chang explained. "A way around the system-key construct. A shortcut, if you will, that bypasses the need for matching keys altogether. Programmers use these backdoors to get into and out of their programs during coding. Many leave one of those secret ways intact, even after they're finished, in case they want to poke around in the future."

"Seriously?" I scoffed. "That's pretty dishonest."

Chang laughed. "Most programmers grew up as hackers. It's in the blood, so to speak."

"That's *awesome,*" Hi said. "So does this system have a backdoor?"

Chang smiled wide, exposing a row of pearly whites. "It does. I recognize this encryption system, and, more importantly, I know who wrote it. He's a weird guy, lives in a Soho loft filled with goldfish tanks."

My pulse began to race. "And you have this backdoor?"

"Yes. For a price."

"We agreed to five hundred," Ben growled.

"That was before. Now you're asking for the crown jewels."

"How much?" I demanded.

Chang met my eye. "Five thousand. Cash. Non-negotiable."

Damn it.

"Fine."

What choice did we have?

⬡   ⬡   ⬡

"They're back." Chang reached beneath his super-desk and pressed a button.

The door buzzed, then swung open. Shelton and Ben entered.

"Any problems at the bank?" I asked.

Shelton shook his head, handed me two bound stacks of hundred-dollar bills. "We're getting close to tapped out, though. I hope this is worth it."

Me too.

I slapped the cash onto the desktop. "Here. Now get to work."

"Already done."

Chang handed me an unlabeled CD in a clear plastic case. "All files, decrypted and ready for viewing. Unread, as agreed."

"The flash drive?"

His blue eyes danced with amusement. "Almost forgot."

Chang was about to remove the drive when something caught his attention.

"Hold up." He scooted to the closest monitor, hands searching for a keyboard.

"Yes?" I asked.

"There's something . . . else on this drive. It's odd. Here."

An image flashed onscreen—a scrambled list of folders and subfiles.

I leaned over the desktop for a better view. "Did you miss those?"

Chang shook his head. "This is a shadow file tree. Those files aren't physically contained on this data stick, but they can be accessed by it."

Shelton joined me by the monitor. "I don't understand."

"This drive *can* access those files," he explained, "but not remotely. The documents listed here are actually stored on a server located somewhere else. To read them, you'd have to insert this drive into that specific server."

Chang eyed me curiously. "This is *extremely* sophisticated. Military grade, or something else that's ultra-secure like medical records, or corporate R and D. *256-bit encryption.* What kind of files are these?"

"That's not part of our deal," I replied frostily.

Chang nodded, but the speculative looked didn't fade.

"So you can't open them?" Ben said.

"No. No one else can, either. What you see are similar to links, but they won't work online. To open those files, you'd have to physically connect to their home network. And I'd bet my PlayStation it's a closed system, which means you'd have to actually be in the server room."

"Can you tell us anything else?" I pressed.

Chang was silent for several heartbeats. "Maybe. Hold on a minute." More like ten.

Chang typed. Grunted. Rotated among his stations. Even consulted a three-ring binder.

"Here's what I got," he said finally. "It's not much. These shadow files were created within the last three months, by a different user from the batch I just decoded for you. But I can't identify either one. Your drive appears to be a legacy key to another system, in another network. Theoretically, it can still access the servers."

I straightened. "Three months old? From a different user?"

That made no sense. Karsten obviously didn't open new files.

Then who did?

And how would *new* files be linked to Karsten's mothballed parvo-virus experiment?

"That's right." Chang shrugged. "But I can't open them. As I said, you'd have to find the server to match the encryption key. What's strange is that, when I got past the encryption, this file tree downloaded *itself* onto your flash drive. That's high-tech synchronization, even though you can't access the content."

"And there's no explanation of what the files are, or where they're from?"

"No. Just a group heading. B-Series."

B-Series? Why did that send a jolt to my nerves?

"If you let me keep the stick," Chang said, "I might be able to find the server."

"No," I said instantly. Then, "No, thank you. We'll take it from here. Can I have the drive back please?"

An odd look twisted Chang's features. Annoyance? Frustration?

Before I could say more, he spun and tapped a few keys. Data streamed across all four monitors, then they all went blank.

Chang removed Karsten's drive and handed it to me.

"Good luck. Change your mind, and you know where to find me."

With a series of waves and mumbled thanks, we made our way out.

All the way down to Ben's car, my thoughts raced.

We had Karsten's files! Finally.

But what was this B-Series? Who was running active files, ones that magically appeared on Karsten's old data stick? Who else even *knew* about Karsten's secret work?

"Success." Ben clicked on his seat belt. "You're welcome, by the way."

I nodded, distracted. Not quite sharing his enthusiasm.

We had what we came for. The mission was a success.

So why did I have a sinking feeling?

CHAPTER 16

Dinnertime snuck up on me.

Whitney pounced as soon as I opened the front door, foreclosing any notion of examining Karsten's files right away.

"You ready to eat, dear?" She wore a pink taffeta dress with matching flats. To dinner. On a Wednesday. At home.

Suppressing a groan, I allowed myself to be ushered to the table.

Kit was sitting on the couch watching *Jeopardy,* drinking a glass of red wine. Whitney continued to putter about, setting out dishes and straightening the place settings. The whole scene felt *very* domestic, like a glimpse into my future.

That thought nearly sent me screaming down the beach.

Coop trotted over and brushed against my leg.

"Hey, dog face." I knelt and rubbed his cold, wet nose.

Cooper yipped. Pawed at my shoulder.

"I know. I left you behind today. Sorry about that."

Whitney was smoothing her dress, a stink-eye on the wolfdog. "The table is set, sweetie."

"One sec."

I scurried upstairs, unzipped my bag, and shoved the CD and flash drive into a desk drawer. Then I trudged back down, bracing for an hour of forced smiles and stilted conversation.

That evening's spread was pork chops with country ham gravy, green beans, and Gouda mac and cheese. We don't eat healthy, but we damn sure eat well.

"Anything interesting going on, kiddo?" Kit dug into his meal. "We missed you at dinner yesterday." He left the question unspoken.

Oh, sure, Kit, lots! The gang and I broke into Lucy and Peter Gable's house last night and discovered a bloodstain the size of Texas, but were chased off by a stalker before we could be 100 percent sure. This afternoon, we took a clue Hi swiped from the district attorney's office—the only piece of evidence in the twins' disappearance—and had a witch look it over. After that we stopped by a hacker's apartment to break in to your old boss's research files. You know, the ones from his secret medical experiment, which accidentally gave me superpowers. How was your day at LIRI?

"No. Same old."

Kit nodded as if he'd expected my response. "I'm just glad the trial is over. Things can finally get back to normal."

"Here, here!" Whitney, hand to chest. Then she folded her napkin and placed it on the table. "Now, Tory, please don't get upset."

"Upset?" Not a good opener.

"You've been distracted lately, so I took it upon myself to help you along with the Magnolia League. I filled out all the paperwork for you, so it wouldn't be a bother."

My eyes closed. Snapped open.

I didn't scream. Didn't stomp my foot. Didn't storm from the table.

At this point, we were past all that.

Instead, I met Whitney's gaze directly. "You anticipated this would upset me."

"Whit's just trying to be helpful." Kit's hazel eyes were pleading.

"Thank you for explaining her actions," I said coolly. "Again."

Whitney's lips parted, but I raised a hand for silence.

Awkward pause. Then I slowly shook my head.

In the end, I *always* lost these battles. Why bother fighting them?

Sighing, I speared a green bean on my plate. "What *exactly* is this going to entail?"

Whitney goggled at my unexpected surrender, but quickly recovered. "Being a Magnolia isn't hardly work at all. You'll *love* it! First-year girls attend two chapter meetings a month, then perhaps join a committee, or help organize a charitable event."

"The deadline is approaching fast, and those ladies are sticklers for rules." Her shoulders tensed, as if expecting a blow. "I went ahead and submitted your application yesterday."

I couldn't help but laugh. "Of course you did."

Whitney nervously giggled with me, but her eyes betrayed her anxiety.

Screw it. Done is done.

"I assume you'll let me know their response?"

Whitney covered her mouth with both hands, as if she couldn't believe her luck. A child who'd gotten a coveted Christmas present. "Tory, you're *assured* of acceptance. Trust me."

Whitney unleashed a torrent of words about all the "rewarding" activities the Magnolia League had to offer. As she droned on and on, something nudged my foot under the table.

Kit's loafer.

I glanced at my dad. He mouthed a thank-you.

My eyes nearly rolled through the ceiling, but I nodded. We both knew this would make life easier.

"And we can go shopping for hats!" Whitney prattled. "I know a *great* boutique on King Street that will have just the thing, plus—"

"You owe me," I whispered from the side of mouth.

Kit nodded ruefully. "I know it."

"What's that?" Whitney, just now discovering she'd been talking to herself. "Tory, you'll still help with the neighborhood party, won't you?"

Ugh. I'd forgotten that gem. Though, admittedly, it wasn't her worst idea.

"Yes, Whitney. Just let me know what you need."

"Wonderful! We should've hosted an event like this *ages* ago." She tapped her bottom lip with a manicured fingernail. "I think invitations would be fitting, even though everyone lives close. We can hand deliver them."

As Whitney ramped back up, something in the living room caught my eye.

Breaking News was interrupting Alex Trebek.

"*Ssh Ssh Ssh!*" I pointed to the television.

"Good evening," intoned the same oily anchorman, with all the grave solemnity he could muster. "There's been a shocking development in the disappearance of Lucy and Peter Gable. In a *Channel Five News* exclusive, we've obtained footage from a *ransom video,* received by police officials mere hours ago, confirming that the Bolton Academy twins have been forcibly abducted."

"Oh my God!" I shot from my seat and ran to the screen.

"A warning to our sensitive viewers." If possible, the anchorman's face grew even more somber. "The following images are disturbing. You may wish to look away."

A grainy image appeared. I watched in horror.

It was a boy and a girl, trapped behind rusty metal bars in a stone chamber. The five-second clip contained a single shot of their dirty, haggard faces.

I recognized both.

We were right.

The enormity of the video sank in.

This was no game we were playing. No lark to kill time, or soothe my frustrated psyche. The Gable twins' lives were hanging by a thread. Two kids I saw nearly every day.

The anchorman's face filled the screen. "Channel Five News has confirmed that a ransom demand of five million dollars accompanied the video."

The program cut to an apoplectic Commissioner Riggins, barking into a half-dozen microphones shoved before his face.

"This tape is part of an *ongoing police investigation,*" he snapped. "Releasing it publicly was *highly* irresponsible. I ask the media to *please* respect the gravity of the situation, and make no unauthorized disclosures that could further jeopardize the safety of these children. I will personally investigate these leaks. And when I find who's responsible, they'll be prosecuted!"

Beside Riggins stood Detective Hawfield, arms crossed and visibly seething.

Big week for Channel Five. They must have a solid source at police HQ.

The anchorman resumed, without the slightest twinge of guilt. "Tune in this evening for up-to-the-minute details of the astonishing Gable twins' kidnapping. Good evening."

Final Jeopardy blipped back onscreen. I sat down, stunned.

Kit was by my side immediately. "You okay, Tor? Do you know those kids?"

"I'm fine." Trying to pull myself together. "We have a few classes together."

"How dreadful!" I was surprised to see tears leaking from Whitney's eyes. "Those poor babies!"

Kit seemed about to say more, but I needed to process.

"I'm going to my room." I bolted upstairs before they could say more.

My door closed with a bang. I heard Kit climb halfway up in pursuit, then stop. A few beats passed, then he slowly descended back to the main floor.

I sat in my chair, mind-blown. Everything was suddenly real, and I didn't like it.

Then do *something about it.*

But what?

Then I knew.

Before, there'd only been one piece of evidence.

Now there were two.

And the Virals needed both if we hoped to help Lucy and Peter.

A plan began to form. The boys weren't going to like it.

But a simple truth was inescapable: we needed a look at that videotape.

And there's no time like the present, right?

CHAPTER 17

The Explorer's dashboard clock read 1:00 a.m.

"Now or never," Ben murmured.

I didn't move. Watched the building across from where we'd parked.

This was unquestionably the riskiest stunt we'd ever considered pulling.

Charleston Police Headquarters is tucked away on the northwestern edge of the downtown peninsula, overlooking the Ashley River. The compound consists of several structures of various size, shape, and level of security.

Some were dark. Others were lit up like Christmas trees.

The boys in blue never fully close for business.

We were casing a two-story compound outside the main cluster. An ugly, dreary pile of bricks, surrounded by a ten-foot chain-link fence topped with razor wire. Though flickering floodlights illuminated the enclosed yard, none burned within the building. A sign at the gate proclaimed it "Annex A."

"We're really doing it this time," Shelton muttered. "We're gonna break into a freaking *police station*. And not some backwoods precinct. Ho, no! That wouldn't be *stupid* enough. This team of geniuses is about to invade the damn HQ."

"We need the ransom tape," I replied. "It's in there."

"Why not hit NASA next?" Shelton squawked. "Or CIA headquarters?"

"We *could* visit Channel Five first," Hi suggested. "They have a copy."

I shook my head. "We don't know if they have the whole recording, or just a clip."

"Tory's right." Ben's fingers drummed the steering wheel. "Plus, our plan is solid."

I watched Ben from the corner of my eye. Worried. While I appreciated his enthusiasm, Ben seemed unnaturally excited to undertake something this dangerous.

An hour ago, he'd picked us up on Morris. I'd barely made it out—slipping past Whitney was significantly more difficult than eluding Kit alone. While Kit slept like a hibernating polar bear, Whitney woke at the slightest floorboard creak. And lately, she'd begun setting our security system every night.

That actually worked in my favor. Whitney's not a tech-savvy person—she thought the alarm couldn't be deactivated without beeping. Not true. A quick read of the instruction manual had introduced me to silent mode.

That night I'd snuck downstairs, killed the alarm, slipped outside, and then reengaged the system from my iPhone. If the bimbo woke up she'd see a steady red light, and wouldn't suspect a thing.

The trickiest moment had been getting by Coop. Even bribed with two Greenie bones, the wolfdog hadn't been pleased to be left behind. Thankfully, he hadn't blown my cover.

"You're sure about this tunnel?" Shelton asked for the fifth time.

"Absolutely." Hi wiped orange Doritos crumbs on his black sweatshirt. We all wore dark, athletic clothing. Our ninja garb, Hi called it.

"Explain it one more time." Sitting there, on the brink, I wanted to visualize our strategy step by step.

Hi sighed theatrically, but repeated the story. "Last fall, my dad had to come down here to reclaim the LIRI hardware stolen from Lab Three. He brought me along to help lug the gear. That afternoon there was a baseball game up the street, snarling traffic around headquarters, so the detective took us on a shortcut."

He pointed to the building across the street. "We went in there. Annex A. That ugly shack has a tunnel to the main building. Even better, the passage connects to the basement, right where evidence storage is located."

"So we enter here, sneak along the tunnel, find and copy the tape, then retreat."

I sounded much more confident than I felt.

"Exactly." Ben was actually smiling. "It's perfect."

"Perfect?" Shelton began ticking points on his fingers. "We don't know how to get inside this building, if the tunnel will be manned, or if the video is actually *in* the evidence room, which is almost certainly guarded, alarmed, and recorded twenty-four/seven."

I tried not to cringe. Shelton was right. Our plan was borderline suicidal.

But it didn't matter. I couldn't get the twins' faces out of my head.

"We'll improvise," was all I said.

"Nope." Shelton wagged his head fatalistically. "We're getting caught, and going to jail. At least they won't have far to take us."

"Enough wasting time." Ben killed the engine. "Light 'em up."

"Do we have to?" Shelton glanced at me with troubled eyes. "Flaring is starting to feel a little like playing Russian roulette. How do we know the powers won't suddenly go sideways on us while we're sneaking past the po-pos?"

"Honestly, we don't," I answered grimly. "But there's no other way to do this. We'll just have to be careful. Keep it simple."

"Which means," Ben said sharply, "you staying out of our heads. No mind scrambles."

Though bristling at his tone, I nodded. "I won't try to merge our thoughts."

"Good. Now let's get moving." Golden light exploded behind Ben's irises. He gasped, then shook like a wet dog.

"See you guys in lockdown." Hi closed his eyes.

"Not funny." Shelton took a deep breath, then shuddered as his power burst to life.

I rolled my neck, then whispered to myself. "Go time."

SNAP.

My flare opened easily. The usual jolt of fire and ice, but nothing like the last time. Waves of pure energy flooded my limbs, powerful and addictive. I almost cooed with the pleasure of it.

Senses boosted to hyperdrive, I stepped from the SUV and scanned our target with preternatural precision. The boys huddled by the rear bumper, waiting for my signal.

Not yet. I wanted to test something first.

Take it slow.

Eyes shut, I visualized the flaming cords in my mind. They danced and spun, seemed almost eager. I harnessed them easily. The cords became tunnels.

I felt an odd sensation, like plunging into freezing water.

Thoughts poured into my head.

So easy this time.

As one, the boys winced.

"Are you reading my thoughts?" Ben demanded, hands clenching into fists. "You *just* said—"

"No." I concentrated on the fiery tunnel leading to Ben. Our connection held, but the mind-meld remained tantalizingly out of reach.

I resisted the urge to try to force it. My flare felt surprisingly stable. I didn't want to risk a meltdown.

The telepathy is imperfect, I sent. *I can't harness your senses, but we can communicate.*

This is plenty weird enough. Shelton nearly ripped an ear from his head.

Coop isn't here. Hi overlaid the thought with an image of my wolfdog chasing his own tail. *Maybe that dilutes the effect?*

I nodded. *This will have to be enough. Let's go.*

Ben stepped into the street. *Follow me.* For some reason, his sending was faintest.

Moving single file, we hurried across and cut left, moving along the fence. An alley ran between the wire-capped chain link and the next building over. We bolted down its length to the rear of the property, which faced the river.

Tucked in the shadows, we peered into the Annex A enclosure, at a parking lot crowded with slumbering snow vehicles. Those don't get a ton of work in Charleston, South Carolina. Ten feet from where we hid, a second gate split the fence. Chained and locked.

Shelton hurried to it without prompting. We crouched, waiting as he picked the lock.

Click.

Got it. Shelton swung the gate wide. We slipped through and darted toward the building.

Look for a door that—

My thought was interrupted by the scrape of claws on asphalt. My flaring nose caught a whiff of wet, musky fur.

We whirled in unison. Two German shepherds were pounding toward us.

Panic flooded my brain as the boys scrambled for hiding places. I froze, unable to move.

Growling, both dogs barreled toward me.

Instinct took over. I flung my thoughts at the charging animals.

HOLD.

Both shepherds stopped short. The larger one—perhaps a grizzly bear in disguise—shook his head, black fur rising along his spine. The other beast cocked his head and yapped, eyeing me with icy brown eyes.

I could sense their thoughts—a jumble of confusion, and thwarted aggression.

The larger dog tensed, preparing to charge again.

Focus on the alpha.

I sent a mixture of impressions and images, trying to communicate as I did with Coop.

No harm. No threat. Leaving your territory.

Grizzly Bear sat back on his hindquarters. Regarded me. Then, slowly, he settled down on his haunches. Brown Eyes whined at his companion, but followed suit.

Pass.

I thought it was Grizzly Bear, but couldn't be sure.

Thank you.

I waved the boys toward the building. Hoped Shelton could get us inside. Quickly.

The guard dogs watched as Shelton reached a set of steel doors, began frantically fiddling with a knob.

Brown Eyes abruptly stood. Drilled me with a look.

Pass. Once.

I felt an emphasis on the second word.

Understood.

After long seconds, the lock yielded. We piled inside and slammed the door shut.

Phase One was complete.

But we were going to need a different way out.

○   ○   ○

What now? Ben asked, his smile gone.

We'd just completed Phase Two—the tunnel had been easy to locate, and blessedly abandoned at that late hour. It'd taken less than five minutes to reach the basement of the main headquarters building.

Where the weak point in our plan reared its ugly head.

Let me think. I peered through a tiny window in a hallway door.

Not only was the evidence room locked up tight, but so was the corridor approaching it. Halfway down its length sat a duty officer, drowsily reading a Dan Brown novel. A security camera perched above him completed the disaster.

"I told you!" Shelton hissed, forgetting to send his thoughts. "And we can't even go back now, unless you wanna be dog chow."

We huddled in the dim hallway, trying not to panic. My mind raced, searching for a miracle solution. At this point, just getting away sounded wonderful.

Then an idea occurred to me.

Hi, where is Hawfield's office?

Hi whipped out his iPhone. Tense moments passed as he surfed the web.

Finally, he looked up. *Major Crimes is on the fifth floor.*

Are you nuts! Shelton's hands shot skyward. *Hawfield knows who we are!*

No, she's right! Hi bounced on his toes. *And nobody that matters will be here this late.*

Ben pointed back the way we'd come. *Elevators.*

With my enhanced vision, I easily spotted the bank of doors twenty yards away.

We go up, I insisted. *But first, snuff the flares.*

Ben reared back. *That's nuts! We can't give up our edge.*

I gave him a hard look. *We might run into someone. We can't risk an officer spotting our glowing eyes, even if it means getting caught.*

Ben crossed his arms. *I'll take my chances.*

I nearly slapped him. *No! It's too dangerous. Stop being stupid.*

A pulse of anger radiated from Ben. He turned and stormed toward the elevators.

I slapped my sides in frustration. Didn't know what to do.

Would Ben really gamble everything? Risk exposure?

Feeling a hand on my shoulder, I turned. Hi gave me "calm down" hands as the golden light faded from his eyes. I glanced at Shelton. He'd also powered down.

Deep breath.

SNUP.

I shivered as the shock waves dissipated. Losing my flare made me feel small and weak. A terrible hollow feeling, that seemed worse each time.

"Let me." Hi hustled up the corridor.

Shelton and I waited, unable to pierce the gloom, not speaking for fear of discovery.

I counted seconds in my head.

"Come on," a voice finally whispered.

Shelton and I jogged to the elevators. Ben stood at the doors, his eyes their normal dark brown. Wordlessly, he punched the up button.

We waited, pulses pounding. A door beeped, then opened. The car was empty.

The four of us piled inside. Hi pressed five. The doors slid shut.

"Hope nobody else needs a lift," Shelton whispered.

"We can make something up," Hi hissed. "Say we lost our pony."

I snorted. "And came to report it at one a.m.?"

"Better than breaking in to steal evidence," Hi countered. "Maybe we loved that pony."

My heart rose in my throat as we passed each floor. One. Two. Three. The elevator slowed. I was close to losing my dinner.

I imagined the doors opening to an office full of detectives working overtime. Heads turning. Confused eyes gradually growing suspicious. Hawfield, outraged, dialing Kit's number.

Four. Five. The doors hissed open.

Before us was an open space filled with interlocking cubicles, surrounded by glass-enclosed offices lining the walls. Every light was off. No one was there.

I gasped in relief. Shelton actually fell to his knees, while Hi rubbed a hand across his face. Ben chuckled nervously, wiping sweat from his brow.

"Hurry." I moved along the row of offices. The one I sought was third from the end.

Hawfield, Fergus.

Rounding the standard issue gray metal desk, I considered where to start. I woke his computer by tapping the space bar. No good—the system was password protected.

Then I noticed an iPad on the desktop. I flipped the cover and pressed the home button. The display winked to life. A collection of icons covered the screen.

The right one was obvious: GableRansomVideo.

"That's it!" Hi squealed. "But how do we get it?"

I thought furiously. Had no idea.

"Give it here," Shelton demanded.

He opened the iPad's web browser and navigated to Gmail.

"Brilliant," I breathed.

"Won't be so brilliant if they trace what I do," Shelton said. "But I have a blank Gmail account for joining websites, so I don't get spam. I'll use that."

He typed quickly.

"Tony Domo?" Hi scoffed. "Great name, genius."

"Can it. I was in a hurry."

Shelton logged in, attached the file, and mailed it to himself. Then he logged out, closed Safari, and opened Utilities to erase the iPad's browser history.

"Best I can do," he said nervously. "As long as no one suspects, no one will check the hard drive and notice what I did."

A squeaking noise in the hallway.

"Someone's coming!" Ben shoved everyone deeper into Hawfield's office.

We dove behind the desk in a ragged dog pile. Froze. The sound grew closer.

I stared at the tiny slice of doorway I could see. A yellow bucket wheeled into view. Passed, followed closely by a worn pair of Nikes. The squeaks sounded for another few seconds before fading completely.

We let out a collective breath.

"Let's get the frick out of here!" Shelton moaned.

"Deal."

Sticking my head through the door, I scanned the hallway. All clear. We bolted for the elevator. Painful moments passed as we waited for the car to arrive.

Adrenaline jolted me as the door opened.

Empty again. All the gods were smiling on us.

"What now?" Hi asked, once inside. "We can't go back through the tunnel."

"Now we go for broke." I pressed *L*.

The boys flinched, but didn't argue. They understood.

I pulled out my cell, tapping keys until I found what I needed. Then I cupped the iPhone tightly in my left hand.

We rode in silence.

The car stopped. The doors slid open.

Squaring my shoulders, I strode into the lobby.

Several officers lounged behind a counter running the length of the room. Opposite them, a man in handcuffs was slumped on a wooden bench, a huge welt forming on his forehead. Beside the suspect, an officer was calmly filling out paperwork.

On the next bench over, a pair of elderly ladies were seated, waiting, with matching scowls on their faces. Farther down the line, a trio of disheveled college students were scrolling their cell phones.

I spied a row of glass doors at the opposite end of the room.

Hesitate and you're finished, Brennan.

Straight from the elevator.

Across the lobby.

Through the doors.

The boys at my back like white on rice.

We walked swiftly, but not unduly so. Everyone stared straight ahead.

Behind the counter, an officer glanced up as we passed. His mouth opened, a confused expression on his face.

The phone beside him rang.

With a last look our way, the man shrugged, then reached to answer.

We exited the building, skipped down the steps, and then hurried around the corner.

I hit disconnect, ending my call to the CPD intake desk.

Together, we sprinted down the sidewalk.

CHAPTER 18

We scrambled into the bunker an hour later.

Ben had driven almost all the way there, something we *never* do. But I couldn't wait.

We had Karsten's files. We had the ransom video. Sleep wasn't coming anyway.

Shelton dropped into the workstation chair. "What first?"

I weighed options. The danger to the twins was more immediate.

"The ransom video."

We gathered behind Shelton as he logged into his fake Gmail account. "It's an MP-four file. Twenty seconds long. Probably shot by a handheld digital video camera. HD mode. Nothing embedded in the recording. No private streams."

I nodded, clueless as to what Shelton was talking about. But I trusted his expertise.

"Play it," Ben said.

Shelton double-clicked the file, then expanded to whole screen mode.

We watched in silence.

The shot was eye level. A dirty stone chamber, bisected by a line of rusty metal bars. Harsh light poured from somewhere off camera. Beyond the bars, a boy and a girl were huddled together on the floor, squinting in the radiance. The room didn't appear to have a ceiling. Water dripped from unseen heights above.

"It's them," Hi breathed. "They're looking right at the camera."

Shelton shivered, rubbed his arms. I understood.

It appeared the twins were looking right at their captor. I couldn't imagine the feeling.

"Turn up the audio," Ben said.

Shelton adjusted the QuickTime player settings, then fiddled with the desktop speakers. "No can do. There isn't any."

As we watched, the camera moved left to right across the chamber, as if being carried. The focus remained on the two miserable teens in the center of the cell.

Lucy and Peter didn't twitch a muscle, but their eyes tracked the camera.

After twenty seconds, the screen went black.

"Again," I breathed.

Shelton clicked play a second time. The clip repeated.

When it ended, I began chewing a thumbnail. Unfortunately, nothing about the video jumped out at me. The scene was horrifying, no question, and confirmed that the twins had been abducted. But from an investigative standpoint, the tape seemed like a dead end.

"There's nothing useful," Hi said. "The kidnapper knew what he was doing."

"Roll it again. And watch for details," I instructed. "Everyone take a quadrant. Look for any kind of hint where this was filmed, or by whom."

After agreeing on who was eyeballing what, Shelton replayed the recording. I watched the northwest quarter of the screen. Came up empty.

"I got nothing," Ben said.

"Same." Shelton and Hi. Jinx.

"Rotate sectors clockwise," I said. "We'll watch this a million times if we have to. There has to be *something*."

"Won't the police already be doing this?" Shelton asked. "With, like, professional editing equipment, and a video expert?"

"You ready to give up on these two?" I touched the image frozen on the monitor.

"No." Shelton shoved his glasses into place. "No, I'm not."

We watched again. Rotated once more, and repeated the process.

I was scanning the southwest section of the screen when a thought struck me.

"Those bars look old," I said. "Like they've been there forever."

Hi nodded. "Good point. This . . . cage likely wasn't built for this kidnapping."

"Run it again," Ben said. "Everyone examine the bars."

The scene replayed.

"Holy crap!" Hi yelped.

"What?" I said immediately.

"Shadow!" Hi jabbed a finger at the center of the screen.

Shelton turned to face Hi. "Say what?"

"Run it half speed. Watch as the cameraman crosses the room. There!"

Hi was right. As the shot moved, a shadow briefly appeared on the floor, lengthened, then shrank back and disappeared.

"That's the kidnapper!" Then my spirits sank. "But how does a shadow help?"

"If we can isolate it," Hi said excitedly, "we could conceivably esti-mate the person's height and weight, maybe even gender. It's a place to start, at least."

I clapped my hands. "LIRI has amazing AV equipment—half the vis-iting researchers film documentaries of their work."

"What's that?" Ben pointed to a bar at the edge of the shot. With the tape paused, the chamber's background light was striking the steel at an oblique angle. Squiggly lines ran a foot of its length.

My pulse thumped. "Is that *writing*?"

Shelton boxed and enlarged the image. "It is! But I still can't read it."

We strained our eyes. Manipulated the image this way and that. Even considered flaring. But the grainy squiggles wouldn't form anything legible.

I pounded the desktop in frustration. "We need to see those words."

"We'll have better luck at LIRI," Hi promised. "We can play around with their equipment and really enhance the shot."

"Tomorrow," I said firmly. "Right after school."

"If we're gonna do that," Shelton said, "then let's check Karsten's files now."

"Good idea." I handed over the CD from Chang.

Shelton inserted the disk and opened the drive. A directory listed hundreds of files.

"Wow," Hi said.

"This might take a while," Shelton agreed.

My arms crossed. I'd waited too long for this moment.

"Then we'd better get started."

"This is pointless," Ben complained.

5:30 AM. We'd been skimming files for three straight hours.

I could barely keep my eyes open, but snapped at Ben nonetheless. "This is what we've been searching for—the entire record of Karsten's parvovirus experiments!"

"Which we can't make any sense of," Ben fired back.

Hi rubbed his face. "I mean, it's all interesting. Lab cultures. Data sets. Karsten's research protocols and stated objectives. But most of this material is way beyond me."

Shelton nodded wearily. "It's great to understand the *mechanics* of what Karsten did, but I can't see how it helps us. Our infection was unanticipated. Totally unplanned. There won't be a record of *that,* which is what we really need."

"This stuff helps, though." I stole the mouse and double-clicked a file. "Here. Karsten emphasizes that XPB-19 is contagious to humans. He knew!"

"*How* does that help?" Ben demanded. "How do we *use* any of this information? Without Karsten to explain his work, these files might as well be written in Chinese. They're useless."

"We don't know that." Voice stubborn. "There are *hundreds* of pages here, and we've barely skimmed half of them."

"These aren't the records we need! You want *answers,* Victoria?" Ben made air quotes with his fingers. "Well, here's some real talk: In order for this data to be *any* use, we'd have to have a basis for comparison. We'd need records of *our current condition,* right now. That means submitting *ourselves* to medical testing, by someone who knows what they're looking for. That sound good to you?"

I bit my tongue, suddenly discouraged.

Ben continued, relentless, biting off his words. "Unless you're ready to throw on a white gown and become a full-time lab rat, these files are totally useless. End of story."

I stared daggers at Ben, who glared back.

My God. Is he right? Have I been fooling myself all along?

Hi raised both palms. "It's almost dawn, guys. Let's call it a day before we kill each other. We can get back to this tomorrow."

I tore my gaze away. Nodded sharply.

This had been one of the longest days of my life. I was exhausted.

We crawled outside and piled into the Explorer. Ben drove in silence.

Nearing the complex, he switched off his headlights. Dropped us off fifty yards away. Then he sped down the blacktop, heading off the island.

Shelton, Hi, and I crept to the rear of the building. Mouthing good-byes, we split up and slunk toward our respective units.

At the back door, I dug out my phone and deactivated the house alarm. Slipped inside.

Coop was standing in his doggie bed when I reached the main floor.

Maybe I was tired. I missed the signal.

Turning the corner, I ran smack into Whitney at the bottom of the stairs.

"Tory!" Her eyes widened. Then, taking in my clothes, narrowed.

Whitney's arms crossed over her white satin robe. "Sneaking out again? Your father is going to explode!"

My sluggish mind groped for an excuse. Struck out.

I stood there, gaping like an idiot.

Whitney was right—Kit was going to murder me.

Panicking, I blurted the first thing that came to mind.

"Please don't tell! I was meeting a boy."

Why did I say that!?!

Whitney's eyes nearly popped from her skull.

"A boy?" she hissed. "At this hour?! Who on earth—"

"Jason Taylor."

It felt like someone else was speaking. My mind was a melted slushy, suggesting ideas it thought Whitney might enjoy.

Whitney paused. Frowned. Finally, "Very well. I won't tell your daddy, but this does *not* happen again, young lady. Do you hear me?"

I nodded, too tired to process what was happening. "Yes, ma'am. Thank you."

Then I gave her a quick hug. Whitney, tensed, then returned it.

For some reason, I felt bad.

You're manipulating her to get out of trouble.

"Now up with you!" Whitney shook her head. "It's nearly dawn already, and you won't be missing school tomorrow."

I nodded. Climbed to my room.

My reserves were gone.

I was asleep before my head hit the pillow.

CHAPTER 19

Thursday

Morning came way too soon.

"Ghaaah." I slapped my alarm clock, hoping it would break.

Head pounding. Nasty taste in mouth. Eyes glued shut.

I'd never felt more drained.

My door swung open. Whitney stuck her head inside.

"Rise and shine," she said coolly. "I'll expect you downstairs for breakfast in twenty minutes. No exceptions." She withdrew with a knowing glance.

Our encounter an hour before came crashing back. Nightmare.

Why in the world had I mentioned Jason? How long would she hold her tongue?

From this moment forward, I'm at her mercy.

The thought made me want to crawl under my covers and never resurface. I imagined the day ahead, and the long hours before I could sleep.

"Blargh."

○   ○   ○

Sixty minutes later I was in uniform, aboard *Hugo*, and motoring toward downtown.

I sprawled on a bench in the stern, staring at our trail of wake.

Face slack. Mind numb. Body exhausted.

Shelton sat beside me, head in his hands. We hadn't exchanged two words. Hi was inside the passenger cabin, flat on his back and dozing.

My thoughts wandered. I replayed the horrifying ransom tape in my head. Composed a silent prayer for Lucy and Peter.

We'd put the Gamemaster behind bars, but a new evil had taken his place. I felt swamped with hopelessness. The world was dark, and full of monsters.

My focus drifted to Karsten's secret files. Ben's angry words.

Was he right? Was the information on the flash drive useless? I was forced to admit he'd made a compelling argument. Karsten wouldn't have any notes specifically pertaining to our condition.

Don't give up hope. Work the problem, and good things will come.

But I was zonked. Just wanted to sleep. To shut the world off. Check out.

An idea bloomed. Drained as I was, I didn't immediately dismiss it.

I straightened in my seat. *Why not?*

Because it might be hazardous, my rational mind shot back. *Because it's exactly what you were blasting Ben about, which makes you a total hypocrite.*

But both logic and pride were sorely overmatched.

I was dog-tired. Miserable. If my canine DNA could provide some relief, I wanted it.

Stupid stupid stupid.

Deep breath. Eyes shut.

SNAP.

The power scorched through me. I tried to hide the transformation from Shelton, fighting to keep still as my body thundered and raged.

As the flare unleashed, my weariness fled. The headache disappeared. Energy infused my muscles. My mind sharpened along with my senses. It felt wonderful.

This is bad. Dangerous.

At that moment, I didn't care. Just sighed with pleasure.

"Tory! Are you crazy?!"

Shelton shoved his sunglasses onto my face.

I started, suddenly aware of how careless I'd been. My eyes scanned the boat. Thankfully, no other passengers were on deck.

Shelton's gaze bored into me. "Has *everyone* lost their minds lately?"

"Sorry, you're right. But, Shelton, my fatigue just . . . melted away. I feel *great*."

"Really?" His expression grew hopeful. "Okay, watch my back."

I slipped on my shades and handed his back. Shelton swapped them with his eyeglasses.

"This feels wrong."

"I know." But I held my flare anyway.

Shelton's thin frame shuddered. He gasped, grabbed his head.

Slowly, his breathing eased. Shelton's head came up, a smile spreading his lips.

"I take it back. This feels fantastic."

"Which worries me. Flaring is becoming addictive."

The cabin door opened and Hi stepped out. He stared as though we'd grown horns.

"I knew it." He joined us on the bench. "Explain yourselves."

"Light one up," I said ruefully. "You'll understand."

His eyebrows rose, but Hi dug out his shades. Seconds later, he gasped as the inferno erupted inside him.

"*Ahhhh.*" Hi linked his hands behind his head. "That's nice. Does this mean we don't need to sleep anymore?"

"Of course not." Exactly the thinking I feared. "I'm no flare expert—who is?—but I know *everything* comes with a price. When you burn energy, it's gone. Freeing the wolf probably taps a hidden reserve. Useful, obviously, but we can't cheat the laws of physics just by using our powers."

"I don't know, Tor." Hi tapped his feet. "I feel pretty damn super right now."

"This is what Ben was talking about," Shelton added.

My head whipped. "Huh?"

Shelton's fingers found his ear. "Nothing. Just something he mentioned."

I glanced at Hi, who looked away.

"Boys?" I stood and faced them. "Something to share?"

"It *was* a secret." Hi aimed a kick a Shelton, who dodged easily. "Ben made us swear not to tell you."

I crossed my arms. Waited.

"Ben flares first thing every morning," Shelton said. "He says it centers him. Makes him strong. He said *we* should do it, too."

Hi shrugged. "Maybe he's right. Right now, tell me you don't feel great. I might go beat someone up."

"No." I felt certain. "Ben is being incredibly reckless."

Hi spread his hands. "Right now, who are we to judge?"

Ouch. Hi had a point.

"Snuff 'em," I ordered. "Now."

SNUP.

The power vanished. I nearly groaned at the loss.

Still, I felt better than before. Some lethargy crept back, but not much. I couldn't deny that flaring had chased away most of my exhaustion.

But I didn't trust it.

Nothing is that easy. Every action has consequences.

Hi and Shelton removed their sunglasses.

"I feel fresher," Hi said. "Fact is fact. Maybe Ben's not as crazy as you think."

"Ben's gambling blindfolded," I said firmly. "He's gone way too far. Flaring in public. Flaring for pleasure. Flaring just to face the day! He's totally out of control, taking risks we *all* might suffer for. It has to stop."

Shelton slid his prescription specs onto his nose. "So what are you going to do?"

"Talk some sense into him. Right now."

○   ○   ○

I took a city bus from the marina to Mount Pleasant, then connected to a local line. A few more stops, and I was standing outside Wando High.

Which was crazy.

Hi and Shelton would cover for me at Bolton, but I didn't have a clue where to find Ben. This was not the greatest plan ever concocted.

I have to talk to him. Things have gotten out of hand.

I was testing various excuses to summon Ben from class when I spotted him.

Ben was loitering in the parking lot, chatting with two other guys. He wore his standard black tee and jeans. His taller companion sported a purple ski cap despite the eighty-degree weather, while the other boy had an inch-thick wallet chain hanging from his cargo shorts.

"Cutting class," I muttered. "That idiot."

Ben did a double-take when he spotted me, then slowly shook his head. As I drew near, he whispered something under his breath. His moron buddies exploded in laughter.

I'll kill him. Then murder him afterward.

"What the hell are you doing?" Not the most diplomatic of greetings, but my temper was long gone. "Is your first class Parking Lot Maintenance?"

Ben waved a hand at me. "You see what I mean?"

Wallet Chain chuckled as he toked a cigarette. "That's not very nice, sweetheart."

"You'll never land a man like that," added Ski Cap. "This ain't Beantown."

"Ben?" Seething. "May I speak to you privately?"

Ben rolled his eyes. "Give me a sec, guys. I've been naughty."

I waited until the stoners were out of earshot.

"Great crew you've assembled." Dripping with sarcasm.

"Leave them out of this," Ben warned. "What, I can't even *have* friends, now that I've been kicked from the Ivory Tower?"

"Maybe go to class. You might find a better peer group in there."

Ben snorted. "I'm pretty sure *you* have class right now, too."

Touché.

"What are you doing here?" he demanded. "We're packmates and all, but you're not my mother. I've already got one of those, thanks."

I took a calming breath. Yelling at Ben would get me nowhere.

"Hi and Shelton told me you've been flaring every morning. To feel good." Hiding my guilt at having just done the same.

It was . . . an experiment. I won't do it again. I won't!

Ben snorted, tucking his long black hair behind his ears. "Remind me to compliment their secret-keeping skills."

"Ben!" I forced him to meet my eyes. "That *can't* be a good idea."

"Why not? For all we know, flaring might be the healthiest thing ever. We don't know." He pointed a finger. "*You* don't know."

Valid point. But my instincts were clear.

I chose a different tack. "Every time you flare in public, you put our lives in danger. Not just your own. Mine. Hi's. Shelton's. The whole pack, Ben."

"I'm careful." Dismissive. "You might not believe this, Victoria, but I'm not an idiot."

"Then don't *act* like one! Show some restraint. Show some *character.*"

I regretted the last word even as I spoke it.

"Oh, I see." Ben looked away. "This is still about what I did."

"No, it isn't." *Was it?*

"I've apologized." Ben scuffed the pavement with a shoe. I could feel him shutting down. "A hundred times. I can't make you accept it."

My lips froze. No words came.

I didn't know what to say. Honestly didn't know if I'd forgiven him.

Ben looked me square in the eye. "I can't undo my mistakes," he said quietly. "No one can. If you can't get past it, there's nothing more to say."

He turned and headed for the building.

"Ben. Wait."

He didn't stop. In seconds I was alone in the parking lot.

"Damn it."

Walking back to the bus stop, I was more upset than ever. This trip had accomplished nothing. I might've screwed things up even worse.

I couldn't get through to Ben. He wouldn't listen.

What'd you expect? Technically, you're not even talking to him.

My steps slowed.

When was the last time Ben and I had spoken alone?

The hurricane. The hospital.

When he admitted his feelings for me.

The realization jarred me to a standstill.

That morning's fight had been our first private conversation in *five* months.

I never said anything back. About any *of it.*

Because I don't know what to say.

Suddenly, the hairs on my arm stood at attention. With a slap of awareness, I realized *it* was happening again. The ephemeral feeling had returned, lodging at the edge of my conscious thoughts. I could barely detect its presence.

I stopped dead, extending my arms like wings, as if achieving outward balance might create the same within me.

No good. The sensation abruptly winked out, leaving no trace.

"This is getting *really* annoying," I muttered.

My mind raced, struggling to record some data about the mysterious feeling. Make even the slightest link to something I could recognize. Once more, I failed.

Wrapped in such thoughts, I nearly missed the BMW idling across the street.

Tinted windows blocked any view inside the vehicle. Its jet-black hood gleamed in the early morning sunshine.

Something about it felt . . . off.

The car was blocking a fire lane, close to nothing in particular. No stores. No restaurants. No businesses of any kind. There was no reason for anyone to park there.

Unless you're watching the school.

Two dots connected in my mind. I'd seen that car before.

Yes. Switching buses by the library.

An identical BMW had circled the bus stop, then pulled into a McDonald's across the highway. The shiny ride had caught my eye. I'd wondered, in passing, why no one had gotten out to make an order.

I halted with a sudden disturbing thought.

Was I being followed?

Before I could consider more, the BMW swerved into traffic and sped away.

CHAPTER 20

I shoved my lunch away.

No appetite. The visit to Wando High had been a disaster.

Hi glanced at my sandwich, one eyebrow raised.

I waved permission. He slid my tray before him with a grin.

"I *told* you it was a bad idea," Shelton said between bites. "You can't push Blue like that. He just doubles down on whatever he's being stubborn about."

Hi made a gagging noise. "Aw, what is this? Alfalfa sprouts. *Blech.* Pass."

The tray came back my way. "Keep your horse food."

"It was worse than that," I admitted. "I hurt Ben's feelings, too. He thinks I don't trust him because of the Gamemaster."

Hi swished his mouth with Diet Coke. "Well, do you?"

"Do what?" I asked, raising my voice to be heard over the cafeteria din.

"Trust him. Because last I checked, he was headlining your no-fly list."

"I don't know." Rubbing my forehead "I mean, yes, I trust Ben. It's not like I think he'd betray us again. Or that he'd known what his lies would lead to."

I paused, trying to sort out my feelings. "It's not a trust thing. It's more about . . . forgiveness. I *want* to let it go, believe me. I just can't seem to." I blew out a breath. "Every time I think about what Ben did, the anger bubbles back up."

Shelton nodded, but didn't speak.

I leaned back in my chair. "How'd you guys get over it so fast?"

Hi shrugged. "It's Ben. I've only got three real friends. I can't afford to lose one over some Greek tragedy."

My eyes narrowed. "Greek what?"

Hi slapped both hands on the table, fixed me with an intense stare. "Ben did it for love of a woman, Victoria. One he can never possess."

My face burned. This topic we *never* discussed.

Shelton chuckled. "You're such a dope, Stolowitski."

Hi balled up his lunch bag and took aim at a nearby trash can. "It's true, though."

Throw. He missed by a good six feet.

"Foul!" Hi turned back to me, his face serious. "You wanna know why I forgave Ben so quickly? Because I felt sorry for him. Can you imagine being in his shoes?" Hi held up an index finger. "He took one little shortcut, to impress a girl he liked, *and it almost got his friends killed.* Almost got the *girl* killed. That's you, by the way."

Hi sat back in his chair. "I can't imagine the guilt he must carry around."

"It eats at him," Shelton agreed. "All the time. Though he'd never let you see."

I didn't respond.

To be honest, I hadn't thought about how Ben's betrayal affected *Ben*.

Something new to consider.

Hi leaned forward. "Our pack is only five strong. We *have* to forgive one another, even when it's bad. How else are we gonna survive whatever comes next?"

Shelton nodded like a bobblehead. "Ben's not just some guy, he's family. *Pack.* You don't throw that away."

"I know!" My hands rose ineffectually. "I wish it were that easy. There's more to—"

I cut my words short as Hiram's gaze flicked to something over my shoulder.

"Hey, guys." Jason's voice was right behind me. "Hi, I rebounded your miss. Give it more arc next time. Follow through with the wrist."

He set his tray down beside mine.

My fingers found the bridge of my nose. I didn't have time for our usual dance.

"Jason!" I snapped. "Private conversation! Do you mind?"

"Not at all," he said smoothly, smiling, but unable to hide the hurt in his eyes. "I was on my way out anyway. Later." Jason strode toward the exit, a pace too quickly.

Shelton and Hi both gave me a look.

"What?" Then I covered my face with both hands. "Argh! I can't stop screwing up today."

"He'll be fine," Shelton offered. "I think."

"Don't sweat it," Hi said. "Jason always bounces back. That guy's like a puppy dog, he can't stay mad at you. Let's get back to that beemer. You really think it was following you?"

"I don't know anymore." I slumped in my seat. "You shouldn't trust anything I say this morning. I'm cursed."

"The Fairy Dust witch!" Hi whispered, waggling his eyebrows. "She got you."

"Blargh."

"I'm keeping an eye out anyway," Shelton stuffed his lunch bag into his backpack. "If I see a black BMW on my six, I'm running first, asking questions later."

"We're still going to Loggerhead this afternoon, right?" Hi glanced around, then dropped his voice. "For the . . . home movie thing?"

I nodded. "We might as well deal with what we can. Let's take the afternoon shuttle. I'll think of an excuse for Kit, though I'm open to suggestions."

"Ben?" Shelton asked.

"Not today. I think the two of us need a little distance."

The bell rang. We gathered our things and headed for the door.

"Tell Kit we're cutting a music video," Hi suggested as we walked. "Something real gangster, so we need to smash-cut our dance routines. Lay down some visuals. We could offer to let him freestyle rap over the second verse."

I gave him a thumbs-up. "Foolproof. Anyone need a locker stop?"

Two head shakes, so we proceeded directly to class.

Fourth period. AP English Language and Composition. We had Mr. Edde again for second semester, which wasn't bad. He knew his stuff, and wasn't nearly as uptight as some of the other faculty. He'd shaved his Afro, however, which was a crime.

Ella was in this class, too. There were no assigned seats, so we'd taken to sharing a table by a large bay window looking out over the soccer field. Hi and Shelton manned the one directly behind us.

Jason was also on the roster. Spotting him enter, I waved enthusiastically, beaming from ear to ear. He stopped and raised a hand—a confused smile on his face—before taking his seat by the door.

Hi's right. Jason never stews on anything. So different from Ben.

The next group to enter was less pleasant.

The Tripod, in formation.

Ashley, Courtney, and Madison glided to the very back of the room, which they considered theirs. All three sat together, though the tables were designed for two. Mr. Edde had given up trying to separate them.

At first, the Tripod's appearance in an AP class had stunned me.

Not so much Ashley—I knew she was whip smart, as all deadly predators must be. But Madison seemed indifferent to education, even before her . . . funk. And Courtney was downright idiotic.

Not for the first time, I wondered at their marks. Mr. Edde was not an easy grader.

"Scouting the enemy?"

I jumped as Ella's bag thumped onto our table. How did she always sneak up on me?

"Just wondering what they're doing here."

"Their parents must be humored, I'm sure." Ella dropped into her chair, her stormy gray eyes twinkling with amusement. "At least until they rope a husband who'll let them lounge by the pool all day."

I snorted. "If that's the case, they'd love my Annoyance-in-House."

"Why?" Ella tossed her braid over her shoulder. "What'd Whitney do now?"

I ducked too late, took Ella's glossy black rope right across the nose.

"Be careful with that!" But I giggled at her favorite trick. I'd toyed with the idea of growing my hair out just as long, then repaying the favor.

I'd look like a carrot-colored homeless person. Not gorgeous like she does.

I shoved hair envy aside. "Whitney signed me up for the Mag League. I've been reading about the organization, and it sounds like a never-ending cotillion. *Not* pleased."

"You're not alone." Ella's eyes rolled. "Mommy dearest thought it best as well."

"Really?" I perked up immediately. "Oh thank God!"

Ella smiled sarcastically. "I'm glad our mutual imprisonment cheers you so."

"Oh, it does."

I couldn't chase the smile away. At least Ella would be there with me.

Who knows? Maybe it'd be fun. We could turn this thing into an all-out snark fest.

Once again, I thanked my lucky stars for having met her.

It was *so* nice having a girl to talk to.

Grinning like a fool, I accidentally let my gaze meet Ashley's. She smiled sweetly. Without another option, I nodded as though I'd sought her out. Then I quickly glanced down, pretending to search for a page in my book.

"Do *not* be afraid of that girl," Ella whispered, without looking up.

"Can't help it." Eyes on my text. "She's terrifying."

"She's nothing. A spoiled little princess who thinks terrorizing a high school actually means something. I wish she'd pull that crap on me."

"Not likely."

I risked another peek at the Tripod. Ashley was scolding Madison, who nodded meekly. Courtney was staring out the window, toying with her long blond hair.

"They *do* give you a wide berth," I said. "Why is that?"

Ella scowled as she dug in her bag for a pen. "It wasn't always like this. Freshman year, I dodged them every time I walked the halls."

She slapped a Uniball on the table, then squeezed my hand. "Soccer did the trick. It gave me confidence. I realized I was *letting* those bitches get inside my head. The whole thing was stupid. So I stopped avoiding them. Quit ducking every time they snapped their fingers. Pretty soon, they stopped testing me. Sound familiar?"

It did. The Tripod had quit harassing me only after I'd shown some backbone.

Well, a bit more than that.

Not for the first time, I wished I'd met Ella sooner.

Chance told me. He gave the same advice.

Suddenly, I wanted to tell Ella about the Gable twins. Ophiuchus. The ransom video. The black BMW. For a single deranged instant, I wanted to tell her about my powers.

But I didn't. Couldn't. Ella was a true friend. Maybe even a "best" one.

The *last* thing I wanted was for her to see the crazy part of my life. To drive her away.

"Something wrong?" she asked. "You've gone totally pale."

"Blame my Irish roots." Trying to play it off. "I'm just tired."

The second bell rang. Mr. Edde rose and walked to his whiteboard.

Wiping the troubling thoughts from my head, I tried to concentrate on *Paradise Lost*.

At least *it* was something I could control.

CHAPTER 21

We marched single file through LIRI's front gate.

A blazing sun hung in the western sky, without a single cloud to keep it company. Temperatures in the mid-eighties kept the tropical air muggy and hot. Forest sounds surrounded us as we headed for Building One.

Hugo had taken us directly to Loggerhead Island, so we hadn't changed from our school uniforms. Trooping through the woods, my sweat glands began a formal protest under my heavy wool blazer. I wasn't the only casualty—Hi lumbered beside me, red-faced, panting like a dog. The hike from the dock had him close to combusting.

Outside the perimeter fence, a troop of rhesus monkeys prowled the treetops, hooting challenges from the heights. The isle itself is a wildlife preserve, home to dozens of animal species, including a large population of our simian observers.

Inside the chain-link barrier, white-coated scientists filled the courtyard, moving purposefully between buildings, or relaxing on stone benches. On a weekday in spring, the institute bustled like a beehive. Guest researchers arrived daily from around the globe.

The LIRI compound consists of a dozen glass-and-steel buildings, arranged in two rows facing each other across a manicured central common. The larger edifices contain offices, conference rooms, administrative centers, and, most importantly, six state-of-the-art veterinary research labs. The smaller ones are storage facilities, vehicle depots, and equipment sheds.

My father, Kit, managed the whole thing. Still getting used to that.

We passed through sliding glass doors into Building One. Four floors high, it was easily the largest structure on Loggerhead. The Flagship, as Kit called it, contained the most offices and workspace, including the director's suite, security headquarters, and three of the labs.

Upon assuming the directorship, Kit had massively increased security. Along with expensive equipment and systems upgrades—state-of-the-art video cameras now covered every inch of the grounds—LIRI also employed three full-time guards. At least one was on duty 24/7, manning a kiosk in the lobby.

I crossed my fingers as we entered, hoping we could avoid one in particular.

Thank God for small favors—Sam was on duty. Blessedly, Hudson was somewhere else.

Security Chief David Hudson ran his department like a Shogun warlord. An ex-military, by-the-book ball-breaker, the prickly man wasn't a fan of unsupervised teenagers on Loggerhead.

Kit had overruled him on that point, granting us permission to visit the island.

So long as we respected Hudson's rules. Of which there were *hundreds*.

And we did. Grudgingly. Usually.

Hudson's two underlings couldn't have been more different.

Carl Szuberla was a short, enormously fat bowling ball of a man. Though a bit moody—and definitely not the sharpest knife in the drawer—overall he wasn't so bad.

Sam Schneider was older than Carl, somewhere in his sixties. Rail thin, and bald as a cue ball, he was much sharper than his portly coworker. Sam had a sarcastic tongue that rivaled even Hi's. I rarely saw him without a hunting magazine in his claw-like fingers.

As we approached the desk, I kept an eye out for Hudson. The man could materialize out of thin air, and I was hoping to avoid him altogether.

Sam, I could usually handle. While not as easy to fool as Carl, he preferred doing as little as possible. A clever mind can exploit that fact.

Sam spied us approaching.

"Hello, Tory." Setting down his copy of *Field & Stream*. "Come to complicate my day, maybe get me fired?"

"Hi, Sam." I flashed my cheeriest smile. "Don't be silly. I'm here to see Kit."

"Director Howard won't be expecting you, of course." Sam sat back and crossed his arms. "Because that'd be too easy."

I shrugged. "Everyone likes surprises, right?"

Sam snorted. "It's been *my* experience that absolutely no one likes surprises. I'll call up."

He lifted the receiver and dialed an extension. Spoke to someone on the other end. Hung up. "Your father isn't free at the moment, he's with the accountants. They're probably cutting my salary."

I'd known that. Kit had complained about the meeting over breakfast.

"Okay. We'll just head up to his office and wait."

Sam's expression soured. "I'm not supposed to permit that. Which you know."

"Come on, Sambo!" Hi winked. "Live a little. What are we going to do, rob the place?"

The guard crossed his arms. "Wink at me again, Hiram, and I'll throw you to the wolfpack." But he was already reaching for a clipboard. "Sign in. And let's not get lost, hey?"

I scribbled my name. "Thanks, Sam. You're the best."

"Clearly not, since I'm letting you in anyway. Now scram before Hudson gets back."

Needing no more prompting, we hurried to the elevator. Once inside I pressed two, thankful that the car's location wasn't displayed in the lobby.

The director's suite is on the fourth floor. We were headed for the photo lab.

Our luck wasn't perfect, however.

When the doors opened, Mike Iglehart was waiting impatiently.

I suppressed a groan. For some reason, this bozo always gave me a hard time.

That day was no different.

"Miss Brennan." Curse or greeting, hard to tell.

Iglehart had thinning black hair, combed horizontally across his scalp. He examined us critically, tiny, close-set eyes staring down a long nose.

"Hello, Dr. Iglehart." Unsure what else to say, I moved past him into the corridor.

"Wait."

I paused. Turned. The boys bunched at my back.

"Yes?"

I could tell Iglehart was itching to interrogate me.

Behind him, the elevator doors began sliding shut. Iglehart stuck out a hand to keep them from closing.

An awkward moment stretched.

"Nothing. Never mind." Iglehart stepped into the elevator as the doors began closing a second time. We watched to make sure he didn't suddenly reemerge.

Shelton grunted. "That guy is so weird."

"Keep moving," Hi warned. "By now, half the building knows we're here."

At the end of the hall was a tinted glass door. Audio/Video Editing and Production.

I looked left. Right. The coast was clear.

We slipped inside and locked the door.

The small room had a horseshoe-shaped counter running along three walls. Expensive-looking equipment lined every inch. Boom microphones. HD monitors. DVD players and burners. A massive soundboard. Behind the high-tech workspace, a table and chair arrangement hugged the rear wall.

"You guys know how to use this stuff?" I asked doubtfully.

"Yep." Shelton was rubbing his hands together.

"Of course I do." Hi sounded offended. "How else would I record *my debut album*?"

"Prove it." I swept a hand toward the mountain of hardware. "Get to work."

"Why don't you just have a seat?" Shelton pointed to the rear table. "Back there, for now. We'll call you when ready."

I thought of some choice words, but held my tongue.

"Fine. Your show."

With nothing to do, I opened Words With Friends on my iPhone.

I usually crushed Ella, but this time she had the upper hand.

Shelton and Hi chatted excitedly, examining components and hashing out a game plan. Shelton inserted his flash drive into the closest USB port.

Unable to contribute, I concentrated on my letters. V V Q O C A L. Ugh.

I tried to get comfortable. It might be a *long* afternoon.

◇   ◇   ◇

"Tory?" Shelton called.

My head jerked.

"Whaa?" More yawn than speech.

Not surprisingly, I'd drifted off. Lack of sleep was definitely taking a toll.

Hi pointed to one of the monitors. "We might have something."

Groggily, I pulled my chair next to theirs. "Show me."

"Using PhotoSpy, we were able to isolate the shadow on the ransom tape." Hi maximized a window, revealing a grainy white outline on a black field. "We calculated its dimensions by using what we know of Lucy and Peter—since the twins appear in the same image, we can use their measurements to create a scale for quantifying the shadow."

"That's great, guys."

"Not really," Shelton said. "Unfortunately, we don't know the distance between the cameraman and the light source. Without it, our scale is imperfect. What we *can* determine doesn't tell us much—the cameraman is between five foot six and six foot eight and weighs one hundred to three hundred pounds."

I gave him a flat look. "That's practically useless."

Shelton nodded. "We know. That's not why I called you over."

Hi pressed more keys. The steel bar with squiggly lines appeared onscreen.

"We had more luck with this," Shelton said. "Check it out."

He signaled Hi, who tapped a sequence of buttons. The image passed through a sequence of filters. Some made the scrawling loops sharper. Others made them impossible to see.

"The program ran hundreds of these," Hi said. "We think this one's a winner."

Another keystroke. The image snapped into tight focus, the once-fuzzy lines resolved into letters. Something was definitely printed on the bar.

"So close," I hissed, squinting and angling my head. "But still too small to read."

PART THREE

JIGSAW

CHAPTER 29

Kit's footsteps receded down the hall.

 With an ear pressed to my bedroom door, I heard him mumble something to Whitney. Her response was inaudible. Seconds later the TV clicked on.

Beside me, Coop nuzzled my hand. I absently scratched his back.

I knew Kit was worried. Who wouldn't be? His teenage daughter just had a nervous breakdown at a crime scene.

Retreating onto my bed, I grabbed my iPhone. Checked email. Voicemail. Text messages. Chat. Nothing from the other Virals. I hadn't heard from anyone since this afternoon.

Clock check—8:00 p.m.

Coop settled down beside the bed, his eyes never leaving me.

The holes in my memory were slowly filling.

I recalled flashing lights. The mass of police officers. Mr. and Mrs. Francis, red-eyed on their silly little couch. My mad dash up the stairs. A rush of blood to the head.

Ella had been taken. Ella was missing.

I felt panic bubble up inside me once more.

Calm. Breathe.

I glanced at the light blue pill resting in my trash can. Maybe I should've swallowed it.

No. I need a clear mind to be of any use.

I knew I was barely keeping it together. Could feel the shrieking desperation, just below the surface, that threatened to engulf me. To blind me. To turn out the lights a second time.

Ella has been taken. *Ella* was missing.

I grabbed my phone. Still nothing.

On the Francises' porch—as three EMTs were guiding me from the property—Shelton had whispered he would gather the pack. Hi had waved from across the front yard, where he was sitting between two officers, waiting for his mother to arrive. Apparently he'd body-blocked the first cops to chase me through the house. The police were none too pleased.

I owe you one, Hi. You bought enough time.

That strange, unnerving playing card. Its ghastly image was seared into my retinas.

A golden sea monster. Some horrid snake-fish hybrid, all sharp teeth and vicious claws. Hi's intervention had given me precious seconds to examine the clue.

The *link,* I should say. There was no doubting that whoever kidnapped Lucy and Peter Gable had also abducted Ella. The snake-fish card was a smoking gun.

No one could compare it to Ophiuchus and *not* see a connection. The items were clearly of common origin.

A madman's signature.

The twisted calling cards of a psychopath who steals children from their homes.

On its own volition, my mind leaped to Rex Gable. The man seriously gave me the creeps.

But would he really imprison his own children? Did he grab Ella, too? Why?

I was forced to admit it didn't make sense.

What would Rex Gable have to do with Ella Francis?

Yet . . . Rex Gable *was* at the art show. He'd have seen Ella there with me, radiant in her rebellious green cocktail dress.

And the black BMW. The type of car Rex Gable might own. *It* was at the opening, too.

My hands found my face. Rubbed slowly, up and down.

I didn't know what to think. My brain felt like scrambled eggs.

Against my will, I pictured Ella, locked in that awful dungeon with the Gable twins.

Or worse, all alone.

Cracks in my calm resurfaced. Anxiety threatened to overwhelm me.

Coop popped onto the bed and curled up beside me. He rested his giant head on my knee. I dove forward and hugged his body close.

Knew that someone was looking out for me, always.

The tide of dread receded, but didn't fully disappear. Disturbing thoughts about Ella kept exploding inside me, like popcorn on a hot stove. But Coop's warm, solid presence helped keep the demons at bay.

I hadn't felt like this since losing Mom.

Stop it. Ella's missing, not . . .

I shook my head to dispel the terrible thought.

Do something. Work the problem.

Go to the police? With *what*, exactly? My suspicions? A few wild theories?

We had next to nothing concrete. Not really.

A bleach-stained area in an otherwise spotless house. No help there.

The authorities had surely identified the Ophiuchus card by now. No sense revealing Hi's sticky fingers just to pass along stale info.

And how could I possibly convey the feeling I got from watching Peter Gable's eyes?

The writing on the steel bar. That's definitely *intel the police could use.*

Moving to my desk, I powered my MacBook and googled "Philip Simmons Ironworks."

Dozens of hits. The links momentarily distracted me from my grief.

Philip Simmons was a renowned African-American blacksmith and ironworker. Scrolling Wikipedia, I discovered he'd recently passed away at age ninety-seven. He began his career at a small shop on Calhoun Street, before moving into the specialized field of ornamental wrought iron in the 1930s. All told, Simmons fashioned over five hundred decorative pieces—gates, fences, balconies, and window grills—many of which still grace the area's richest mansions and estates.

I clicked a few more sites, impressed. In 1982, the National Endowment for the Arts awarded Simmons its National Heritage Fellowship, the highest honor the United States can bestow upon a traditional artist. The South Carolina legislature gave him a "lifetime achievement" award, and commissioned several public sculptures for museums and the city of Charleston. Simmons was inducted into the SC Hall of Fame in 1994, and received the Order of the Palmetto—South Carolina's highest award—in 1998. Some of his pieces are displayed in the Smithsonian.

I leaned back in my chair. "Not bad."

This man was no common grunt. Though Simmons began his career making penny nails and horseshoes, he became a world-famous artist. A *real* one—not like that fop Jean-Paul Delacourt and his horrible interpretations. Philip Simmons was a true master at shaping metal.

So how did steel bars bearing his name end up forming a dank prison?

I surfed a bit more. Late in life, Simmons had been in extremely high demand. His works literally blanket the Lowcountry. Without more to go on, his mark was useless for locating the twins' dungeon.

Still, I knew the CPD had more resources than Google. This was a tip they could use.

But how would I explain having a copy of the ransom tape? Impossible. Commissioner Riggins would have a stroke.

In all honesty, I doubted they'd even let me through the door. Who was going to trust a high schooler's video analysis? The silly girl who'd fainted while contaminating a crime scene.

I'd get handed a second blue pill. And this time, they'd check under my tongue.

Fine. No police. Then *what*?

The card from Ella's room. Find out what it is.

I reached for my iPhone. Ran a search. Placed a call.

"Yes?" The same melodious voice.

"Miss Gordon?"

"Speaking." A tad hesitant. "May I help you?"

"This is Tory Brennan. We met the other day in your shop. You told me and my friends about Ophiuchus, and the zodiac?"

Silence.

I forged ahead. "I have another question, about a different symbol. Would it be possible to pay for a session over the phone?"

No response. But I heard breathing on the line.

"Miss Gordon? Hello?"

"Now's not a good time."

I felt the brushback pitch sail by my chin. Ignored it.

"I know it's after business hours, but I'd appreciate if we could just talk. I'm willing to pay double, if that helps."

"It's not the money. Look, why don't you—"

"Clara?" My voice shook. I was suddenly on the brink of tears. "I'd really, *really* like to do this now, if you don't mind. I've had a horrible day. Can you please help me?"

There was another pause. Then, "What would you like to know?"

"Thank you. How should I send payment?"

"Never mind that." Brusque. "Ask your question."

"I've encountered another symbol, similar to the first one we showed you."

I described the card from Ella's room in exacting detail.

"That is Cetus," Clara said. "Known as the Sea Monster in Greek mythology, he was slain by Perseus while saving Andromeda from Poseidon's wrath. He's commonly referred to as The Whale today. Cetus is in the same boat as Ophiuchus—omitted from the zodiac."

"There's *another* missing sign?"

"Yes. Cetus is located in a celestial region known as the Sea, because of the many water-associated constellations nearby. Pisces. Aquarius. Capricornus. Others as well."

"Is Cetus a sign, though?"

"He has claim to be. The constellation passes *very* close to the ecliptic. Once a year—at the boundary between Cetus and Pisces—a sliver of our home star strays into Cetus for not quite a full day. March fourteenth. The planets also appear in Cetus on rare occasions. Thus, his inclusion in the zodiac is arguable, though not as clear-cut as Ophiuchus."

I thought a moment. "What does Cetus mean to people?"

There was a sigh on the other end. "It's hard to say. What you describe is a seventeenth-century depiction of Cetus, that of a dragon fish. In other times, Cetus has been portrayed as simply a large fish, or whale, or shark."

"But who would care about him now?" Frustration tinged my voice. "Who would follow Cetus *today*? Who would carry his symbol around in their pocket?"

"I'm not sure, Tory." Gordon sounded disappointed that she couldn't answer. "Sailors, maybe. Cetus is often a ship's name, chosen to express a lack of fear of the sea. But he's usually viewed as a bad omen, or a bringer of misfortune. Superstitious mariners associate him with bad weather, pirates, lost cargo, pretty much anything negative. On some ships, merely saying his name can trigger reprisals."

Sailors? What?

"Is there anything else you can tell me?" I pressed.

Another pause. I could almost see Gordon debating whether to say more.

"Clara, please."

"Just this." She spoke quickly, as if wishing to dispel a bad taste. "In most legends and myths of the ancient world, Cetus is associated with wickedness and ferocity. Some believe his sign represents pure evil. Unrelenting depravity and corruption."

Her words jarred me. What kind of monster were we dealing with?

Click.

"Hello?"

The line was dead. Surprised, I hit redial. The call went straight to voicemail.

She hung up. Without getting paid.

Why would Gordon do that?

Flopping back against my pillows, I replayed the conversation in my mind.

She'd been hesitant to speak. So unlike her friendly demeanor when we'd first entered Fairy Dust. Upon reflection, Gordon's reticence seemed more than annoyance at the late hour.

Why did I get the sense she'd been frightened?

A gong sounded on my computer.

"Finally!"

I leaped for my desk, startling Cooper from the bed.

Entering the Virals chat room, I found all three boys present.

Uh-oh.

They'd met there ahead of time, before alerting me. To *discuss* me.

"I'm fine." Wanting to nip any sympathy in the bud. "What I'd like is to focus on this case. No emotion. No distraction. We need to help Ella, *now*, in any way we can. And the Gable twins. Will you help me?"

For a moment, none of them spoke. Prepared speeches seemed poised on their tongues.

"Okay," Hi said simply.

"I can do that," Shelton promised.

"Anything you need." Ben's voice crackled with anger. "Let's get this bastard."

"Then listen up." I gave a quick summary of what I'd learned.

When I'd finished, Hi piped up. "I also learned something that might help."

"Please." Nodding encouragingly. "Anything."

"I know where Ella was snatched from." Hi rubbed his left shoulder. "After I *accidentally* tripped those officers inside the Francis house—"

"Thank you for that."

"No problem. Anyway, the police took me out on the lawn. They were probably all so terrified of me, they couldn't concentrate. Who can blame them?"

I made get-on-with-it gestures into my webcam.

Hi's voice grew serious. "The cop assigned to babysit me was a talker, said that Ella was last seen at her job the night before. She took a break, went outside, and didn't come back. Never got home."

A surge of adrenaline. This was useful information. Ella waitressed two evenings a week at a pizza joint called the Flying Tomato.

"Great job, Hi. That's our next move. We'll turn that place upside down."

"Tonight?" Shelton asked. Though this time, his voice carried no reservations.

I considered it. Wanted to agree. But police would be swarming that restaurant right now. Plus, there was no way I'd get past Kit and Whitney in the next few hours.

"No. But let's go early tomorrow morning, before they open. Agreed?"

Shelton nodded.

"You got it," said Hi.

"In." Ben jiggled his keys. "I'll be there first thing."

I logged off and lay down on my bed. Coop jumped up beside me. As I tussled his scratchy chin, some of the weight lifted from my shoulders.

For the first time since waking, I felt a measure of control.

Lying there in the dark, the panic began to recede. Transform. Become something else.

Anger.

A slow-boiling rage filled me inside, head to toe.

I captured the feeling. Harnessed it. Enslaved it to my purpose.

Someone out there had attacked my friend. Stolen her. Put her life in danger.

That person is going to pay.

Coop's head rose from his paws.

He regarded me with lidded eyes, then gave a low, dangerous growl.

"That's right, boy." Stroking his head. "That's damn right."

CHAPTER 30

Saturday

The Flying Tomato was closed and shuttered.

No police tape. No squad cars keeping watch. Whatever the police might've discovered the night before, they hadn't sealed the premises.

The restaurant was on Tradd Street, two short blocks from the Francis home. Ben pulled into a public lot around the corner on King. We walked the last fifty yards, not wanting to advertise our presence.

The sign was garish—a giant ripe tomato, wearing white sunglasses and sneakers, flying off a half pike. A funky, hipster hangout. I knew Ella loved working there.

She'd taken the job against her parents' advice. Getting out of the house, meeting new people, and making a little money had appealed to Ella's sense of independence.

She made minimum wage, plus tips. Ella got *plenty* of those.

Ella thought a girl should work, even in high school. I totally agreed, and had harbored secret hopes of joining the Flying Tomato staff once old enough to drive.

That dream was out the window now.

The pizza parlor was a white one-story structure with red shutters. A long front porch ran its length, set with tables for eating outside. We entered a gravel lot adjacent to the building. At eight o'clock on a Saturday morning, there were no cars present.

"Ready?" Ben fought to keep the eagerness from his voice.

I nodded. "Light 'em up."

For once, I didn't argue the point. We'd flare, and leave no stone unturned.

When it came to Ella's safety, I wasn't holding back.

SNAP.

A crackling sensation, followed by a blast of scorching heat.

Sweat erupted from my pores. I held my face in my hands, trying not to scream as every hair on my body stood at attention.

"Too much!" Shelton moaned, rubbing his temples.

Beside me I saw Hi wobble, then collapse. Yellow light strobed from his eyes.

Something is wrong.

The inferno inside me continued to build. My arms shook. I couldn't feel my legs. Staggering like a drunk, I fought to control my breathing.

I saw Ben wheel and swing his fists, as if fighting an invisible foe. His eyes flickered between golden and brown.

He stumbled. Then, hand on his knees, Ben vomited on the ground.

Pressure built inside my skull. I felt like a balloon inflated well past the point of safety.

Desperate, I squeezed my eyes shut, willing the flare to level. Instead, the pain amplified.

In my subconscious, the flaming cords that connected us thrummed out of control. Their forms were disjointed, indistinct. Unbound, they flailed and twanged wildly.

An atonal warble filled my ears. I could barely track the lines, much less control them.

This isn't right. We have to let go!

I don't know if I sent the message, or if the boys simply arrived at the same conclusion.

"Screw this," Hi gasped. "I'm shutting down."

"True that!" Shelton howled.

Both stiffened. Convulsions racked their bodies, but, moments later, they released twin sighs of relief.

SNUP.

My own flare died.

I sagged, nearly crumpling in relief. The agony receded.

When my head cleared, I heard Shelton screaming at Ben. "Release it, Blue!"

"*No.*" Ben spoke through gritted teeth. "*I'm* in charge . . . not some . . . dog DNA . . ."

He shuddered, falling against the side of building.

I ran to his side. "Ben, stop it! You have to let go!"

Ben's face swung to me, eyes slitted. His jaw and back were rigid. A vein pulsed in his neck as he grimaced, panting, on the verge of passing out.

"Ben, please." I took his hand, voice suddenly calm. "You need to stop. We'll figure this out together. I promise."

Ben looked away. For several heartbeats he continued to fight. Then his hand squeezed mine as his body went slack.

He staggered, nearly dropped. Shelton and I caught him, then eased him to the gravel.

For a full minute we sat in a clump, catching our breath, no one speaking.

Finally, "I don't know *what* that was."

"That's never happened before," Hi wheezed. "It's like my flare was attacking me."

"Oh, man." Shelton was shirt-cleaning his glasses with jerky motions. "We got problems, ya'll. I knew our powers were getting wilder, but that was a whole 'nother level."

Ben rose, brushed dirt from his jeans. "Let's try again."

"Are you crazy?" Hi struggled to his feet. "No thanks, pal. One barbequing was enough for me."

"Ben, be reasonable." I tried not to scold. "Whatever just happened, it was serious. Maybe even deadly. We have to consider this carefully."

Ben seemed about to argue, but turned away. His shoulders rose and fell.

"Fine." His back to us. "For now."

We dusted ourselves off. A quick scan of the neighborhood confirmed we were still alone. Which was fortunate—our group seizure would've been tough to explain.

"We'll do this old-school," Hi said. "Using only the power of our massive brains."

Shelton chuckled. "A throwback."

I smiled, trying to mask my anxiety.

What the hell just happened?

Every fear I'd harbored about the nature of our mutations came roaring to the surface.

Was our short circuit merely an aberration? Some odd quirk, never to return?

Or was it the beginning of the end? Was my body rejecting the canine DNA?

Or worse, was the new genetic material . . . taking over?

We don't have time for this now.

My mind returned to the task. Ella was *missing*. Our flare problems would have to wait.

"Shelton, please open this restaurant." Striding for the door. "There's no time to waste."

○   ○   ○

"I'm out of ideas." Hi was leaning against a red-brick oven. "And no leftover pizza *anywhere* in here? Unreal."

We stood inside the cramped kitchen. For the last thirty minutes we'd turned the place upside down, examining every square foot of the restaurant. Dining room. Kitchen. Pantry. Storeroom. Office. Even the two bathrooms. Nothing was out of the ordinary.

"We should bounce," Shelton urged. "Somebody might show up to make spaghetti sauce any minute."

Both boys glanced at me.

I punched my leg in frustration. I hated quitting, but they were right. This was serving no purpose.

"We didn't check the Dumpster," Ben said from across a counter. "Or anything out back."

"The cop said Ella went outside," Hi added. "Maybe she was snatched behind the building?"

I snapped a nod. "Shelton, lock up behind us."

Slipping out the back door, we found ourselves in an alcove paved with concrete. A large Dumpster was hard against the building. Beyond it were three rolling recycling bins and a pair of rusty folding chairs. A wooden fence enclosed three sides. The fourth was open to the gravel lot where we'd had our flare meltdown.

Hi pointed to the chairs. "Cigarette station. I don't suppose Ella is a smoker?"

"The Lady Griffins soccer captain?" I scoffed. "Not likely."

Hi began lifting bin lids while Ben rooted in the Dumpster. Without a better plan, I began a slow circuit of the enclosure. Looking for what, I had no idea. A tightness was building in my chest—that crushing feeling of helplessness, creeping back in.

"Hey, Tor." Shelton was kneeling beside the chairs. "What's this look like to you?"

I was hurrying to his side when we heard the screech of tires on loose stone.

Hi dropped into his battle crouch. "Oh crap!"

Ben stepped away from the Dumpster. Shelton and I moved to his side.

All eyes watched the corner of the building.

Nowhere to run. If someone came back here, we'd have some explaining to do.

Footsteps on pebbles. Approaching.

A familiar face rounded the corner. The last person I expected to see.

"What?" The only words I could manage.

"You're in a position to question?"

Chance wore tan shorts and a gray polo. I couldn't recall seeing him so casual before.

"You shouldn't be here, Claybourne." Ben's voice was menacing. "Leave."

Chance barely glanced at him. "I don't take orders from you. I assume *you've* stopped by for a breakfast calzone?"

I stepped in front of Ben. "Why are you here, Chance? Did you follow us?"

For a moment, Chance's gaze roved the group. Finally, "Yes."

My breath caught. "Why?"

"I heard about Ella on the news." His tone softened a degree. "I'm sorry, Tory. I know you two had become friends."

Tears threatened. I fought them back, surprised at how close to the surface my emotions lurked.

"We thought maybe we could help." I left it at that.

"Help how?" Chance pressed. "What can *you* offer that the police can't?"

"Mind your own business," Ben said darkly. "For once."

"No." Chance gave a quick headshake. "No, I think we're past that."

I could feel the tension rising. Shelton hid behind my shoulder. Hi was acting nonchalant, but his tapping foot gave him away. And Ben . . .

"I know what you were doing at the aquarium." Chance either didn't sense the danger, or didn't care. "You were snooping in Marcus Karsten's old files."

Ben tensed. The charge in the air became palpable.

Then, like a lightning strike, the odd sensation returned. For one blinding instant, I felt lines of connection blasting from my mind and looping around the others. Ben. Hi. Shelton. Even Chance. Then my mind twitched and the feeling completely evaporated.

What was that!?

"I don't know how you tracked them down," Chance continued, oblivious. "Or what led you to the aquarium. Questions for another day." His voice hardened. "But there were *other* files on that server you had no business viewing."

I struggled to regain my bearings. "I don't know what—"

"Save it, Tory." Chance's pupils dilated. "You copied my B-Series files. *You* know it, and *I* know it. I want them back. Every last megabyte."

Suddenly, I saw it. Beneath the cool exterior, Chance was furious. And scared. Maybe even terrified.

No more lies.

"No." I was pleased my voice didn't quaver. "Those files involve Karsten's secret work. We have an interest in that."

His cheek twitched. "The files are encrypted. You'll never get in."

"We'll see about that."

Chance's gaze bored into me. I met him, stare for stare. As best I could.

"I could go to the police," he said softly. "Breaking and entering. Wire fraud. Tampering with Candela property. I have you *on tape*, red-handed. One phone call and you're done."

Bluff.

"You won't do that." Spoken just as calmly. "You don't want the cops to know about the B-Series, either. Those files are *your* dirty little secret, aren't they? Like father, like son."

I saw the punch land.

Chance's eyes betrayed him. My guess was dead-on.

"I can destroy you." The heat rose in Chance's voice. "You're *nothing* in this city. I'm rich. Powerful. *Respected.* Cross me, and you'll pay dearly. Your parents, too."

That was the line. Chance crossed it.

Ben charged forward and shoved him to the ground.

Chance tumbled backward, taken totally by surprise. Ben stood over him, chest heaving. Lifting Chance by his shirt, Ben cocked his other fist.

I raced forward and grabbed Ben's elbow. His head whipped to me, nostrils flaring.

"No." Holding his gaze. "That's not what we do."

Ben snorted. "Whatever." But he dropped Chance and walked away.

Chance roared to his feet. "Try that again, boy!"

Ben spun, a smile splitting his face. "Gladly."

"Stop it!" I placed myself between them, one arm outstretched toward each.

Ben had surprised Chance, but he was the smaller of the two. This could get ugly, fast.

Shelton and Hi moved to Ben's flanks, began whispering in his ears.

My hand touched Chance's chest. "Be the bigger man," I said softly.

Livid eyes met mine. Then rolled.

"Once." Swatting my hand from his chest. "This *one* time, Tory. For old time's sake."

"You're lucky, Benjamin." Chance nodded toward me. "You have a guardian angel."

"Another time," Ben promised. "We'll see who's lucky."

Chance turned my way. "You're upset about Ella, and not thinking clearly. We'll revisit this issue later. But those files are mine, and I want them back. That isn't a request."

Without another word, he strode from the alcove. I trailed him around the building—to make sure he actually left—and watched Chance climb into a car.

"Well, well."

The other Virals approached behind me.

"Well what?" Hi asked. "Did you want to sock him, too?"

I pointed. "Chance has nice wheels."

The boys followed my finger.

We watched a gleaming black BMW tear from the parking lot.

CHAPTER 31

"H im!" Hi shouted dramatically.

"It adds up." I shook my head, sliding facts into place. "Chance has plenty of spare time, and has been suspicious of us for months. Given everything he knows, following me isn't the craziest thing in the world. Plus, he was at the art gala that night."

"So the mystery car isn't connected to the kidnappings?" Shelton asked.

I hesitated.

Surely Chance wouldn't have anything to do with . . .

"No." I dismissed the notion. "Looks like Chance was simply keeping tabs on me."

"Because he knows too much." Ben aimed a finger at me. "And you don't seem very surprised, Brennan."

I flinched. "Chance *may* have mentioned a few of those things at the aquarium."

A bit guiltily, I told the boys about our showdown in the corner office. When I'd finished, they gaped at me, equal parts anxious and angry.

"How could you keep that from us?" Hi sputtered. "Chance knows about Karsten!? About Cooper!? He knows about the virus we caught!?"

"This is so, *so* bad," Shelton moaned. "That punk could expose us at any time!"

"He's a threat." Ben had a look in his eyes that left me cold. "If Chance suspects we were infected, combined with what he's seen this last year—"

"Calm down." Trying to do so myself. "Chance doesn't have all the pieces yet. He knows Coop was infected with XPB-19, and he knows we have the wolfdog. But that's it."

"You said *yet*," Hi pointed out. "That implies he'll put it together eventually."

Deep breath. "Chance suspects we caught the supervirus. And given what he's witnessed over the last year, I think he believes it affected us somehow. But he has no idea *how*," I added quickly. "He doesn't know the whole truth. And, most importantly, he can't *prove* anything, or tell anyone. Not without exposing Candela's involvement with illegal experiments. Which he obviously won't do."

"We're supposed to trust *Chance freaking Claybourne* with our deepest, darkest secret?" Ben growled. "That's the plan?"

"Give me some time to think it over," I pleaded. "Come up with a solution."

Ben fixed me with a dangerous stare. "Okay, Tory. But don't take too long. I won't have Chance running around, endangering my freedom. My *life*. He needs to be dealt with."

I suppressed a shiver. Didn't want to understand what Ben was implying.

"It's time to jet," Hi said. "People might start showing up here soon."

I nodded, took a step toward the street.

For a brief moment, my thoughts returned to the spike of interconnectedness my mind had experienced. The frequency was increasing, the intensity escalating. Yet the attack—that's what I was forced to call them at this point—came and went without warning. The onset seemed completely random. I couldn't even *guess* at a pattern.

There has to be a trigger. Something that sets off the effect.

"Wait!" Shelton pointed to the rear of the Flying Tomato. "Almost forgot."

"You found something?" My concern for Ella shifted back to the forefront. A deeper contemplation of Viral side effects would have to wait.

"Maybe." Shelton led us back to the alcove. "I'm just trying to figure out what *that* is."

On the ground between the folding chairs was a fist-sized chunk of red-orange rock. Pockmarked, misshapen, with a rough, bubbly exterior, the lumpy stone seemed oddly out of place.

Shelton knelt to scoop it up.

"Wait."

I moved closer and dropped to one knee. Hi and Shelton snagged the chairs and set them aside, exposing the multi-hued rock to the morning sun.

I stuck my nose inches from the rock. It had an odd, sulfurous scent.

Something was stuck to the stone's surface. A shiny filament, rising on the breeze.

Gently, my fingers extended, capturing the slender line. I held the wisp before my eyes.

A single hair. Black and glossy.

I carefully stretched the strand between my fingers. It was over a foot long.

Ella.

"We've got something." My voice was steady, but my heart raced as I removed a plastic vial from my pocket. "Hiram, please grab a large plastic baggie from my evidence kit. It's in the car."

As Hi hurried off, I carefully inserted hair into vial. Then, dropping to my elbows, I examined every centimeter of rock I could see without touching it.

A tiny rust-colored oval marked the left side, with a thin streak descending from the center of the discoloration, as though made by a dripping liquid.

I didn't need Coop's nose.

"I found a hair. And maybe blood."

Shadows fell across the stone. I glanced up to see Shelton holding latex gloves. Hi had the ziplocks. Ben handed me a cotton swab and stopper. "Anything else?"

Despite the circumstances, I smiled. "Just one thing. The green packet in my kit."

I pulled on the gloves. When Ben returned, I opened the packet and laid out several items. After moistening the tip of the swab with a squirt of filtered water, I gently rubbed it against the stain. Then I removed a thin plastic strip from a white pill bottle.

"This is called a Hemastix strip," I explained, "which contains the chemical tetramethylbenzidine. TMB for short. It's like a dipstick test for human blood, and works better than Luminol on trace samples. Bottom line—if this strip changes color, it's a presumptive positive for blood."

"Presumptive?" Shelton asked.

"Best we can do. But with the hair attached, and this stain appearing on an out-of-place rock at a possible crime scene, I think that paints a pretty clear picture."

"Any more toys you're holding out on?" Hi grumbled. "I don't know you anymore."

"Thank Aunt Tempe for this one," I replied. "She stocked my evidence kit. But an entire bottle of Hemastix strips only costs like thirty bucks."

As precisely as possible, I rubbed the dampened swab against the yellow material at the end of the strip. In seconds the patch turned blue-green.

"Bingo." I placed the used strip into a second vial. Then, nodding to

Hi, I lifted the rock in my gloved hands and placed in the plastic bag. Sealed it tight.

Hi shook his head. "Man, Charleston has the worst cops in the world. How could they miss this?"

"It's just an ugly rock," Shelton countered. "I'm not sure why *I* noticed it."

"So we take this stuff downtown?" Ben asked.

I was about agree, then stopped myself. "Why?"

This seemed to take the boys aback.

"What are *we* supposed to do with it?" Shelton countered. "The cops can run DNA tests, and figure out whether that's Ella's hair. And . . . blood."

His voice faltered as the implications hit home.

"I know it's hers already." I had zero doubt. "And those tests won't help us *find* her."

Hi scratched his head. "Then . . . what?"

"The rock." Ben's eyes found mine. "We should track the rock, not the DNA."

"What? That could be from anywhere," Shelton whined. "The rock may not even be a clue. The kidnapper could've scooped it from a roadside ditch."

"It's all we have." I stared at the bagged hunk of stone. "The police already know Ella was abducted. They don't need DNA to confirm it. An investigation is already going full swing."

Hi nodded slowly. "But if the rock can be traced to somewhere specific . . ."

"What about prints?" Shelton said. "If the kidnapper hit Ella with that, then—"

I shook my head. "Such a basic mistake? I don't see it."

"We can examine the rock ourselves first, *then* give it to the police," Hi suggested. "No harm, no foul. Everybody wins."

"Examine it how?" Ben cocked his head. "You mean LIRI?"

"With Kit and Hudson already on our case?" I snorted, packing up my kit. "Not a chance. Not after the video debacle. Plus, to learn anything that way we'd need the mass spectrometer, or the gas chromatograph. But you can't even power those machines without a dozen permissions. We wouldn't last five minutes."

"Then let's find an expert," Hi said. "Some weirdo rock junkie who can eyeball this bad boy, and tell us what it is."

I tapped my nose. "My thoughts exactly."

Shelton's face lit up. "CU has a geology department. We're close to the campus, too. Maybe somebody's working on a Saturday?"

"It's worth a shot." Zipping up my bag. "Let's get moving. Today, there's no time to lose."

CHAPTER 32

Charleston University's Department of Geology and Environmental Sciences was eight blocks away, on Coming Street.

We drove past Ella's house on the way. It was all I could do not to cry.

Ben found a spot out front. We entered a three-story brick building and took the elevator up one floor. Stepping into a small lobby, we asked a passing student for the office of Professor Wiley Marzec.

Marzec was younger than I'd expected—no more than forty. A bit thick around the middle, with a round, friendly face and a mullet of brown hair. He wore lime-green shorts and a brown T-shirt that said "Rocktastic." When he spoke, his voice filled the room.

"Come in, come in!" Half rising, Marzec waved to a pair of wicker chairs facing his desk. His office was small, but cozy, lined with wooden bookshelves holding an assortment of stones, fossils, and thick text-books. Something called the International Stratigraphic Chart was taped to one wall. A fantastic geode rode his desk as a paperweight.

"Cool!" Hi zoomed to the sparkling rock.

"I know, right?" Marzec waved permission for Hi to touch it. "It's amethyst, which is the purple version of quartz. And check out that red streak circling the core. That's pure hematite under the crystalline surface. Found it at Thunder Bay, up in Canada. All the other rock-jocks are jealous."

"Dope." Wisely, Hi didn't attempt to pick it up. "Five bucks?"

"Not on your life." Marzec smiled as he turned to me. "Tory, I presume?"

"Yessir." Slipping into a seat. "And thank you so much for seeing us on short notice."

"My father's name was Sir." Wiley leaned back in his creaky office chair. "I'm Wiley. Or Professor Marzec, if you must. Now, what can I do you for?"

"We found a rock that seemed out of place." I snapped for Shelton, who was standing behind me. Hi had filled the other seat, with Ben looming over his shoulder. "We were hoping you could tell us what it is."

Shelton handed me the ziplock. Hesitating only slightly, I passed it to Marzec.

"Ah!" Marzec smiled wide. "A phosphate nodule. Were you guys down by the river?" His fingers found the bag's seal. "May I?"

"I'd prefer you didn't," I said quickly.

Marzec's brows quirked, but he set the bag on the desk and peered through the plastic.

"You said something about a river?" Hi prompted. "Which one?"

Marzec's whole focus was on the stone. "Copper. Wando. Edisto. Any of them. But I was mainly thinking of the Ashley." He sat back. "What do you know about phosphate mining in the Lowcountry?"

Our blank faces gave him his answer.

Marzec glanced at the ceiling in thought. "Where to start?"

"How about the Cliff Notes version?" I suggested.

"Sounds good." Marzec tapped the plastic bag. "What you have is called a phosphate nodule. A real beauty, too, must weight five pounds. Can't you smell that odor? These rocks are found throughout the

Charleston Basin, and along the banks of the tributary rivers. Their ages range from the Oligocene to the Pleistocene epochs. In South Carolina, phosphate deposits run parallel to the coast for about seventy miles, extending south from the Wando to the Broad River, and then inland for approximately thirty miles."

My heart sank. That sounded like a *lot* of real estate.

"What exactly *is* phosphate?" Shelton asked.

"Let's start with phosphorus." Marzec's voice became professorial. "One of the seventeen nutrients required by all living plants and animals, it's absolutely *crucial* for growing food. If the dirt you're farming lacks phosphorus, that deficiency will severely limit production. To compensate, farmers use various fertilizers to correct any shortfall and increase crop yields."

"Soil needs phosphorous to grow crops," I summarized. "Got it."

"Exactly. Phosphorus is *essential* to life—there's no substitute for it in agriculture. The element readily combines in nature, forming crucial organic compounds. For example, it's a vital component of nucleic acids—DNA and RNA molecules—from which all life springs. It's also a key component of phospholipids, plasma membranes, and solid structures like bones and teeth."

"Need phosphorus to live," Hi said. "Roger that."

Marzec winked, perhaps acknowledging his long-winded style. "I'll cut to the chase—phosphorus itself is highly reactive, and doesn't appear naturally in its elemental form. Instead, it occurs in phosphates—charged groups of atoms. Basically, a phosphorus atom hooked to four oxygen atoms."

"Okay." This was getting more technical than I'd expected.

"You can't mine pure phosphorus," Marzec simplified. "It doesn't exist anywhere. Instead, you have to look for phosphate rocks—like this one—dig them up, then break the stones down."

"Okay." I shifted, not totally sure I understood. "Phosphate rocks contain phosphorus, which is essential for making good fertilizer. So people dig them up for sale."

"Perfectly stated." Marzec spread his hands. "This was a *major* industry in the late 1800s. The amount of available farmland was limited, which meant the same tired plots had to be replanted over and over. Overuse was leaching essential nutrients from the soil. Farmers were desperate for a way to get those minerals back. Enter phosphate mining."

"They needed prehistoric rocks to make fertilizer?" Hi asked. "Nothing else worked?"

"Before the mining boom, farmers were dependent on guano for fertilizer. But that had to be imported, and was very pricey. Finding high-quality fertilizer buried right beneath their feet was a godsend for local sharecroppers."

"Wait. Guano?" Hiram's eyes narrowed. "You're saying—"

"Yes." Marzec grinned. "Farmers were buying the droppings of seabirds and bats, which are high in both phosphorus and nitrogen."

Shelton crinkled his nose. "Man, farming is just nasty. For *real.*"

"Are phosphate rocks widespread?" I asked.

"Actually, no." Marzec jabbed a thumb at a multicolored map behind his desk. "There are large deposits in central Florida, certain regions of Idaho, and along the North Carolina coast. Smaller ones in Montana, Tennessee, and, of course, here in the Lowcountry. Phosphate rock was so prevalent along the Ashley River that many landmarks in that area still bear its name."

"Ashley Phosphate Road," Ben said. "I've driven there."

"Correct." Marzec stroked his chin. "The banks of the Ashley River were *riddled* with phosphates. Once their utility was discovered, mining companies sprang up along the waterfront. For the next fifty years, strip mining for phosphate rock was *the* major industry in that area. By

1885, South Carolina was producing *half* the world's supply. Some folks got rich, although Mother Nature won't be sending them any thank-you cards. Entire sedimentary layers were dug up, ripped out, and then barged downstream."

There was a pause as Marzec seemed to run out of steam.

"Is phosphate mining still a big business today?" I prompted.

"Oh no." Marzec took a long pull on a Diet Coke. "Most of the local deposits quickly tapped out. By the 1900s, the vast majority of operations had shuttered. Fertilizer production had all but ceased in these parts by the 1930s."

I shifted again, thinking hard. "So are these phosphate sediments still prevalent near the riverbanks?"

"I wouldn't say prevalent." He tapped the bag once more. "Honestly, I'm surprised you found a pure nodule of this size just lying around." Marzec eyed me curiously. "Where *did* you pick this up?"

"Wake-boarding off Folly Beach," Hi inserted. "I was attempting a heel-side five-forty when I wiped out. Found this little guy bouncing in the surf."

"I see." I could tell Marzec was skeptical, but he let it pass. "Well, any other questions?"

"No, Dr. Marzec." I flashed my very-grateful smile. "Thanks so much for your time."

"Delighted." Marzec scratched behind his ear with a snort. "I've been working here five years, and you're the first non-students to ever ask me a thing. Come back anytime."

We gathered our things, Hi gently scooping the rock from Marzec's desk, then exited with another round of thanks. I waited until we were safely inside Ben's SUV before speaking.

"What do you guys think? Marzec kept mentioning the Ashley River."

"But these rocks were everywhere," Hi said. "He listed every other river in the area, too."

Shelton shook his head. "We could maybe narrow our search to locations near a riverbank. But that's still miles and miles. And for all we know, the kidnapper just picked up the stupid rock while out driving around. It might not lead to anything."

I looked at Ben. He glanced away.

No one wanted to say it straight out.

"So we're still nowhere." My voice trembled slightly.

Silence filled the car.

I could sense the boys wanted to comfort me. Had no idea how to.

"Let's go home," I said softly.

○   ○   ○

"Tory, where have you been?"

There was real concern in Kit's voice as he sprang up from the couch.

I elected for half truth. "The boys and I went to where Ella worked. I thought maybe we could spot something."

"Oh, honey." He wrapped an arm around my shoulder.

I felt tears welling behind my eyes. Forced them back.

Kit released me. Held me at arm's length so he could look into my eyes.

"If you want to cancel this barbeque, just say the word. Whitney will be fine."

The block party. I'd completely forgotten.

Of course we can't have a stupid cookout today. My friend was abducted!

"It's fine." A glance at the clock. "Tell Whitney I'll be ready to help in an hour. Where's Coop?"

"He's asleep on your bed." Kit ran nervous fingers through his curly brown hair. "Are you sure, kiddo? I don't know if this party is a good idea."

"It's okay. Better a dumb cookout than nothing. Maybe it'll keep my mind off . . . things."

Kit nodded slowly. "Only if you're certain. And we leave the minute you want to."

I forced a smile. "Thanks, Dad."

He tried to hide his surprise. I never called him that.

Then I saw today's *Post and Courier* sitting on our dining room table. I started. "What is that!?"

Kit tracked my eyes, then winced. "There's a story. Maybe now's not the best—"

Ignoring him, I grabbed the newspaper. A giant picture dominated above the fold.

Two playing cards, side by side. Ophiuchus. Cetus.

A banner headline screamed: "Zodiac Kidnapper Baffles Police."

Eyes wide, I read the full-page story. Then I slammed the paper on the table.

"The police don't know *anything*!" Sides heaving. "But the press has it all the next day!"

Kit grabbed the newsprint and dumped it in the recycling bin. "Forget that nonsense. I'm sure the police have leads they aren't sharing."

I shook my head angrily. "Someone has leaked every major development in these cases so far. Yet the cops don't have a *damn* clue."

"Tory, I understand how upset you are, but we have to trust—"

"*I* know more than those bozos!"

Kit stopped short. "I'm sorry?"

Careful!

I buried my face in my hands. Worry for Ella was compromising my judgment.

Then I made a decision.

"Kit?"

"Yeah, kiddo?" Watching me closely.

"Please sit with me. I have some things to tell you."

We each pulled a chair from the dining table. Sat facing each other.

Deep breath.

It's the right thing to do.

"We need to visit police headquarters. Today. I have evidence they need to see."

CHAPTER 33

Kit led me inside the lobby of police headquarters.

My eyes shot to the intake counter—thankfully, a female officer was on duty.

I released a pent-up breath. At least I wouldn't be recognized from our late-night visit two days ago. This meeting was going to be bad enough.

Shelton, Hi, and Ben were a few steps behind me. I'd argued that we didn't all need to be there, but Detective Hawfield had seen things differently.

Ruth Stolowitski had Hiram by one elbow, a murderous look on her face. Shelton's father, Nelson, had accompanied his son. Ben came alone.

Kit spoke to the desk officer, then waved us toward the elevator bank.

"Fifth floor," I told him.

He raised an eyebrow.

"Lucky guess."

Arriving at the Major Crimes department, we were greeted by a junior detective who led us to a conference room with a circular table large enough for everyone to sit.

At least they didn't throw us in the box. That's something, right?

Moments later, Hawfield walked in. He wasn't alone.

"You've *got* to be kidding!" Hi blurted.

Carmine Corcoran's scowl was as deep as ever. He'd lost a few pounds, but was still a large man, with muttonchop sideburns and a bristly black moustache. His hair was graying at the temples, making him appear more distinguished than his forty-five years merited.

Ruth popped the back of her son's head. "Mind your manners, Hiram."

"Why does *everyone* do that?" Hi muttered. "And that was child abuse. In front of the police, I might add."

"Sergeant?" I tried to decipher Corcoran's insignia. "Or is it still Security Director?"

"It's *Captain* Corcoran now, Miss Brennan." Spoken with evident satisfaction. "I was asked to rejoin the force after foiling those felonies last summer. I've moved up in the world."

"You're welcome." Hi dodged another matronly swat.

Corcoran shot Hiram a hooded glance, but didn't rise to the bait. He'd been the officer in charge during our investigation of the skeleton on Loggerhead Island last spring, and had worked private security during our pursuit of Anne Bonny's lost fortune the following summer. Neither encounter had been overly pleasant.

Corcoran was on the short list of people I wouldn't mind avoiding forever.

But here we were. Our luck never seems to improve.

Detective Hawfield pulled out a chair and sat. "Let's get down to business, shall we? I thought it prudent that Captain Corcoran attend this interview, since he has some . . . experience with the witnesses."

I'll say.

Hawfield spread his hands. "This is your meeting. Please begin."

Kit glanced at me. Reaching into my pack, I removed the bagged phosphate nodule and placed it on the table. Then I set two vials beside it—one containing the long black hair, the other holding my Hemastix strip.

Hawfield frowned immediately. "What is that?"

"Evidence in the kidnapping of Ella Francis." I was surprised at how calm my voice sounded. "We discovered it behind the Flying Tomato this morning."

"Bubby, what *is* this?" Ruth squawked.

Hi held a finger to his lips. "Quiet, Ma! Just listen."

Hawfield's hand found his forehead. "You're telling me that you've handled evidence from a possible crime scene? That you removed it?"

I nodded. Corcoran made a noise in his throat I choose not to interpret.

"In our defense, the rock was just sitting there." Shelton looked to his father. "The cops missed it the night before. What if it rained? Or some dog got it? We couldn't just *leave* it."

Nelson put a comforting hand on his son's shoulder.

"You had no business there in the first place," Corcoran huffed. "Like moths to a flame, the four of you. Like it or not, your actions have tainted the crime scene."

"We didn't touch the stone," I said coolly. "It's been sealed in that evidence bag since we discovered it. Shelton's right—we couldn't just leave it lying outside."

Hawfield raised a hand for quiet. He seemed to have regained some of his equanimity. "Why do you believe this stone is evidence?" he asked.

I rotated the bag to expose the rust-red blemish. "The rock seemed out of place. Examining it, I noticed two things. This red stain on its side, and a twelve-inch black hair stuck to its surface, which I think might belong to Ella."

My voice broke on her name. Kit reached over and squeezed my hand.

Hawfield gave me an appraising look. "I assume the hair is in that test tube?"

"Yes. The other vial contains a Hemastix strip I used to assess for blood. It came back presumptively positive."

Hawfield reached over and collected the three items. "I can't condone what you've done. Proper procedure is for a citizen to alert the police—"

"It's a disgrace!" Corcoran spat, folding his beefy arms. "By handling these items, they're now useless in a court of law. Any lawyer worth a bag of Doritos could have them withheld."

"Maybe," I snapped. "But I'm more worried about *finding* Ella and the twins. Your people missed this completely. Without us, you wouldn't even have it."

"We do multiple sweeps! We'd have found it eventually."

"Done is done," Hawfield said calmly. "We'll need statements explaining what you found, where, when, who handled it, all the details."

I nodded.

"Good. Now, is there anything else?"

"We showed the rock to a geologist."

"More hands?" Corcoran lifted his palms to the ceiling. "Great Lord in the morning!"

Ignoring Corcoran's dramatics, I related our visit to Professor Marzec and the information he provided. Hawfield took careful notes, then rose and left the room. We waited in uncomfortable silence for his return.

"Okay." Hawfield sat heavily in his chair. "Is there anything else we need to discuss?"

I thought about the bloodstain at the Gable house. The labeled bar in the ransom video. Both pieces of information could be useful to the investigation.

But explaining *how* we obtained that evidence might land us in juvie.

I looked at Corcoran. He glared back. That made up my mind.

"Just one other thing. I think you should look into Rex Gable. The twins' stepfather."

"*Excuse* me?" Corcoran sat forward, red-faced. "What are you implying, young lady?"

"Some of his actions since the twins went missing seem . . . questionable." I couldn't mention his phone records, but was trying to push them in that direction. "I'm just saying that Rex Gable might merit additional consideration."

"Of course," Corcoran scoffed. "The evil stepfather is the culprit. Thank goodness we have Nancy Drew on the case."

Kit straightened. "Now wait just a min—"

"Dr. Howard, we've been down this road before." Corcoran shook his head. "These kids have gained a little notoriety recently. So now, suddenly, they think they're expert crime fighters. I think the celebrity status has gone to their heads."

My temper exploded. "And *I* think you're still the same stupid, brain-dead—"

"Everyone, please!" Hawfield looked like he'd rather be anywhere else on the planet. "Let's not lose our composure. Miss Brennan, we'll take your opinion under advisement."

I knew what that meant. But what else could I do?

"We done here?" Ben's first words.

Hawfield and Corcoran wheeled on him as one.

Abruptly, I got a bad feeling.

"Mr. Blue." Hawfield's voice became less cordial. "Are you able to give an account of your whereabouts on Thursday evening?"

Ben's eyes narrowed. "Why?"

"Please answer the question."

"I was in Mongolia. Surfing."

"Don't get cute, son." Shifting his bulk, Corcoran attempted to loom menacingly. "You might've wriggled off the last hook, but you've got no more get-out-of-jail-free cards."

My eyes widened. "Are you suggesting *Ben* had something to do with Ella's disappearance?"

"I'm not suggesting *anything*," Hawfield said curtly. "I simply asked a question."

Ben's face reddened, but he answered. "I was at home. Watching TV."

"Was anyone with you?"

Ben shook his head. "My mother works second shift this week."

Corcoran crossed his arms. "What about the morning of March twenty-eighth?"

"No idea."

Corcoran leaned on the table. "Think. Harder."

Ben's face went rigid. I could see him shutting down.

"That's enough." Kit put a hand on Ben's shoulder. "We came here voluntarily, to provide information regarding Ella's abduction. Not to be interrogated. If you want to ask Ben any more questions, you'll need to speak with his parents first."

Then my father steeled his voice. "And let me be frank—accusing this boy of having anything to do with the kidnappings is offensive and grotesque. I expect better from our police."

Captain Corcoran snorted, but said no more.

Hawfield rose quickly. "Thank you for coming down. If you'll follow me, we can knock out those statements . . ."

◯   ◯   ◯

I walked outside and stretched. The paperwork had taken over an hour.

Ben sat on a bench nearby, staring at nothing.

"Hey."

"Hey." He slid over, making room for me to sit.

After a slight hesitation, I did.

For several moments, neither of us spoke. I sat very still, feeling awkward, watching a gaggle of children play hopscotch in the riverside park across the street.

"They think I know something," Ben said sourly. "That I might be working with someone again. 'Craving the spotlight,' Corcoran said."

"I wish you had an alibi."

His head spun. "Why? *You* don't think I had anything—"

"Ben, no! I just meant that it'd be easier. That they'd go away."

Ben held my gaze. His shell was crumbling. I saw raw emotion hiding behind his eyes.

"Because if you thought I was capable of something like . . . like *that*, I might . . ." His voice cracked. "I couldn't take it."

He looked away. The harbor breeze ruffled his silky black hair.

My hand found his, almost by its own volition. "Ben."

"What?" He didn't turn.

"I want you to know that I forgive you. It's past time I told you that."

He tensed. I squeezed his hand, letting him know I meant the words. I did. I couldn't be mad at Ben anymore. It was like being mad at my left arm.

And right then, I needed my arm back.

Ben's head dropped. Then, shockingly, his shoulders began to shake.

"I never meant for . . . It wasn't supposed to . . ."

"*Shhh.*" I scooted close, wrapped an arm around him. "I know. I know."

I heard snivels, desperately masked. Ben's whole body trembled. Then he relaxed.

"I'm sorry about the flaring." Wiping his cheeks with his palms. "I can be such an idiot sometimes."

"Sometimes?" I joked, trying to lighten the mood. "I understand. Let's just tone things down for a while, until we figure out what's wrong."

"Okay." He sat back, too embarrassed to look at me.

Our hands parted. My arm slipped from his shoulder.

"I just wish we could *do* something." Ben punched his thigh. "For Ella, and Lucy and Peter. Some whacked-out monster has them, and we've got these incredible gifts. But right now, they don't mean anything. We're nowhere. I've never felt so . . . *useless.*"

"Helpless." I hugged myself close. "It's like I can see Ella drowning, but can't save her."

Unbidden, thoughts of my friend flooded my mind. Her mischievous smile as we whispered secrets in calculus. The two of us laughing at the terrible artwork. A quick give-and-go we'd executed on the practice field.

Ella Francis had become one of my closest friends. Maybe even a best one.

My own walls caved. Tears trickled from the corner of my eyes.

Then strong arms enveloped me.

"Don't cry." Ben's hot breath on my cheek. "We'll find her. And the twins. I promise."

"Don't make promises you can't keep," I hiccupped. "People *always* do that."

"I mean it." Firmly spoken. "I won't *let* us fail. Not at this."

The sobs broke free. I burrowed into Ben's chest, letting everything go. I cried and cried and cried, unthinking, releasing a week's worth of pent-up emotion in a few hot seconds.

Ben held me, silent, softly rubbing my back.

A thought floated from somewhere far away.

This isn't so bad.

I pushed away, gently breaking Ben's embrace. Looked into his eyes. His face was a whisper from mine.

I thought of Ben's confession during the hurricane. How he'd wanted to be more than just packmates. Emotions swirled in my chest, making me dizzy. Off balance.

"Ben . . . I . . ."

"Tory?"

My father's voice sent us flying apart as if electroshocked.

Kit was descending the steps, an odd look on his face.

"Yes?" Discreetly wiping away tears.

I saw a thousand questions fill Kit's eyes, but, thankfully, he kept them shelved.

"I hate to do this, kiddo, but Whitney's party starts in an hour. She's trying to be patient, but, frankly, that isn't her strong suit."

"No. Right." I stood, smoothing clothes and hair. "Mustn't keep the Duchess waiting."

Kit frowned. "Say the word, and we cancel right now. No question."

"No, sorry. I was just being flip. It's really fine." Forced smile. "Might be just the thing."

"All right, then. We need to get moving."

Kit glanced at Ben, still sitting on the bench, striving for invisible.

A smile quirked my father's lips. "And you, Mr. Blue? Ready for a good ol'-fashioned backyard barbeque? My daughter will be there."

Ben's uneasy smile was his only response.

CHAPTER 34

The party was surreal.

The weather that afternoon was perfect. Sunny, mid-seventies, with a light breeze sweeping in off the breakers. Everyone wore shorts, sandals, and shades, luxuriating like house cats in the warm April sun.

The food was top-notch. Whitney had chosen JB's Smokeshack for catering, and the local barbeque hotspot totally delivered. Spare ribs. Smoked chicken. Pulled pork. Cornbread. Okra casserole. Cabbage. Yellow potato salad. Apple cobbler. I'd shoveled down two plates, and was considering a third.

The whole neighborhood turned out. All twenty of us. Lorelei Devers spread a blanket on the grass, and in moments five more appeared beside hers. Ruth and Linus Stolowitski sat on their stoop, greeting everyone who passed by. Kit bounced here and there, tweaking the sound system, hauling bags of ice, and making sure food and drink flowed smoothly. Tom Blue brought out an old croquet set, and soon half the guests were playing.

Younger kids scampered about, invited by Morris Islanders with family in the area. They ran laughing across the common, or tossed

Frisbees and plastic horseshoes. All told, perhaps fifty people were milling about, smiling and stuffing their faces.

All but Coop—Kit made me lock the wolfdog away. Probably for the best.

Above it all lorded Whitney, a queen bee managing her hive. She seemed everywhere at once, greeting new arrivals, stocking the napkin dispensers, even organizing the parking lot. All while wearing a face-splitting smile, and giggling like a schoolgirl, totally in her element.

But even Whitney's effervescence couldn't shake the pall hanging over the festivities. Most conversations inevitably gravitated to the kidnappings. Heads shook in dismay. Theories were exchanged. And dozens of surreptitious glances were cast the Virals' way.

Everyone knew the missing kids were our classmates. Some had learned that Ella and I were close.

I tried to avoid notice.

Though I played the dutiful daughter—wearing a sundress, shaking hands, even helping little ones find a bathroom—inside, I cringed. The whole thing felt like a betrayal.

While I was sipping raspberry lemonade, Ella was imprisoned somewhere.

I couldn't shake the feeling that I should be doing more.

At least my emotions were in check.

After my crying jag with Ben, it felt like my feelings had simply shut down, or somehow switched off. The well had run empty. I'd gone numb.

In a way, that was good. I felt more capable of rational thought than I had in days.

After the party's first hectic hour, the boys and I had settled down at the edge of the lawn, where the grass gave way to sand, and eventually surf.

I finished scarfing a bowl of banana pudding and pushed it aside. "We need to discuss our options."

Hi rolled to a sitting position. He wore an orange Charlotte Bobcats tee and navy shorts.

"We're stuck," he said. "The rock is our best clue, but it doesn't lead anywhere."

Shelton set down his sweet tea. He wore white on white—polo shirt and cargo shorts. Hi had dubbed it Shelton's "Carlton" look. I didn't get it.

"I can't crack those B-Series files," he admitted. "The encryption is light-years out of my league. 256-bit keys. The universe will end before anyone forces through *that*."

"Just do your best," I encouraged.

"My best won't get the job done. We need to call Chang."

"No." On this point I was certain. "We can't trust him. We don't know what's in those files, and Chang's already proven he's a loose cannon. We go it alone."

Shelton sighed. "I'll keep looking. Hope for divine intervention."

"I know you can do it." Trying to buck him up. "Eddie Chang's not half as smart as the great Shelton Devers."

"I don't know," Hi said. "That dude's pretty sharp."

"Thanks," Shelton grumbled.

"Now," Hi continued, "if she'd said *me*, I'd be on board. I'm super intelligent."

Ben reached up from where he was lying with his eyes closed. Smacked Hi's dome.

Hi rubbed his head. "I'm getting pretty tired of that move."

"Then quit being a dope." Ben's lids remained shut.

"Hey, sure. No problem. I just need to—"

Hi lunged for Ben, intending a flying body slam. Ben caught Hi in midair and tossed him downhill in one quick motion. Hi tumbled, rolled, and dropped over the berm onto the sand.

"That was dumb," Hi informed the blue sky.

"Yep," Ben agreed, settling back on his elbows.

Hi began dusting himself off. "I shouldn't have spoken before I pounced."

"Wouldn't have mattered." Ben rose and walked to the berm, then extended a hand to help Hi climb up. They sat back down as if it never happened.

Boys.

○   ○   ○

The party was winding down.

Caterers began loading their truck as Kit disassembled the tent. Mr. Blue packed up his croquet mallets and headed for the driveway.

Shelton and Hi had already gone inside, leaving Ben and me alone.

Somehow we found ourselves down on the dock.

We sat in companionable silence, tossing sunflower seeds into the surf. The sun dipped in the west. Seagulls rode late afternoon thermals, cawing into the wind.

Ben started talking about Wando High. I countered with news of Bolton. Before long, we'd exchanged our stories, catching up on the last five months in each other's lives.

I hadn't realized how much I missed Ben. How badly I wanted him back at Bolton.

"Think there's any chance they let you back in?" I asked hopefully.

"Headmaster Paugh?" Ben laughed. "Don't bet on it. That's okay anyway. For all I bitch, Wando's a pretty nice school. I'll be cool there. I really don't skip much, FYI. I'm not sure what I was thinking that morning. I barely know those guys."

"The Rhodes scholars I met in the parking lot? They aren't both Harvard bound?"

"Ease off, Brennan." Spoken with a smile. "Not everyone is born a genius. The world needs us ditchdiggers, too."

"You're not a ditchdigger."

"Hey, I *like* digging holes. Don't try to change me."

Several minutes passed quietly as the sun slowly dropped toward the horizon.

Ben broke the silence. "Why do you think our flares have gone crazy?"

"Wish I knew." I tossed an oyster shell into the water. "Maybe our powers are still evolving. We don't really understand the extent of our mutations."

"Maybe the wolf is tired of hiding," Ben said quietly. "Maybe he wants a permanent seat at the table."

My head shook on its own volition. "I feel like it has to do with *us,* though. Like, maybe our pack is screwing things up somehow. Not connecting right. It's hard to explain."

Ben nodded. "I've never understood what you do. Honestly, it freaks me out."

I snorted. "You don't say."

"Oh, come on. How would you like it if I read your thoughts? If you couldn't keep a single secret."

"I *don't* keep secrets from you."

"Everyone has secrets." Ben's voice was suddenly serious. "Even you."

My back stiffened. Ben had repeated Chance's words nearly verbatim, and it jarred me.

He was right, of course. I was keeping several secrets from Ben.

Like how comfortable it felt to be alone with him. How much I'd missed his reassuring presence. His quiet strength.

Why keep that a secret?

Ben changed the subject. "What should we do about Chance?"

"Another crap sandwich." I made sure to catch his eye. "We're *not* going to hurt him, or anything like that. That isn't on the table."

He waved my words away. "I know that. Heat of the moment. Forget it."

"We've dealt with Chance before. Usually, he can be reasoned with. We just have to find out what he wants."

We avoided talking about Ella. At this point, what more was there to say?

Ben removed his shoes, plunged both feet into the lapping saltwater. Then he leaned back against a post, sighing contentedly.

The little-boy maneuver brought a smile to my face.

I reflected on how often I misjudged Ben. How often he came through when it mattered.

My breath suddenly caught. Were my feelings toward him changing?

Did I just miss my good friend, or was this something more?

I didn't know. Wasn't sure I wanted to find out.

Ben and I were *pack*. Nothing could be closer than that. Could it?

That dangerous train of thought was broken by a buzzing in my pocket.

Incoming text. I unlocked my iPhone and read.

"Who's that?" Ben asked absently. "Did Hi finally figure out how to take screen shots?"

"It's Jason," I answered without thinking. "There's a party in Old Town, though he's selling the thing like it's some kind of prayer vigil."

Water splashed.

I looked up.

Ben was retying his shoes, a closed-off look on his face.

"Have fun." He rose quickly. "We can talk more tomorrow."

"Ben, wait!" Popping up as he strode by me. "I'm not going!"

Ben waved without turning, heading for his father's door. I watched him disappear inside.

Ugh. Never forget how moody that boy is. Always a live wire.

Then I laughed without humor.

My best girlfriend was missing. No ransom tape had appeared. I had no idea how to help.

Boy problems were less than meaningless.

Determined to accomplish *something* for Ella's sake, I hurried for my own home.

CHAPTER 35

I stared at online pictures of the zodiac cards.

The paper's website had posted full-color shots, much more detailed than the photocopy we'd stolen from the DA's office. Both Ophiuchus and Cetus were shown in vibrant clarity.

Not that it mattered—the images told me nothing about the kidnappings.

I slumped back in my desk chair, wondered again who was passing this stuff to the press. The leak obviously had access to the evidence.

Rex Gable might fit that bill.

But the pieces had yet to make sense.

Why antique zodiac cards? What did they mean to the criminal? What message were they intended to convey?

Clara Gordon's words ran through my mind.

Cetus often represented unrelenting evil. Is *that* what we were facing?

A chilling thought struck me. Ella had been snatched outside the Flying Tomato, not at home. Which meant this lunatic had broken into her bedroom and left the card there.

Why take the risk? Such brazen disregard for danger was unnerving.

Suddenly curious, I searched the Internet for the location where Lucy and Peter were kidnapped. Found nothing. Score *one* for police secrecy, at least.

I tapped my lip, thinking. Had the twins also been abducted away from home?

If so, the criminal had separately planted the Ophiuchus card as well.

I shivered, recalling the shadowy form that had watched us rifle the Gables' basement.

Had that been the kidnapper?

Another thought. How had the criminal taken *both* twins at once? The Gables weren't exactly athletes, but they were healthy teenagers. How could one individual overcome both kids at the same time? Or were they grabbed separately?

I need more details about the Gables.

Idly, I spun in my chair. Coop's head rose from his paws. Noting my attention was elsewhere, the wolfdog settled back down to nap.

Something else was bothering me.

Why was Ella abducted at all? It didn't seem to jibe with the first crime.

The twins were taken for money. That was crystal clear—there was a ransom tape and a demand for five million dollars. Uncharitably, I wondered if Rex Gable had made any effort to gather those funds.

Would he actually pay? My gut said no.

Of course, my gut also suspected him of committing the crime in the first place.

Which, admittedly, didn't make a ton of sense. At least, not if money was the motive.

But there's been no ransom tape for Ella.

No million-dollar demand, at least not yet. And, based on what

I'd seen of Ella's parents, they would *definitely* pay. Anything. Gladly. Whatever it took to get their daughter back safely.

So why nothing from Ella's captor?

If it wasn't for the zodiac cards, the kidnappings wouldn't seem connected at all.

The phosphate nodule was more important than I'd thought—it was tangible evidence of an assault, assuring that Ella's case was treated as a crime from the beginning.

Take away the cards, and I'm not sure the police would've linked the disappearances.

Three Bolton Prep kids missing, in the same week?

Okay. The cops would've investigated any possible connection. But that didn't change the fact that Ella's disappearance seemed entirely different from that of the twins.

There was still too much I didn't know.

Had the police responded to the ransom demand? Contacted the twins' kidnapper? Was there a way to do so?

When was the payoff required? Where? Who was supposed to make the drop?

I slapped my leg in frustration. I needed more on the Gable case.

That investigation was the only link to our adversary. Find the twins, and I'd find Ella.

I was considering options for stealing a police case file when a fanged unicorn appeared on my screen. Shelton. Requesting a meeting.

I was logging into our chat room when a second message popped up.

Shelton wanted to meet at the bunker. Said it was important.

Clock check—8:00 p.m.

Saturday night. I can pull that off.

Grabbing keys and iPhone, I tapped my thigh for Coop to follow.

"C'mon, dog brain. This time, you're more than welcome."

○   ○   ○

"I'm a genius," Shelton announced smugly.

A smile split my face. "You cracked the encryption."

"What? Oh, hell no." Shelton waved the idea away. "Keep dreaming. But I found something else you're not gonna believe."

The four of us were gathered around the bunker's circular table. Hi was munching on a sleeve of double-stuffed Oreos. Ben watched with distaste, his feet up and hands behind his head.

I sat next to Shelton, who'd brought his laptop from home.

Coop was gnawing a rawhide in the back chamber.

"Spill it," Ben commanded.

"I wasn't getting anywhere with those B-Series files." Shelton opened the computer and typed quickly. "So I decided to poke at something else for a while. Get my mind right. My first thought was of Rex Gable's phone records."

Shelton spun his laptop to face the group. "Check out this nugget in what Chang sent us."

His finger tapped a word at the top of Chang's email.

"Bellweather." I looked at Shelton in confusion. "What does that mean?"

Shelton smiled triumphantly. "It's the name of Rex Gable's favorite hunting dog. I found a random reference online."

Ben's feet hit the floor. "You dragged me out here to talk about a dog?"

"Kind of," Shelton said slyly, "since that dog's name is Gable's password for his cellular account."

"Hey, genius," Hi said, mouth encrusted with chocolate crumbs. "We already *have* those records. You're looking at them right now."

"Use your brain cells, Stolowitski. For how many different accounts do you use 'Westeros' as the password?"

"For everything!" Hi blurted. "And now you've ruined it, jerk!"

Suddenly, I understood.

"What'd you find?" I asked excitedly.

Shelton made a sweeping gesture toward his laptop. "Rex Gable has a Gmail account."

He pulled up an inbox. Dozens of emails, filed in separate folders.

"Shelton, that's awesome!" Trying to decide where to start. "We can divide—"

"Ahem."

I blinked. "You've already found something, haven't you?"

Shelton's face grew serious as he punched more keys. Then he spun the computer to face us once more.

Onscreen was a single email.

From: Rex Gable. To: Rex Gable. No subject. No message.

One attachment. An MP4 file.

Noting our attention, Shelton double-clicked.

The twins' ransom tape played in its entirety.

Hi scratched his head. "I don't get it. Of course Gable has the ransom tape. They're his own stepkids, for Pete's sake."

Shelton tapped the *date* of the email.

Monday, April 1.

I had it in a flash. "That's the day I testified! We ran into Detective Hawfield the next morning, in the DA's office. Commissioner Riggins, too. At that point, neither of them were treating the twins' disappearance as a crime."

Ben followed my drift. "Which means they hadn't seen the ransom tape yet."

"Which *means*," Shelton finished, "Rex Gable had a copy at least a full day before the police. Maybe even two!"

"He mailed the clip to himself," I said aloud. "Why do that?"

"Because *he* filmed the dang thing, like you said!" Shelton was so amped his voice cracked. "He's the kidnapper!"

My fingers drummed the table. "You could be right."

"*Could* be?" Shelton sounded incredulous. "That's a smoking gun, girl!"

"Not necessarily," Hi countered. "Maybe the kidnapper emailed the tape directly to Rex Gable first, and he panicked for a day, not knowing what to do. Or maybe the kidnapper told Gable he *couldn't* go to the police."

"But why did he email it to himself?" I repeated.

"I do that sometimes," Ben said, "when I don't wanna risk losing an important document, like a paper for school. Uploading it to Gmail is like a free backup in case my computer dies."

I nodded, thinking aloud. "Shelton still could be right. Gable uploads the file and sends it to himself, backing it up externally, like Ben said. Then he destroys every other copy. Now the tape is out there in the cloud, but *not* on his hard drive or camera. It creates a level of distance. So long as he's not a suspect, the police won't check his personal email."

"Still, not very smart," Hi said. "I mean, *we* found it. If we're right, Rex Gable's an idiot. Why not delete that email after sending it on to the police?"

"He *did* delete it," Shelton answered. "But the fool never emptied his trash. I found that message in his deleted items folder. I figured that would be the most interesting place to start."

"You're *killing* it tonight, Devers!" Hi tossed him a high five.

I shook my head in wonder. "Could Rex Gable really be that dumb?"

I didn't think so, but it was surprising what silly mistakes people could make.

Maybe the man was simply computer illiterate, and forgot to cover this one track.

And we found it. But what to do now?

Suddenly, I was furious.

That bastard. His own family! And then grabbing Ella for no reason . . .

"Wait."

I flattened my palms on the table. Thought hard.

The boys quieted.

"Rex Gable wouldn't hold his own stepkids for ransom," I said. "That makes no sense. There must be another motive."

"I can think of a few," Ben said quietly. "None of them good. Maybe Rex wanted Lucy and Peter out of his hair. Permanently."

Ben's statement was like a ten-foot icicle through my heart.

If Rex Gable was the kidnapper, and he didn't want his stepkids found, then Ella . . .

"But why take *her*?" Louder than I'd intended.

"That part, I can't even guess." Hi sat back, face ashen. "What does Ella Francis have to do with the Gable twins? If a stranger snatched Lucy and Peter, then grabbed Ella later to up the stakes, why haven't we seen a second ransom video?"

Hi was echoing my confusion from earlier. I was still just as puzzled.

"The police need to know," Shelton said. "This email will make Rex Gable a suspect."

"Screw those jokers." Ben moved to the window bench. "I'm done talking to them. About anything."

"Today's meeting didn't exactly go well," Hi conceded. "That douche-bag Corcoran would rather arrest *us* than anyone. If he finds out we're conducting an investigation, breaking into other people's emails . . ." He spread his hands. "I just don't see how to do it."

"Dealing with Corcoran is pointless," I said. "He clearly isn't interested in anything we have to say."

"I haven't even checked Gable's inbox yet," Shelton said. "If the dumbass left a copy of the ransom video in his trash folder, who knows what other mistakes he's made?"

"First order of business." I brought my hands together. "We review every single email."

"Tomorrow." Ben shrugged at my disappointed look. "Sorry, but my mother said I have to be home in an hour."

"Same here." Hi wadded up his cookie trash and stuffed it in the wastebasket. "With a kidnapper on the loose, I can't believe my mother even let me outside. I had to convince her it'd be pretty tough to grab all four of us at once. But she'll be waiting by the door already."

I looked at Shelton.

"I'm free bright and early," he offered.

"Okay." I exhaled slowly. "I'll do what I can tonight, then we'll finish in the morning."

"You're staying out here?" Shelton asked. "Alone?"

"No big deal. I don't want Kit seeing what I'm up to."

"I don't like it," Ben said. Behind him, Hi looked uneasy.

"No one knows this place exists." I pointed to the other room. "And there's an eighty-five-pound predator in there that loves me. I'll be fine."

They relaxed. Coop might be a big sloppy puppy to us, but to the world at large, my pet was a dangerous-looking beast. A better body-guard didn't exist.

"You can leave my laptop here when you're done," Shelton said.

"Text me when you get home," Ben requested. "Please don't forget."

I hid a smile. "Will do. Bye, guys. And *please* sleep. We've got a ton to do tomorrow."

Hearing movement, Coop padded into the chamber. Watched the boys crawl outside. Satisfied that I had no intention of following, he curled into a ball at my feet, closed his eyes, and began snoring.

"My hero."

I cracked a Diet Coke. Opened the first email.

"Watch your back, Rex," I whispered. "You can run, but you can't hide."

CHAPTER 36

U gh. Enough!"

I closed the laptop and shoved it aside.

Coop rose, stretched, and shook his muscles loose, the tags on his collar jangling loudly. He yipped once, then slipped through the exit.

"Right behind you." I turned off the floor lamps and killed the power. Pulling on my windbreaker, I crawled from the bunker behind my canine escort.

Outside, the night air was heavy and wet, with traces of rain lingering on the ocean breeze. Heavy squalls had swept across the island during the two hours I'd worked alone, delving through Rex Gable's Gmail, message by message.

I was well into the previous year's emails, but had found nothing of interest. A few hundred remained, but I wasn't optimistic.

The moon was three-quarters, waxing, reflecting enough light to see without a flashlight. The tall grasses bordering the overland trail would be soaked, so I elected to walk along the shore instead. A slightly longer route, but not much, and watching the crabs skitter and dance as we approached would entertain the mutt.

With Cooper trotting beside me, I split a stand of prickly pears, then ran-walked down the dunes to the beach. I paused a moment to bang sand from my shoes. Coop was already scampering for the tidal pools, snuffling everything in sight.

I love the ocean.

An odd thing to discover, having grown up in central Massachusetts. But I knew it now—wherever life took me, whatever career I might choose, ultimately I'd settle by the sea.

I scooped up a stick as we strolled, in no particular hurry. Catching Coop's attention, I tossed it into the darkness ahead. He fetched it four consecutive times—a new record—before loping inland with the prize between his teeth.

Coop has the chasing part down cold. Bringing things back is always touch and go.

I took two more steps, then nearly stumbled.

The feeling had returned.

A now-familiar sensation swelled inside my brain, its accompanying sense of oneness arrowing outward in an expanding, spiraling circle. For a fleeting moment, I felt connected to all things around me.

My mind opened like a flower. Inviting. Welcoming. Searching?

Then the sensation vanished once again, leaving no trace.

I held my body still, hoping that, this time, maybe, some clue would reveal itself.

None did. After a few moments, I sighed, resumed my walk down the beach.

"Makes no sense," I whispered to myself. "None."

Shaking off the disorientation, I heard a rustling in the dunes directly to my right. Figured Coop had found a rabbit hole.

"Leave the bunnies alone!" I called.

But Cooper's head poked from the cattails fifty feet ahead.

His canine eyes found mine—two golden disks gleaming in the darkness.

My steps slowed. "How'd you get way up there, boy?"

Vines crunched. A rush of air beside me.

Something black and heavy swooped toward my head.

I barely had time to react, diving to my left as an object hummed past my forehead.

Hitting the ground, I tucked and rolled sideways as a hulking shadow crashed onto the space I'd just vacated.

A muffled curse. The dark shape rose, turning this way and that.

Instinct took over. As I scuttled away on my butt, the wolf *forced* its way out.

SNAP.

Fire exploded inside my chest.

The flare unfolded without being called.

Raw energy flooded my system, pooling and spreading, like a nuclear reaction spiraling out of control. The adrenal jolt was too powerful to withstand. I collapsed on the wet sand, my body convulsing, every muscle cramping at once.

I glimpsed the shadow streaking toward me—a sinuous figure in black, wielding some sort of club—before my eyes simply blanked.

The power was too much.

I lay there, helpless, my senses shutting down one by one.

A gust of wind. A throaty growl. Then a tearing sound, followed by a strangled scream.

"Coop!?!"

The thump of metal on flesh, followed by a yelp of canine pain.

Heavy breathing. Another terrified shout. Then footsteps pounding away.

I tried to rise, but the inferno inside left me paralyzed. Exposed.

SNUP.

The power fled as quickly as it came. I don't know if I consciously dispelled it, or if the flare simply withered and died.

Slowly, I came back to the world.

Legs standing over me. A rough tongue against my cheek.

As my vision refocused, I saw that Coop was straddling me, hackles raised, eyes fixed on the dunes.

"Good boy," I rasped.

Coop's gaze dropped for a moment. Another quick face lick.

Then he snapped back to attention, growling as he scanned for threats.

My brain slowly reassembled. I nudged the wolfdog aside and rose to my knees.

A deep breath as I worked the cobwebs out, then I stood.

Reality came crashing home.

Someone had attacked me. Here. On Morris Island.

Miles from anywhere a stranger should be.

Facts molded into conclusions.

I'd been targeted. There was no other reasonable explanation. Not for an attack on this deserted beach, at this late hour. Not out here in the middle of nowhere.

Coop nuzzled my side. I knelt, hugged him close.

"You saved me, dog face." Kissing his snout. "My hero, for real."

Coop took a step forward, then winced.

"You okay, pal?" I ran my hands along his sides, then down his legs. When I touched his left forepaw he yelped and stepped back.

I gripped his collar. "Let me see, boy."

Gently, I examined the paw. Two nails were smashed, and there was some mild swelling. A small gash ran along one side, cutting into the pad beneath.

Coop whined as I probed, but I held firm.

"Nothing broken, but it looks painful as hell." I glanced left, then right, assessing our position. It was another two hundred yards to the townhouses.

"We'll take it slow." Stroking Coop's head with my hands.

I thought about the assailant returning. Recalled the ripping sound, and cries of pain.

Coop gave worse than he got. That bastard is probably still running.

We covered the next hundred yards at a glacial pace. Coop was favoring his leg, and with each passing step I worried he'd need a trip to Dr. Abendroth.

Get home. Get inside. Get safe.

Then Coop froze.

His body tensed as his head swung toward the dunes.

Eyes wide. Ears erect and forward. Coop bared his teeth and growled.

I crouched beside him. My eyes darted to the lights of my complex just ahead.

Should I scream? Would anyone hear me?

In the gloom of the island's interior, six glowing circles appeared.

Red. Quarter-sized. Floating in close-set pairs.

As I watched two spheres vanished, then reappeared a dozen yards away.

I stood very still, spellbound.

The paired lights inched closer. I heard the slightest shifting of sand.

Abruptly it hit me.

Eyes.

Three pairs, spread out among the dunes.

The realization chilled my blood.

In all my life, I'd never seen red eyes like that. Not on any creature.

Coop lunged forward, barking wildly. Then he yelped as the injured paw took his weight.

The scarlet orbs stopped moving. Hovered in the blackness.

I stared. They stared back.

Coop went ballistic. On three legs, he began limping toward the dunes, howling and baying at the silent red circles. Ropes of saliva dripped from his jaws.

Floodlights flickered on at our complex. One. Then another. Then a third.

Each successive halogen dispelled more of the shadows.

As the illumination spread our way, the eyes vanished.

The beach felt suddenly empty. I counted to ten. Nothing reappeared.

Whatever had been watching was gone.

○   ○   ○

"Everything okay, honey?"

Kit was standing on our front stoop. "What's gotten into Cooper?"

"He hurt his paw."

My voice trembled. I hoped Kit would attribute its shakiness to concern for my pet.

"Poor guy."

Kit stepped down and took a quick look. "Yikes. How'd you manage that one, fella?"

He was clubbed, protecting me from a masked attacker.

"Coop stumbled by the rocks."

Kit eyed the stairs, then, squaring his shoulders, lifted the wolfdog and carried him up.

"*Oof.* What are we feeding you? Dinosaurs?"

Kit muscled Coop into the house and over to his doggie bed. Then he collapsed to the floor, wiping sweat from his forehead.

"Note to self," Kit panted. "This dog is too big for carrying."

Cooper licked his face.

I stood by the stairs, unsure what to do. A part of me knew I was still in shock.

I'd been attacked.

My powers had nearly killed me.

And then strange . . . *something* had stalked me in the darkness.

Unless I'm hallucinating. Oh, crap, am I hallucinating?

"Kiddo?" Kit was watching me. "You okay? I don't think his paw is broken. Rest and ice oughta do the trick."

I shook my head to clear it.

Kit couldn't know what just happened. Ella needed me. The last thing I could afford right then was my father restricting my movements.

"I'm just tired." Feigning a yawn. "I'm trying to think of how we'll get Cooper upstairs."

Kit's face fell. "Tory, I'm not sure I can manage that. I nearly died just now."

Sensing the issue, Coop rose. Limped to my side. Nipped at my palm.

Against all odds, it triggered a smile. I knelt and hugged my dog, ruffling his fur.

"We'll go slow. One step at a time."

No matter what, I wasn't leaving Coop downstairs, alone.

Not tonight. My protector deserved better.

Bu as we maneuvered my wolfdog up the stairs, riser by riser, the dark thoughts returned.

I'd been targeted. Someone had come for me in the night.

And there could only be one explanation.

I didn't know how or why. I couldn't fathom the connection.

But the truth was as plain as the smashed nails on Cooper's swollen paw.

The Zodiac kidnapper was now after *me*.

CHAPTER 37

Sunday

We reassembled in the bunker ten hours later.

I'd asked Ben to pick us up in *Sewee,* not wanting to walk across Morris that morning. I knew my attacker wouldn't still be hiding in the sand hills, but those glowing red eyes were fresh in my memory.

If they actually existed. If my brain hadn't gone fishing after the flare disaster.

But Coop had seen them, too. And gone ballistic.

Coop saw something, *but he was injured. It could've been the kidnapper considering a second pass.*

I'd left my canine protector at home that morning. His bum wheel needed bed rest.

Coop hadn't liked the idea, but I'd been firm.

"I'm on high alert," I'd assured him. "I'll be safe with the boys."

"Gift cards?" Hi's complaining brought me back to the present. "Why not just hand me a note that says: I don't care enough to make an effort."

April 7. Hiram Stolowitski's sixteenth birthday.

"When exactly were we supposed to shop?" Shelton was scrolling Rex Gable emails on his laptop. "It's been a hectic week, bro."

"I bought you *Assassin's Creed* six weeks before *your* birthday," Hi shot back. "Waited in line all afternoon. The guy behind me smelled like fish tacos, but *I* stuck it out."

Ben clapped Hi's shoulder. "If it helps, I didn't remember to get you any gift. Tory and Shelton picked that up. I signed the card though. See? Ben. Right there."

"These are the memories that scar," Hi huffed. "I'm gonna be so complicated when I grow up. I'll probably film documentaries."

I sat forward at the table. "Okay, so . . . like, don't freak out."

That got their attention.

"About?" Ben took the seat across from me, next to Hiram.

"There was an incident last night." Oh so calm. "I'm perfectly okay, but on the way home someone attacked me on the beach."

"What?!" Three stunned voices.

"*That's* why you didn't text," Ben muttered.

Keeping my emotions in check, I described the chain of events. All but the part about mysterious red eyes. I needed to gnaw on that one. Were they even real?

"That's the *last* time you walk home alone." Ben's voice simmered with anger. "Thank God for the mutt. He's okay?"

"Coop's paw took a hit, but otherwise he's unhurt." I held up my palms in surrender. "Hey, no more arguments here. You three can sleep on my bedroom floor if you want."

"You think the attack was random?" Shelton's gaze slid to the bunker's entrance, perhaps worried that storm troopers might barrel in at any moment. "I find that hard to believe."

"Not a chance." Hi shook his head. "The Gable twins, then Ella. Now you. All Bolton Prep students. But what's the connection?"

"Linking me and Ella is easy," I said, "but what ties either of us to Lucy and Peter?"

No one had a theory.

"And your flare actually took you out?" Shelton hugged his knees. "Not cool."

I nodded grimly. "Full-blown backfire. I collapsed like a fainting goat. My eyesight even cut out. If Coop hadn't been there to defend me . . ."

Ben's fist hit the table. "Worst possible timing."

I rubbed my eyes. "And that weird feeling keeps coming on out of nowhere. Like a ghost. It's happening more often, and the sensation is getting stronger."

"Great," Shelton huffed. "Another mental health issue to worry about. Still no idea what it is? Why the vibe comes when you're *not* flaring?"

I shook my head helplessly. "None."

"That's background noise." Hi tapped the table with his index finger. "We gotta catch the psycho kid-grabber. Like, right now. If the bastard came after Tory once, he might do it again."

"Let's go over every scrap of evidence." Shelton closed his computer. "These emails are going nowhere. If Rex Gable wrote anything else that's incriminating, he did a better job hiding it than the ransom tape."

"We should focus on locations," Hi insisted. "Find where the kidnapper is holed up."

"But *how*?" Ben rose and leaned against the bunker wall. "We don't have anything to go on. Should we just drive around, shouting Ella's name out the windows?"

"Wait." A thought was winging in my brain. "We know about the phosphate nodule, but never really investigated its source."

"I looked some yesterday." Hi moved to the computer workstation. "Check this out."

Hi pulled up an old map detailing the Charleston Basin and its tributary rivers. Labeled along the riverbanks were the locations of old phosphate mines.

"You thinking mineshaft?" Shelton watched from over Hi's shoulder. "Like, they're being held underground somewhere, near one of the rivers?"

"That's not how those operations worked." On the second monitor, Hi opened a magazine article. "I read this a few nights ago. The phosphates being mined weren't buried very deep. Maybe six to ten feet. The miners would dig trenches by hand alongside a deposit, then remove the topsoil in layers to expose the rock. Then they'd strip it all out and move to another spot."

"So they weren't underground mines." Shelton scratched his chin. "What then?"

A line in the article jumped out at me.

I pointed. "This says that a major drawback of strip mining was how badly it scarred the land." I read from the screen. "Dozens of beautiful plantations were destroyed to make way for the phosphate mining operations."

Ben glanced at me. "Yeah. So?"

"These mines were dug on old plantations along the riverbanks. Some of *those* probably had expensive manor houses. Ornate gates. Fancy kitchens. Sprawling barns."

Ben shrugged. "Still not following."

"Professor Marzec seemed surprised we'd found such a large nodule. That makes me think these rocks aren't that common. Maybe the kidnapper found it at a place where phosphates were actually brought to surface, and a few old samples were still kicking around."

"Okay." Shelton was fiddling with his glasses. "So the rock used to attack Ella likely came from near an old phosphate mine. I buy that. But this map shows *hundreds* of locations."

My voice grew excited. "But we have another piece of info as well."

Blank stares.

"The writing on the prison bar in the ransom video! We know who forged the steel."

"Philip Simmons!" Hi was already typing. "If we can find a map of his works, then cross-check *those* locations with old phosphate mining operations—"

"We can narrow the possible locations." Ben shook his head in wonderment. "Incredible. It's nice having a genius around."

"It's only genius if it works." But I flushed at the compliment.

"Got it." Hi had found exactly what we needed—a map of greater Charleston pinpointing the works of legendary ironworker Philip Simmons. "I love Internet more than pizza. Maybe."

Hi and Shelton exchanged places without a word.

We'd entered a Devers area of expertise.

"I'll superimpose the Simmons map over the mining chart." Shelton cracked his knuckles. "Won't take a minute."

Shelton opened GIMP and got to work. I watched impatiently as he merged the two images to create a unified picture.

When he finished, I stared at the screen, enthralled.

Only five places overlapped.

Hi was glancing from map to article. "The three locations on the Stono River are all out. Everything around there was demolished in 1943, to make way for the private airport on Johns Island."

"When did phosphate mining stop?" Ben asked suddenly.

It took a moment for Hi to find the answer.

"The 1930s," he said finally. "The industry peaked in the 1880s, then slowly ran out of steam over the next four decades. It was barely limping along by the turn of the century."

Ben looked at me. "Simmons wasn't born until 1912. And he must've spent a long time learning his trade, right? He wouldn't have run his own shop for at least twenty years, probably more. Which means the 1930s."

Hi frowned. "So?"

"Metal bars marked by Philip Simmons probably didn't even exist *during* the mining boom," Ben said. "I bet the bar in the ransom video was formed after all the phosphate mines had shut down."

"We should look for a plantation that survived the mining craze!" I blurted, then clapped my hands in excitement. "An estate that was still intact when its mine shut down, and wealthy enough to require expensive ironwork services sometime afterward."

"Of course!" Shelton nodded eagerly. "That would account for both a Simmons steel bar *and* phosphate rocks in the same location."

I squeezed Ben's shoulder. "Who's the genius now?"

He snorted, looked away.

Hi was now shoving Shelton aside. "Leave this part to the birthday boy."

Retaking the keyboard, Hi began running searches, pausing now and again to scan an article. Without a way to help, the rest of sat down at the table to wait.

An eternity later, Hi spun to face us. "Ladies and gentlemen!"

We rushed to his side.

A website was open, detailing the historic contributions of one Philip Simmons.

In the mid-1980s, Mr. Simmons repaired iron railings on the riverfront steps during a plantation-wide beatification project. But that was not his first encounter with the estate. As a young man, Simmons knew many of the African Americans living on the plantation, and would visit often and provide what services he could.

I checked Shelton's combined map.

The location was perfect—hard against the Ashley River, a phosphate mining operation had occupied the same grounds from the late 1800s until the early twentieth century.

I checked the website's header. Something about the name felt right.

"Drayton Hall," I whispered.

"There are two other possibilities," Hi pointed out. "A cotton plantation on the Edisto, and a horseback riding retreat a few miles farther inland."

Perhaps my head was still scrambled from the night before.

But I could practically hear Ella calling to me.

Trust your instincts. Trust yourself.

"No." My finger touched the screen. "This is the spot."

"And we're going there. Right now."

CHAPTER 38

A fancy tourist mansion?"

In the rearview mirror, I could see Hi shaking his head.

He'd said it before at the bunker, and I'd had the same response.

"However unlikely, that's where the evidence points." I twisted in my seat to catch his eye. "If this isn't the right spot, then we'll scout those other two locations."

He nodded unhappily. "All I'm saying is, how in the world would a kidnapper hold three high school kids hostage at a place you can buy a ticket for, six days a week?"

Hi did have a point. Frankly, a strong one.

"Drayton Hall is a huge plantation." Shelton was sitting beside Hi. "And some areas aren't open to the public. Maybe the kidnapper is using one of them?"

"Gimme facts." Ben was at the wheel. "I wanna know what we're getting into."

We'd crossed James Island and were driving northeast up Ashley River Road, about fifteen miles beyond downtown Charleston. Civilization slowly fell away—the Explorer cruised through a dense forest of magnolias and live oaks, which hugged the road on both sides, creating a tunnel effect.

No sound. Little movement outside the confines of our packed SUV.

The surrounding woods had a creepy, claustrophobic feel, as if the trees intended to keep all human life confined to the narrow two-lane blacktop knifing through their domain. Though the forest had a cold aesthetic beauty, the area didn't give off a friendly vibe. I couldn't imagine anyone living out here.

Shelton read from his iPhone. "Drayton Hall is a classic eighteenth-century Ashley River plantation in the heart of the Lowcountry. *Blah blah blah.*" He began skimming the description. "A marvelous example of Palladian architecture . . . survived both the Revolutionary and Civil Wars . . . National Historical Landmark. The seven-bay double-pile plantation house was built by John Drayton in the late 1730s . . . completed in 1742 . . . using both free and slave labor. *Ugh.* C'mon, man. Slaves?"

"Forget the house," Ben advised. "What about the grounds?"

"Don't rush me." Shelton scrolled his cell. "Six hundred and thirty acres. The plantation grew rice and indigo. The estate's been kept in pretty good shape, although some of the oldest buildings are gone. The phosphate mine was close to the river."

"That's our focus," I said. "Old phosphate nodules probably aren't scattered over all six hundred acres."

"There!" Hi pointed to a narrow road cutting into the forest.

An elegant wooden sign announced the entrance to Drayton Hall. Ben turned onto the long driveway—a slender black strip in a sea of brown and green. It looked like a path to the end of the world.

"Man! I thought *we* lived in the middle of nowhere." Hi's nose was pressed to his window. "I've changed my mind, Tory. This *is* the perfect place to hold someone prisoner. I'm keeping it on file."

Ben eased down the lane, keeping our speed low.

I didn't blame him. It felt like we were invading a foreign country.

"There's an administrative center, a library, and a gift shop. Not what we're looking for." Then Shelton's eyes lit up. "But there's a *bunch* of stuff near the water. A garden house. Barn. The old mining works."

"Perfect." Pulse racing.

Could we actually have solved this riddle?

It seemed like such a long shot, yet something inside me was certain. *This* must *be the right place.*

"Can we wander around alone?" Hi asked. "Because I doubt any kid-napping cages will be on the official program."

Shelton nodded. "Eight bucks for grounds only."

Half a mile in, the woods ended. A trio of ponds slipped by as the road cut sharply left, then back to the right. Ahead, an expansive lawn ran a hundred yards to the foot of Drayton Hall itself.

The stylish manor house was three stories, brick, with twin front staircases leading up to a white-column-flanked front door. The roof was elegant red tile. A balcony opened on the second level, just above the main entrance.

A workers' platform was attached to the building's left side, with cans of paint stacked on each of its four tiers.

"Pretty," I said. "And whoever's in charge of maintenance is earning their keep."

The access road ended in a small parking lot beside the administration center. There were no other cars. We exited the vehicle, and Shelton hustled over to buy four tickets.

Seconds later his voice called out. "You're not gonna believe this!"

We hurried to where he stood by a pair of locked doors.

A sign was taped to the glass: "Closed for renovations. See you this summer!"

Ben turned on Hi and Shelton. "All that fancy googling, and you didn't catch that part?"

"No, guys!" My eyes widened. "How long has the plantation been shut down?"

They all took my meaning.

"Three weeks." Hi was squinting at his phone. "And it's out of commission for another two months."

Shelton stomped over. "Where'd you see that?"

"Home page. Clear your cache once in a while, dummy. Is this your first smartphone?"

"This *could* be the place." Ben was suddenly all business. "The timing works."

"The river." My intensity matched Ben's.

Ella might be here.

Trapped in a cage, somewhere on this sprawling estate.

The thought made me both anxious and determined.

I would *not* fail my friend.

The twins, too. If their stepfather is responsible, we might be their only hope.

Shelton's eyebrows rose above the level of his glasses. "Should we . . . you know . . . take the dog out for a walk?"

I shook my head, avoiding Ben's eye. "The last time I tried, I nearly lost consciousness. That makes two disasters in a row. We can't risk it today—this mission is too important."

Ben was first to respond. "I'm with Tory. We don't need superpowers to search the grounds. We can always revisit the issue, if necessary."

Hi and Shelton nodded, looking relieved.

At skipping the flares, or the lack of a fight?

Shelton scored a map from a nearby bin. "We should start at the house. A wide lane runs from its back door, dividing the property in half."

I waved him forward. "Lead the way."

We cut through a screen of magnolias, entering the football field of grass that served as the estate's front yard.

"Nice digs," Hi said. "But I'm not mowing this lawn. It'd take days."

We walked up to the manor, then circled the building to an arrow-straight path stretching from its rear.

"It leads to the Ashley." Shelton peered ahead, hand-shielding his eyes. "This road was how they moved materials and supplies up to the house. Back in the day, the river was the best way in and out of here."

We followed the sunken lane toward the water, moving in and out of shadows cast by azalea trees lining both sides.

I felt hemmed in. Constricted. As beautiful as it was, I didn't like it there.

But it's perfect for hiding something you don't want found.

"Eyes peeled," I warned. "If we're on target, what we're looking for will be up ahead."

In minutes we reached the riverfront. Beyond a few broken-down sheds and the remains of an ancient garden, we'd seen nothing along the trail.

Water gently lapped the high bank. Only the occasional birdsong broke the silence.

The stillness was unnerving. Even on Morris, it was never *this* quiet.

"Where is everybody?" Shelton's shoulders were tense. "This place feels like the dark side of the moon."

"There's not another house for miles." Hi kicked a pebble into the stream. "I guess that's what six hundred acres buys you—total isolation. And Sunday must be a day off for the workers."

Ben was surveying our surroundings. "You could hide *fifty* dungeons on this property."

I took a deep breath, trying to formulate a plan. "Shelton, you mentioned structures by the river?"

Repositioning his glasses, Shelton consulted the handout. "Barn and garden house to the left. Mining stuff and cemetery to the right."

"Let's split into pairs," I said. "Hi and I will check the mine and graveyard. You two take the garden house and barn. We'll meet back here in twenty."

Ben waved away my suggestion. "Shelton and I will check the mine."

"You heard her say 'graveyard,' too, right?" Shelton squawked. "Not my speciality, Blue."

I started to protest, but Ben cut me off. "You were *attacked* yesterday, Tory. And *your* flares seem wonkier than the rest of ours. We'll handle this one. You and Sweet Sixteen can sweep the gardens."

Hi tugged my elbow, whispering, "He's right. Let him have this."

I swallowed my pride. "Fine. But promise. If you see anything suspicious, you'll regroup with us before you act. No exceptions."

Ben nodded, looking relieved. "Deal. See you in twenty."

Snagging Shelton by the shoulder—who muttered "graveyard?" one more time before relenting—Ben headed west along the riverbank.

Sighing, I turned to Hi.

He smiled wide. "Heigh ho, heigh ho, off to the barn we go?"

"Blargh."

We moved eastward and reached the garden house in moments. What was left of it, anyway—three crumbling walls surrounded a few well-tended flowerbeds. A winding path led from it down to the waterfront, which was screened from view by a stand of weeping willows.

Fifty yards farther on was the barn, its wooden exterior cracked and weathered.

My jaw clenched. I was on a goose chase.

I spun to face him. "These structures aren't even maintained."

He looked away. "They, uh, don't look too . . . sturdy."

My eyes narrowed. Hi was in on it, too, eh?

Shelton must've been acting reluctant, so I wouldn't suspect their plan. I was being shielded from harm. Sent to investigate the unlikely spots. Kept away from the phosphate mine.

Snap decision. "You check this path. There might be caves by the waterline."

Irritably, I gestured to the barn. "I'll buzz that relic, then we head to the mining area."

"Search the river for prison caves. Got it." Hi gave me a thumbs-up. "By the way, worst birthday ever."

I hustled forward, making little effort to conceal my movements. I'd been tricked—sent from the danger zone by my macho companions—but I refused to waste all day on this sideshow.

The barn was surrounded by live oaks, its planks cut from the same wood. Drawing closer, I realized the building wasn't the owl-invested wreck I'd suspected.

An area before the entrance had been floored with wooden beams and bound by a low wall. Inside, a dozen sawhorse tables and benches were arranged in rows. Wood cuttings depicting wild animals had been nailed to nearby tree trunks. A large chalkboard hung beside the door into the structure itself.

It clicked.

An outdoor pavilion. The barn had been converted into a low-tech schoolhouse, perhaps for use by visiting school groups.

The barn door was new-looking and properly seated. A single window to its left was draped from the inside, blocking view of the interior.

I stood a dozen yards outside the pavilion, pondering whether I needed to approach.

Maybe there's a root cellar in there. Or a cold storage room.

Eyeing the damp foundation, I didn't think so. This close to the river was less than ideal for underground storage.

Then I saw it. Just beyond the pavilion were moldy piles of stones.

I hurried across and hefted the closest specimen.

Phosphate rock. I was certain. The smell alone convinced me.

Directly beside the pile was a stretch of muddy, beaten earth. Cutting through the slop were two lines of tire tracks.

My mind flashed to last night's rainstorm.

Someone drove here recently. The tracks were made today.

I rose, adrenaline pumping. My eyes flew to the barn window.

The drape's hem was flipped back in one corner, revealing a tiny patch of unobstructed glass. Enough to see inside?

Dropping the nodule, I crept forward. With each passing step, it became more clear.

A light was burning inside the barn.

Then I heard something.

Voices. Arguing?

I stopped dead. Strained to listen.

No good. The noise was too indistinct to make out.

Dropping to a crouch, I crab-stepped forward, vaulting the pavilion's low wall.

A board creaked beneath my feet. I froze, heart banging wildly.

The voices continued, undeterred.

One male. One female. Most *definitely* arguing.

Should I get Hiram? The others? What if the speakers moved?

Ignoring the condition I'd forced Ben to accept, I scurried to the base of the windowsill.

Oh so carefully, I rose on the balls of my feet.

Peered inside.

had taught me. "My friends will be here soon. You're going to tell us where Ella is."

"You're alone." Hawfield rose unsteadily. "If your pals were here, they'd have come by now. I was wrong after all." He took a step toward me. "You're just a nimble girl with strange eyes. You don't have what it takes to pull that trigger."

He took another step.

I pulled back the slide on the HK45. "Try me."

Hawfield froze. Our eyes locked. One heartbeat, then he took a step back.

Suddenly, my temperature skyrocketed. Sweat erupted all over as my senses lurched into overdrive. Information poured into my brain.

Scents. Smells. Sounds. Impressions.

I felt each Viral pause where they stood. A blast of thoughts nearly wiped my hard drive.

Tory?

Tor, where are you?

Hey, you oka—

Too fast. Too much. I staggered.

Sensing my body was about collapse, I tried the only thing I could think of.

Closing my eyes, I reached out to the other Virals.

The flaming cords thrummed like lines on a ship in a storm. I couldn't grasp them. Couldn't harness the connections.

Something untethered with an explosion of black.

SNUP.

A flash of red exploded in my mind. Pain seared across my forehead.

I felt myself falling, My eyes opened to see the hardwood rising to meet me.

Hawfield was above me, holding the gun. He lifted my dead weight, then flung me over one shoulder.

I tried to resist, but my mind was Jell-O. I couldn't remember how my limbs worked. How to make sounds. I was carried, helpless, through the barn door and out into the trees.

A police car. An open trunk.

Falling. The slam of a lid. Screeching tires.

Then my eyes rolled up and I slipped away for good.

PART FOUR

JEOPARDY

CHAPTER 43

I heard Hi shouting from a hundred yards away.

"What's that fool done now?" I muttered, digging a rock from my sneaks. These retro Jordans might look cool, but they were light on padding.

Adjusting my glasses, I ran in the direction of his howls. Ben and I had already scouted the phosphate mine, and were just finishing a circuit of the old cemetery.

Not my favorite assignment. Freaking graveyards. Next time Tory wants some ancient crypts inspected, *she* can have the job.

"Come on, Devers." Jogging over to join me, Ben cocked his head toward the riverbank. "Sounds like Hiram's about to wet himself."

We found Stolowitski down a ten-foot mud slick, gripping a clump of vines for dear life. His lower body was submerged in the fast-flowing Ashley River.

"About time!" Hi yelled. "Get me out of here. I think I lost a shoe!"

"What in the world?" I almost broke down laughing.

"Where's Tory?" Ben dropped to his butt and scooted down the incline Hi had obviously failed to notice. Halting ten feet from the water's edge, he considered how to get closer without following Hi into the river.

"How should I know?" Hi grumbled, red-faced. "We split up. She was headed for the old barn. *Go check the dangerous riverbank, Hiram. There might be secret caves.* No one said anything about fifty-foot cliffs!"

"You let her go alone?" Ben scolded, slowly working his way down to where Hi was beached. "That defeats the whole purpose!"

"I'm *aware* of that, Benjamin." Hi tried slinging a leg up onto the riverbank, but it flopped back into the roiling current. "But she'd figured out you sent her away from the mine on purpose. *You* try telling Tory what to do when she's pissed."

"I'll pass." But I shook my head at Hi anyway. He looked like a giant fishing lure.

Ben wrapped one arm around a low-slung willow branch, then extended a hand toward Hi, who stared at it dubiously. I shuffled clockwise to get a better view.

"Don't drop me," Hi pleaded. "I can't swim all the way back to the marina."

"Relax." Ben planted his feet and steadied himself. "On three. One. Two—"

Hi leaped too early, but Ben was ready. Locking arms with Hi, he dragged him up onto dry land, then pushed his portly frame back upslope.

"Just carry me," Hi wheezed. "Be my knight in shining armor."

Ben kicked his rear. "Keep moving, you dope."

Hi collapsed at the top, then pointed to a knobby root at the crest of the slope.

"Him," Hi informed me solemnly. "That's the one that got me."

"We waited on the path for like ten minutes," I said, cleaning dirt from my lenses with the tail of my shirt. "Ya'll didn't show, so we checked the graveyard real quick. Where you been?"

"I've been floating in the drink for at least that long." Hi was pull-ing off his drenched socks. One shoe was definitely AWOL. "Tory must've heard me yelling. I think she's punishing me for colluding with you guys."

"Wait." Ben straightened. "No one's seen Tory since we split up?"

"There's nothin' up this way," I pointed out. "That's why we sent her to the barn in the first place."

"Then where is she?" Ben rose, scanning the tree line. "Could she have doubled back?"

"And left Hi to drown?" I felt a hand rise to my earlobe. "No way. She'd have come right by here."

I glanced at Hi, sitting in a puddle on the grass. "You been shouting the whole time?"

"Like an opera singer," Hi confirmed, squeezing river water from his socks.

I was about to say more when it happened.

A slap of cold jolted my system.

Strange buzzing filled my head, like a fax machine attempting to connect.

Ben's eyes went wide. Hi popped to his bare feet, then crouched like a hunted animal.

Suddenly, I knew what was happening.

Tory was flaring.

"It's her!" I whispered, unsure why I'd dropped my voice. "She must be in—"

Something brushed against my mind, making me dizzy.

A blast of heat filled my chest.

BEN! HI! SHELTON! I NEED—

The message abruptly ceased.

Tory!

I tried sending thoughts back, sensed Hi and Ben attempting the same.

Brief contact, then my mind recoiled as if struck. The connection was gone.

Hi staggered against a tree trunk.

"Tory!" Ben shouted, spinning in a wild circle. "Where are you?!"

My brain seemed to spin inside my skull. Then I was on my knees, vomiting in the tall grass. When the world finally righted itself, I felt hands beneath my armpits, holding me up.

"You're okay, buddy." Hi's voice cracked. "Shake it off. We have to find Tor."

Ben was pacing, frantic, at a loss for what to do.

"The barn!" I gulped, straightening my glasses. "That's where she was headed!"

Ben took off without a backward glance. Hiram and I followed, racing through the brush and into deeper woods.

"No shoes!" Hi yelped, hobbling away from a pinecone. "Worst birthday *ever!*"

Ahead, I heard an engine rev.

Squealing tires.

Then the sounds of a car tearing through the mud.

We caught Ben at the barn, which was no hollow wreck after all.

Oh damn. This looks new.

A window had been smashed. The door stood ajar. Ben raced inside, only to reemerge seconds later, firing over to a set of sloppy tire tracks.

Ben screamed in anger and frustration.

And I knew.

Tory was gone.

"I'm telling you, she's been taken!"

Ben slapped the intake desk, causing everyone to jump.

"Take it easy," I whispered, fingers tugging at both ears. "We won't help Tory by getting locked up ourselves."

I imagined Moms bailing me out. Nearly lost my lunch.

The duty officer rose, his face a thunderhead. "Another outburst like that, son, and you'll get your own special room to cool down in. Understood?"

"Yessir," Hi answered for Ben, who was hovering close to tilt. "We're just worried about our friend. She's been missing for at least an hour."

The officer spoke with forced patience. "She's only been gone an hour?"

"Tory was with *us*," I answered quickly. "In the middle of nowhere. No ride of her own, no other way home. We were doing . . . something important. She wouldn't have run off alone."

The officer rubbed his chin. "You're the same kids who came in here yesterday, right?"

I nodded, nervous, not liking where this was going.

"And you don't have any *proof* your friend was kidnapped? You didn't *see* it happen?"

Ben's mouth opened, but I clamped his arm.

"No, sir." *But she didn't just bail without telling us!*

That settled it for the cop. "We've been warned that you four like to tell fantastic stories. Always have something crazy to report. I'm sorry, but without more, I can't help you. Hawfield's orders. We'll call your parents, and they can sort this out."

Ben tensed. I cringed, anticipating an explosion. I kept a grip on his forearm, though my glasses nearly slid off my nose.

"Is Captain Corcoran available?" Hi asked.

I tried not to cringe. *Hiram, why?*

"He might be," the officer answered warily.

"Great." Hi smiled as if the issue had been settled. "Carmine and I go *way* back. Since his Academy days. We'll just pop by his office and fill him in on the new info."

"Now hold on a—"

"Officer—" Hiram's eyes dropped to a shiny silver name tag, "—Shinn, is it?"

The cop snapped a curt nod.

"Great work down here, Shinn. You're a credit to the intake desk. On the ball. I can tell you're heading places."

Hi leaned forward and lowered his voice conspiratorially, forcing Shinn to bend closer as well. "Thing is, Captain CC made us *promise* to bring him any intel we might learn about the Zodiac kidnappings, no matter how trivial. I'd hate to upset such a powerful man by failing to follow his orders, wouldn't you?"

I coughed into my hand, hiding a smile. I saw Hi's play now.

Corcoran was our last chance. Hi knew the captain—and his sour attitude—and was hoping young Officer Shinn did as well. We had to get past this stupid desk.

With a world-weary sigh, Shinn pointed toward the elevators. "Top floor. No stops."

Snagging Ben's arms, Hiram and I hustled him from the desk.

○   ○   ○

"What did I do in life to deserve you kids?" Corcoran grumbled.

I kept my mouth shut, though I felt the exact same about him.

Ben planted his fists on Corcoran's desk. "Tory's been *taken,* Captain. Do your job!"

Corcoran pointed to the chair Ben had vacated. "Sit your butt down, you little cuss. Or else you're out of here. I'll not be scolded by some whippet who can't even shave."

Ben dropped back with an exasperated grunt. I could tell he was nearing the edge.

We all were.

Tory had been snatched, miles from here, by who we couldn't even guess.

And we had no idea how to get her back.

This is the worst.

"Think what you like about us personally," Hi said, "but we've got history together, Captain. Without us, you wouldn't be sitting in that cushy chair at all. You know we wouldn't be here unless we truly believed Tory was in danger."

Corcoran bristled at Hi's mention of the past, but refrained from comment.

I added my voice. "We told you everything we know. Just tell us if you can help."

Corcoran crossed his meaty arms. "Fine. I'll look into it."

"How?" Ben pressed. "What are you going to do?"

"Honestly, boy, I have no idea." Corcoran's forehead wrinkled as he considered options. "If she was grabbed in the woods, as you say, then I don't rightly know where to start. You've given me nothing to go on."

Ben threw his hands up. "You're the *police*! There's has to be someone you can—"

He stopped dead. A faraway look entered his eyes. Then, "Thank you for your time, Captain. Please do what you can."

Ben popped up and strode for the door, motioning us to follow.

I glanced at Hi, who shrugged. Baffled, we hurried after our friend.

Half rising from his desk, Corcoran called to our backs. "Don't do anything stupid, you hear?" But we'd already disappeared down the hall.

Ben mashed the elevator button, then pushed it again and again.

My patience only lasted until the doors closed. "Well? What the heck was that?"

"We made a mistake." Ben stared at the lit arrow, willing the car to descend faster.

"How so?" For once, Hi passed on a pithy quip.

"We came to the wrong place." I saw a glimmer of hope in Ben's eyes. "But if we hurry, we'll still have plenty of daylight."

"So where are we going?" I couldn't help but ask.

"To the one person who'll know where Tory is. Or how to find her."

CHAPTER 44

I awoke in semidarkness.

Blink.

Blink blink blink.

A cool hand was stroking my forehead.

"About time," said a familiar voice. "I was starting to worry."

Lurching upright, I grabbed the dim form hovering over me.

"Ella!" Wrapping both arms around my friend. "You're okay!"

"I wouldn't go *that* far." She hugged me back just as fiercely.

Eyes adjusting to the gloom, I took in my surroundings. Packed earth floor. Dank, moldy stonework. A single lightbulb burning beyond a line of rusty steel bars.

Bars I knew had been forged by Philip Simmons.

Like a bad dream.

I'd joined Ella in the ransom video cell.

"How long have you been here?" I whispered.

"Two days, best I can tell." Ella's long black hair was tied in a makeshift braid. Bits of leaves and twigs poked from the messy tangle. Her face was pale, her eyes red and puffy. I could tell she'd been crying.

"It's hard to say." Ella gestured to the gaping emptiness above our heads. "The light never changes down here, but that bastard feeds me every once in a while. A bucket comes down on a chain. I think we're at the bottom of a well."

Reality crashed in, full force.

I'd been kidnapped by Detective Hawfield.

At the crucial moment, my powers had betrayed me.

What about the boys?

"Was there anyone with me? Did Hawfield mention my friends?"

Ella shook her head. "He brought you alone. That was the first time I'd seen him since he shoved me in here. You were *totally* out. I've been trying to wake you for a while. For a moment, I . . . I thought maybe . . ."

I grabbed her hand, squeezed tightly. "I'm fine. And we're getting out of here."

"I'd like that very much, Tor." Her voice faltered. "I'm pretty scared."

Rising, I gave her another quick hug. "Don't worry. We will. I promise."

Releasing my friend, I surveyed the murky chamber. "What is this place?"

"An actual dungeon," Ella replied with disgust. "Used to punish slaves who got out of line. We're near an old plantation, I think. But deep in the woods, a few miles away."

She must've read my surprise.

"He talks too much," Ella said. "Hawfield explained the cell's origin when he dumped me in here. I think he was trying to freak me out." She shuddered, rubbing her arms. "It worked."

I tested one of the steel bars. The inch-thick metal didn't budge.

"Have you seen the twins?" I asked.

"No." Her eyes grew troubled. "I don't know what he's done with them."

"Oh, they're fine." Bitter words. "Though I wish they weren't."

Seeing her expression, I explained what had occurred earlier in the barn. How the twins had duped us all, then been double-crossed.

When I finished, some of the fire returned to Ella's eyes.

"Those spoiled brats!" She yanked her grungy braid. "How could they be so stupid?"

"The twins got away, but I doubt they'll help us. Those two will just keep running and never look back."

"They better run *far,*" Ella hissed. Then she hiccupped, fighting back tears.

"How did you end up in here?" I asked, trying to distract her.

"The bastard tricked me," Ella said acidly. "It's my fault, I guess. I saw Rex Gable Thursday night. He came into the Flying Tomato, drinking scotch with his golf buddies. He just sat there, laughing and joking, without a care in the world. It *infuriated* me. So I called Detective Hawfield and told him what we suspected. Oops."

Her eyes found mine. "Tory, I told him about you, too. What we saw at the art gala."

"It's okay," I reassured her. "How could you know? Just tell me what happened."

"Hawfield told me to meet him in the parking lot, and not to tell anyone what I suspected. Or that I was meeting with the police." Ella groaned in frustration. "Like an idiot, I did exactly as instructed. I took a break, snuck outside, and met him alone. Ten words into my story, I saw his arm swing, and suddenly I was on the gravel. Next thing I know, he's pushing me down a tunnel that led here."

She covered her mouth. "Tory, I'm so sorry. I led that bastard to both of us."

"*Shh.*" I pulled her close again. "Don't you *dare* blame yourself. *He's* the monster."

Something crunched.

Our heads whipped in unison.

I heard a throaty chuckle. "Aw, how touching."

Hawfield was standing on the other side of the bars, wearing jeans and a red polo. He wiped both hands on his shirt, then powered an electric lantern. With the added light, I could see a narrow opening in the wall behind him.

The way out?

"Two songbirds, trapped in a cage," Hawfield gloated.

I glared at the detective. "You're a psychopath."

"If it makes you feel better," Hawfield said lightly, "I was tracking *your* movements long before this girl called me. But that cinched it—I wasn't ready to pin the whole song and dance on Rex Gable just yet. Hadn't fully covered my tracks. That steak needed a bit more time to marinate, and you two poking around and spreading rumors might've upset my apple cart, so to speak. Couldn't have it."

Ice prickled my spine.

"You were tracking me?"

"Ever since you broke into the Gable house." An expression of true bafflement twisted his features. "Gotta admit, that shocked me. I sat there and watched you and those boys do it, with no idea what you were thinking. You even found the fake bloodstain. Amazing! I won't pretend that episode didn't rattle me. It *did*. I ended up keeping our CSI boys away from that spot while I considered how to deal."

I felt Ella's startled glance. No time to explain. "But we didn't learn anything that night."

Hawfield stepped forward and casually leaned against the bars. His lantern sent shadows dancing up the walls.

Ella and I retreated across the cell.

"See, that's what *I* thought, too." His confusion seemed genuine. "But, next thing I know, I get a call from the witch over in Folly Beach, and she's telling me that the *same four teens* were asking questions about my zodiac card. Who told you about Ophiuchus, anyway?"

Answer him. Trade information.

"We stole a photocopy from the DA's desk."

Hawfield nodded in appreciation. "The fat kid. By the window. Ballsy."

"Why would Clara Gordon call you?" I ventured, hoping to keep Hawfield engaged.

The more he talked, the less he could do . . . unpleasant things.

"Oh, I put her on alert," Hawfield absently scratched his cheek. "All the other psychic astro-quacks, too. I wanted to know if anyone started asking questions about lost zodiac signs. Good thing I took the precaution, too."

It made sense. Hawfield was a more careful planner than I'd thought.

"After that doozy," the detective went on, "I told Bolton's headmaster that you kids were officially 'persons of interest' in the Gable case. That helped me keep tabs as well."

He smiled wide. "Paugh said you girls were close. A fact I took note of."

I shook my head in disgust. "All that work, just to steal some money."

Hawfield snorted. "A *lot* of money. And it *was* work."

"You're sick," Ella hissed.

He waved off the comment. "You were easy to bag, but damn, Brennan, Morris Island might as well be on Neptune. It's near impossible to invent an official-sounding pretext to get out there. I had to go special ops."

The beach. My shadowy attacker.

Thinking of Coop, my temper sparked.

"How's the leg, Detective? Or did my wolfdog bite you in the ass, instead?"

His smirk vanished. "That rabid mongrel should be put down. Maybe I'll see to that, when I'm finished here." The grin returned. "I missed you on the beach, but then you walked right into my arms at the plantation, didn't you? That silly rock. I was careless there. Nearly wet myself when you brought it downtown, but it all worked out in the end. Crazy backflips notwithstanding. You're an agile little imp, I'll give you that. Almost had me in the barn, until you lost your nerve."

My nerve was fine and dandy. It was my brain that short-circuited.

"Why zodiac cards?" Ella's voice sounded small and weak.

"You mean my pals Ophiuchus and Cetus?" Hawfield chuckled. "Seemed like just the kind of occult, hippie mumbo jumbo that would rile the media, but couldn't possibly lead back to me. I have an old book on the stars that my daddy gave me, along with a set of cards he bought at a garage sale. Those two fit the bill."

He laughed, louder this time. "Lost signs! Deadly portents! Just the kind of New Age hooey to get reporters in a lather. Of course, I had to spoon-feed the knuckleheads every step of the way. Journalism is a dying art."

Clever.

Wincing inwardly, I thought of all the time we'd wasted trying to decipher the meaning behind those zodiac cards. Pointless.

"Dropping Ophiuchus by the Gable house was easy." Hawfield sniffled in the damp air. "Planting Cetus at the Francis place took a little more doing, but I pulled it off. But I'm all done with cards now. Don't think I'll bother with Dr. Howard's condo."

The sound of Kit's name on Hawfield's tongue infuriated me.

Did my father even know I was missing? What would the boys tell him?

"You've been sabotaging these cases from the beginning," I said.

No wonder the investigations were inept.

The CPD was being led around by the nose.

Hawfield watched me with amusement. "Of course, Tory. Kinda stands to reason, since, you know, *I'm* the kidnapper. And I've got my bases covered. My colleagues won't trust anything your friends have to say. I've left specific instructions to ignore those boys. They're considered highly unreliable."

"Bastard."

The Virals didn't know who not to trust. And I couldn't get a message to them.

Ella inched closer to me. "So now you're doing this alone?"

"I'll still pin everything on Rex." Rueful shake of the head. "That man doesn't have a friend in the world. Gambling debts up the wazoo, plus the whole trust fund angle with his stepkids. He's the perfect fall guy."

A flaw in his plan occurred to me. I seized on the idea.

"Lucy and Peter are loose. They could blow your cover with one call. There might not be a dollar in ransom coming your way."

"True." The affability drained from Hawfield's voice. "But I doubt the twins are ready to face the music yet. They'll go to ground and keep quiet. For a little while, at least. Long enough for me to collect the dough, I think. But I won't be able to stay in town after all."

The detective shrugged. "Disappointing, but five million bones should salve my wounds. I planned for this eventuality, too. Gotta cover every angle, I always say."

Then his expression hardened, like an invisible mask slipping into place. "You girls are my insurance policy. Double coverage, so to speak. If the twins blab, I've still got *your* lives as leverage. For a bit, anyway."

His last words chilled my heart.

"You'll regret this," I whispered.

"Maybe." He turned to leave. "But not as much as you, I expect."

CHAPTER 45

I'd never driven so fast.

"Slow down, Blue!" Shelton shouted at me, flopping sideways in the backseat as we swerved onto Folly Road. "We won't help anybody if we crash and burn!"

Reluctantly, I reduced speed.

My heart was in my throat. I was close to panic.

Tory was missing.

A lunatic might have her caged like an animal.

My knuckles whitened on the steering wheel. The Explorer accelerated once more.

We had to get her back. *I* had to get her back.

If something happens to Tory . . .

I stomped on the gas, forcing the negative thoughts away.

Find her. Find her find her find her.

"I take it we're heading home." Hi was staring at the passing landscape, his face a sickly green. He didn't do well with speed. "You gonna tell Kit?"

"Not Kit." I swerved to pass a slow-moving truck. "We need the mutt."

"Cooper?" Shelton's head poked between the front seats. "Why?"

"We get the wolfdog." *Swerve.* "Flare." *Accelerate.* "Find Tory." *Pass.*

I swung back into our lane. A bus flew by. Horns blared.

"Great plan." Hi's fingers were imbedded in the armrest. "If we're alive to attempt it!"

The miles roared past, but not fast enough for me. Reaching Folly Beach, I turned left and shot toward Morris Island, crossing the bridge, only slowing as we approached our complex.

Wheeling my Explorer into its usual spot, I spun to face Hi and Shelton.

"Here's the thing." This might be a tough sell. "We can't tell Kit anything."

"His only daughter's been kidnapped!" Shelton shouted.

"Then how do we get Coop?" Hi asked at the same time.

"We have to sneak him out somehow." I tried to explain, though long speeches aren't my thing. "Look, if we tell Kit that Tory's been abducted, we'll have to tell him *everything*. Then he'll march us back to the police, where we'll have to repeat the whole story all over again. After that, our parents will never let us out of their sight, which means we'll be no help to Tory. And they won't know where to look anyway!"

"But *we* don't either," Shelton said glumly.

"Coop will." My voice was more confident than I felt. "He and Tory have that crazy bond. Some mental connection. We all do, but not like those two. The wolfdog will know where to go." *I hope.*

Hi was nodding. "Flaring together, maybe we can sense Tory's location."

"Exactly." I pinned Shelton with a hard look. "But if we tell her father, we'll never get the chance."

Not that I'd let Kit stop me. Nothing is going to stop me.

Shelton hesitated, then, "You're right. But if this fails—"

"We go straight to Kit." I pushed my hair behind my ears and tied it off with a rubber band. "I'm worried Corcoran might've called him already."

"Doubtful," said Hi. "The way the cops just reacted, I doubt they'll help at all."

"More reason to do this ourselves." I took a deep breath. Wiped sweaty palms on my black tee. "You guys ready?"

Two shaky nods. Best I could expect.

Exiting the SUV, we slunk toward Tory's unit. I didn't really have a plan.

Turns out, I didn't need one.

The door to the garage was unlocked. Kit's 4Runner was gone.

Relieved, I hurried to the flower pot where Tory hid an extra house key.

Not many secrets on Morris Island.

Opening the interior door, I was instantly steamrolled by eighty-five pounds of furry beast.

Coop exploded into the garage, bouncing like a live wire. He whined, growled, and pawed the ground, clearly in distress. Then, baring his teeth, the wolfdog fired outside.

"Stop him!" I shouted, clawing dust from my eyes.

"Stop him!?" Hi spread his arms. "How? That's like stepping in front of a freight train with teeth."

Emerging from the garage, I saw Coop's tail as it disappeared down the road.

"Damn!" I didn't know what to do. It's not like we could force him to join us. Not that much dog, all riled up.

Think, Blue! Tory's counting on you!

But I blanked. Felt close to melting down.

Tory was the one who made plans. Not stupid me. Right then, I just wanted to smash something.

Shelton grabbed my sleeve. "Let's flare, quick! Maybe we can call him back."

I nodded swiftly, grateful for a course of action. Closing my eyes, I called out the beast.

In the beginning, I'd struggled to light a flare. Even a year later I still needed to be angry. But after months of secret practice sessions—pushing myself, testing my limits—summoning the wolf had become second nature. Seductively easy. Flaring felt as natural as breathing.

A single thought of some monster hurting Tory . . .

SNAP.

I felt the familiar rush. Relished the surge of energy that came with it. My senses exploded with supernatural intensity.

How can Tory think this is bad? How could anyone deny themselves this pleasure?

I glanced at Hi and Shelton. Both had switched on.

"Now what?" Hi asked. "This is the part where Tory does her thing."

"She talks about glowing lines." Shelton was still panting. "Connecting us, in her subconscious."

Squeezing my lids tight, I tried to imagine what Tory described. Tried to picture Cooper. Tory. Me, Shelton, and Hi. The Virals, together as one. Linked. Body, mind, and soul.

Nothing happened.

Whatever Tory could visualize, it didn't work for me.

Frustrated, I screamed Cooper's name in my head. Imagined chasing him down.

Didn't feel a thing.

"This is stupid." My fingers curled into fists. "How can I summon a dog with my mind?"

"Coop-er!" Hi cupped his hands and shouted into the wind. "Yo, Coop! Here boy!"

Without a better idea, I joined him. Shelton added his voice as well. The three of us called and called, hoping our Hail Mary would connect.

I was about to give up when a gray streak shot from the brush. Coop raced over, favoring his forepaw, bristling from head to tail.

The wolfdog stopped a few paces away. Flashed gleaming white teeth.

Hi backed up a step. "Easy now, killer. We're family, remember?"

The wolfdog was clearly agitated.

It occurred to me that we'd never flared near the mongrel without Tory present.

Unexpectedly, Coop sat. Then, tipping back his head, he unleashed a full-throated howl.

My eyes widened in recognition. "He knows."

I met Coop's golden eyes with my own. Willed him to understand.

Come with us. Help us find her.

Coop cocked his head. Whined. Then he rose and trotted to my Explorer. Pawed the door.

Despite everything, I smiled. "The mutt's in."

"Okay, great." Shelton's hands rose. "But where do we start?"

I looked at Coop. He barked. Scratched at the handle a second time.

The image of a forest popped into my head.

A sending from Coop? From Tory? Some trick of our flare power?

I didn't know. But suddenly, I was certain what to do. "Back to Drayton Hall."

Surprised, Hi and Shelton started to speak at once.

I cut them off. "We go back to where we lost Tory's trail. Let Cooper track from there."

"The kidnapper *drove* away," Hi pointed out. "There won't be any trail to track."

"Not one we can see." I was already moving toward my car. "But maybe the dog has other methods."

I opened the door. Coop leaped inside and settled in the passenger seat.

Turning back to Hi and Shelton.

"You two have a better idea?"

CHAPTER 46

I had a decision to make.

Ella was huddled at the back of our cell, head against the wall, staring at nothing.

I approached the steel bars. Moving down the line, I tested every one. None wobbled or shifted. I wondered how twentieth-century steel had made its way down into a nineteenth-century slave pen. Decades ago, someone must've restored this horrible prison to its original condition.

I didn't want to think about why.

Glancing up into the gloom, I saw a chain hanging fifteen feet off the ground.

"That's how he lowers the bucket," Ella had explained bitterly. "Food comes down every twelve hours. Like we're freaking livestock."

I can make it. Flaring, I can reach that loop on the end.

But not without showing Ella something I'm not allowed to share.

What choice do I have? Am I supposed to take my secret to the grave?

Because, no mistake, that's where this was headed.

I didn't tell Ella what Hawfield had said in the barn. How he intended to "take care of the problem." Why terrify her? Why take away her hope?

Given what I knew, I couldn't hold back. Not with our lives on the line.

"Ella?"

My friend looked up. "Yeah?" Weariness dulled her voice.

"I think I can grab that chain." I pointed into the dim emptiness above. "Climb up."

Ella shook her head. "I tried myself a half dozen times. You can't reach it, not even if you climb the bars first."

"I'm going to try. Can you keep watch?"

"Sure." Ella's voice carried zero optimism. "But it might be better if I stood below to catch you. Or boost you. Or something."

"No. I don't want to be surprised if Hawfield comes back."

"Okay." Ella rose and walked to the bars. "But while I think you're a born soccer player, there's no way you can jump *that* high. Unless you've got moves I haven't seen."

Maybe one or two.

Assuming I don't just black out instead.

I shoved the unwelcome thought aside. There were no other options.

"I have to try. Keep lookout?"

Ella nodded, peered through the bars to where we knew the entrance to be. "All clear."

Come on, DNA. Don't fail me now.

Eyes closed. Mind clear.

SNAP.

As if answering my prayers, the power unfolded easily.

My senses awoke. Amplified. Power flooded my limbs.

For the first time in days, I didn't have to fight to stay upright.

I *flared*, strong as ever before.

No time to celebrate.

Gauging angles, I took two running steps toward the wall. Leaped.

My sneakers hit the stones four feet up. Legs flexing, I pushed off with every fiber of flare strength I could muster, propelling myself backward, outward, toward the center of the room.

I catapulted across the cell. Body soaring, I twisted in midair like a diver, hands flailing toward the black quadrant of space where the chain should be.

Nothing. Panic jolted me. I was going to fall, and hard.

Then my fingertips brushed metal.

I clawed the slippery links.

My left hand slipped free.

But the right one stuck, my fingers wrapping the wet steel in a death grip.

I spun wildly, one-armed, my body pirouetting across the chamber. The metal links cut cruelly into my palm. My shoulder screamed, the bone nearly ripping from its socket.

The hold began to slip.

Arm muscles burning, I propelled forward, throwing my left hand back up onto the slick chain. With both hands in place, I shifted my weight, easing the strain on my joints.

Panting, I held on tight, my momentum carrying me in lazy arcs above the stone floor five yards below.

"Anytime, Brennan." Then Ella glanced over her shoulder. "Holy crap!"

She scurried beneath me, staring up in shock. "You did it! How in the world?"

"Beginner's luck," I grunted, keeping my eyes slitted to tamp their golden glow. "I'm gonna climb up, and see if there's a way out."

"*Go go go!*" Ella bounced with sudden energy. "Then, for the love of God, come back!"

Gathering my strength, I began to haul my body upward, a few links at a time. After five exhausting pulls, I'd ascended high enough to wiggle a foot inside the loop.

I paused, hanging in the fetal position. Breathless. My arms were overjoyed at the unexpected respite. I knew that without the added flare power, I'd never have made it that far.

"Great job, girl!" Eyes blazing, I could make out Ella clearly, fifteen feet below.

I prayed she couldn't see me just as well.

Concentrate. The job isn't done.

Hanging like a spider, I cast my hyper-senses out in a net.

Water was dripping from somewhere high overhead. Looking straight up, I could make out the moldy wooden planks sealing off the ancient stonework. Flaring, I could see how misshapen the boards were, twisted and swollen from years of exposure to sunlight and water. Trickles of illumination filtered through the rotting wood.

A covered well. That must open to the outside.

But the distance was another thirty yards, minimum. I couldn't climb all that way. We were much farther underground than I'd thought.

A cocktail of dank, musty odors filled my nostrils. Mold. Wet stone. Rotting vegetation. I shut off the rancid flow before my stomach emptied.

My fingers burned. The rusty chain bored into my palms. Flare sensitivity was making the ascent doubly painful—my nerves were on fire—but I needed the extra power to keep going.

I couldn't reach the walls—the chain I dangled from was centered in a shaft at least ten feet across. Harnessing my flare vision, I studied the stonework, searching for some other way—*any* way—out of this terrible well.

There.

Ten feet above me, a rectangular hole cut into the stonework.

"I see something," I called down to Ella. "A way out, maybe."

"Okay!" Ella's voice echoed loudly in my enhanced ears.

"I have to get higher."

Taking a deep breath, I gathered my strength for the treacherous assent.

I can do this. Ten more feet.

Reach. Grab. Pull.

Reach. Grab. Pull.

Three more lunges brought me level with the opening.

It was a fetid, black maw, with no hint of light. I glanced up again. The chain ran through a small opening in the wooden boards, but the top seemed forever away.

A look back at the dark gap in the wall.

Neither option was appealing.

Gassed, I opted for crawling over climbing.

Shifting my weight, I kicked out with both legs. Began to swing the chain across the shaft.

Back and forth.

Back and forth.

Slowly, my momentum brought me near the lip of the opening.

Timing was everything.

On the next upswing I flung myself forward, launching my upper body into the crevasse.

My knees cracked against the wall below, skinning painfully as I worm-wiggled into the tunnel mouth. There I paused, gasping for air while I rubbed my bruised and abraded limbs.

"I'm in some type of tunnel," I called down. "I'll see where it leads, then come get you."

"Be careful!" Then, with a slight quaver. "Please hurry back."

"I will, Ella. I promise."

Rising on all fours, I began crawling down the passage.

Grimy stonework passed beneath my hands and knees. I traveled as fast as I dared, flare senses on maximum.

For the first twenty feet, the tunnel sloped gently downward. Then the grade steepened, the passage dropping into a black pool of shadows even my flare vision couldn't pierce.

The floor became covered in a slick wet moss that came loose under my fingers. Wet leaves coated the tunnel's sides, along with a layer of something sticky I didn't want to identify.

I inched down the incline cautiously, testing the greasy surface as I descended.

A loud bang sounded ahead.

Behind me, the chain rattled.

I froze, ears probing, but silence quickly reasserted itself.

Distracted by the noises, I failed to place my next hand with care.

My palm slipped. In an instant my body was tumbling forward. I plummeted down the shaft, unable to halt my headfirst plunge along on its filmy surface.

Seconds later, I rolled from the chute onto more wet stone. Scrambling to my feet, I examined the dark chamber in which I'd been deposited. The room was the same dimensions as the prison from which I'd escaped. But no endless well above, no line of bars across.

Wiping muck from my hands, I attempted to get my bearings.

My instincts told me I'd fallen back to the same depth as the cell holding Ella.

Find a connecting tunnel. Free Ella. Then get the hell out of here.

Straining my flare vision, I spotted an opening at the other end of the chamber. I squeezed through, found myself in a smooth, brick-walled tunnel running in both directions.

A flash of light.

"What the hell?"

I spun toward the voice.

Hawfield was ten feet away, holding his lantern, a stunned expression on his face.

"Damn gymnast!" Hawfield charged, one hand reaching for his gun. His massive bulk filled the narrow tunnel.

I fled in the opposite direction.

"There's nowhere to run!" Hawfield bellowed.

Boots pounded behind me.

Reaching a T intersection, I shot to the right, with no idea where I was going.

Crack! Crack!

Stone chips flew as bullets tore through the space I'd just vacated.

Oh my God oh my God oh my God!

Searing heat rose in my chest. Haloes appeared at the edge of my vision.

No! Not now!

My senses began to overload. I stumbled into another crossroad, cut left.

Footsteps echoed a few paces behind me.

Shock waves traveled my nervous system.

Disoriented, I tripped, landing heavily on the ground.

Rolling, I saw another chute to my left. Cold air drifted from its mouth.

"Game's over, honey." Hawfield loomed above me, sucking in wet, panting breaths.

The detective pulled the slide on the HK45.

Click.

With a last gasp, I scurried for the hole in the wall and shimmied into the adjacent room.

"Get back here!" Hawfield growled.

I rolled sideways as the gun barrel appeared in the opening.

Crack! Crack! Crack!

A deafening roar filled the chamber.

Somehow, my flare hung on by a thread.

I covered my ears, tried to block out the gunshots reverberating in my brain.

Through a cloud of pulverized stone, I spotted salvation.

Stairs. Leading up.

I took them at a dead sprint.

Behind me, I heard the detective force his way through the gap.

"Give it up, kid!" Hawfield craned his neck. "I'll chase you down like a dog!"

The stairs were high and incredibly steep, with a tiny square of light at the top.

Reaching the apex, I felt a light breeze on my face. Heard a sparrow's call.

Ignoring sounds of pursuit, I slithered through an old trapdoor and exited a small cave.

Fresh air. Blinding sunlight.

Tall trees surrounding me, staring down with solemn faces.

I wavered a moment, frozen in indecision.

What about Ella?

No choice. I couldn't do anything for my friend without ducking Hawfield first.

I'll be back, Ella. I swear on my life.

Picking a direction at random, I bolted into the woods.

CHAPTER 47

"Hiram, look out!"

Too late. The leash jerked from my fingers.

"Oh, crap!" I stumbled, nearly face-planted on the pavement. Caught a lone glimpse of Coop's hindquarters disappearing through a line of magnolias.

Shelton smacked his forehead. "Nice job, Stolowitski. He's loose!"

"Told you it wouldn't work!" I shot back, rubbing my wrenched shoulder. "When has Coop ever agreed to my authority?"

Ben held his tongue, but his golden glare spoke volumes.

We were back in the Drayton Hall parking lot. Less than two hours had passed since Tory went missing there, but it felt like a million years.

I wiped sweat from my forehead, could feel my cheeks blazing scarlet. "Hey, next time *you* try to restrain that monster. Coop must weigh eight hundred pounds! It's like walking a grizzly bear."

Shelton rolled his yellow eyes. "What now?"

"What else?" Ben took off after the wolfdog. "We follow!"

"Great. Running." With a groan, I lumbered after him. "Worst birthday ever!"

Ben had driven back to the plantation like an aspiring NASCAR champion. Coop selfishly took shotgun, staring intently ahead, seemingly in agreement with our chosen route. Shelton and I sat in the back, staring out our windows like a couple of weirdoes. Mesmerized. Neither of us had ever ridden in a car while flaring.

So many things to see. To hear and smell. A constant sensory barrage.

I wanted to take the whole world and eat it.

Ben glanced at us once, in the rearview, and chuckled. I guess he'd done it before.

But after twenty minutes of breakneck speed, my canine DNA decided to sledgehammer my brain. Turning onto the plantation's long driveway, my flare suddenly spiked like hot monkey fever, then nearly fizzled out completely. I broke out in cold sweat, nose burning, vision strobing, ears ringing like a hot microphone. It's a miracle I didn't mess my shorts.

Beside me, Shelton winced and rubbed his temples. The car swerved momentarily as Ben gritted his teeth, his face gone paler than a Twilight vampire. Even Coop reacted, shaking his head as if to fend off a swarm of bees.

The wackiness passed as abruptly as it started. I nearly coughed up a lung, but my other body parts seemed to function okay. I was relieved, but more than a little spooked—Tory's recent blackout was fresh in my memory. I wasn't anxious to lose consciousness and roll into a ditch or something. Not if I could help it.

In any case, our Viral telepathic jump circle refused to engage, probably because we didn't have the slightest idea how to engage it. Without Tory, we three bozos were flying blind. No, worse than that—we couldn't even locate the airplane. It was during our last failed attempt that Cooper yanked my arm from its socket and bolted for the hills.

So Shelton and I bombed after Ben, through the magnolias and onto the humongous lawn fronting the manor house, in hopeless pursuit of an enraged runaway wolf hybrid.

Flaring, I spotted Ben easily, fifty feet ahead, dashing eastward across the acre of grass. Coop was thirty yards farther up, bounding at full speed toward the woods on the opposite side.

"Wait!" Shelton pointed the other direction. "The barn's that way, on the *west* side of the grounds!"

"Coop doesn't seem interested!" I shouted as we ran. "What's this way?"

As I spoke, Coop reached the tree line and disappeared among the shadowy trunks.

"Coop's headed for the edge of the property." Shelton attempted to shrug while sprinting. "Far as I know, that's empty forest. The handout doesn't list anything."

"Super." Panting. Wheezing. "I'm excited."

Though my mind is a steel trap, I'm not exactly built for long distance pursuit. I carry a bit too much weight in the . . . everywhere to be an effective cross-country runner. Yet with my powers unleashed, I felt light as a feather. Strong. Fast. Agile. Nevertheless, I was still puffing and blowing a Clydesdale by the time we reached the woods.

Ben waited at the edge of the forest. "The mutt never broke stride. I think Coop knows where he's going."

"Maybe he's tracking her perfume?" I gasped hopefully, turning my head to eject a lethal snot rocket.

Shelton waved at the silent grove before us. "But how do *we* track the wolfdog?"

Ben stared at the snugly massed jumble of trees, as if trying to extract an answer by sheer force of will. Finally, "Follow me." He jogged into the gloom.

I glanced at Shelton, who was looking at me.

"Deserted forest," he said. "No idea where we're going."

I nodded. "A psychopath might be hiding inside. I'm a terrible hand-to-hand fighter."

Shelton shook his head. "This is my life now."

"Hey, at least it's not *your* birthday. Worst one ever, by the way."

His fist came up. I dapped it with mine.

"For Tory," Shelton said.

"For Tory." All joking shelved.

Squaring our shoulders, we hustled into the woods.

◇   ◇   ◇

"Hi!" Shelton hissed. "Hear that?"

"Of course I do." I spoke just as quietly. "My powers are maxed out right now. I can hear your freaking heartbeat."

He nodded, eyebrows up. "Same here."

Then Shelton whistled lightly to catch Ben's attention up ahead.

When Ben turned, Shelton tapped his ear.

Ben nodded impatiently. He brought two fingers up to his eyes, then pointed them left.

"What does that mean?" I muttered, taking a private moment to adjust my sagging shorts. "Look that way? Go investigate? I'm not an army ranger here."

Hearing me, Ben covered his face. Then he whispered, "Just watch my back."

"That's what I've *been* doing." But I zipped my lips at his exasperated glare.

We'd all heard the barking.

Coop? The yips had sounded like Tory's wolfdog, but honestly, it was impossible to tell.

Ben crept forward through the trees. This stretch of forest was particularly terrifying—tall, skinny oaks, with little understory in between. Yet the trunks were tightly packed, limiting how far one could see. The effect was a sensation of being exposed on all sides, while simultaneously feeling hemmed in and surrounded.

I hated it. Beside me, Shelton looked close to passing out.

A furious baying erupted just ahead. Something large crashed though the trees.

Ben froze, unsure how to react. Then he arrowed directly for the commotion.

"Go *toward* the sounds?" Shelton squawked. "That's a classic horror movie mistake."

"Too late now!" Steeling my nerves, I fired after Ben. Shelton trailed a step behind.

The noise rose, a sudden cacophony of barks and whines.

Definitely Coop.

Then Ben yelled at the top of his lungs.

Adrenaline flooded my system.

I vaulted a fallen log, circled a clump of willows, and stormed into a small clearing.

Coop was rolling in the leaves, pinning someone beneath his massive bulk.

Ben dove on the tangle with a voice-cracking whoop.

Raising both fists above my head, I unleashed a primal growl, preparing to launch my full weight onto whatever I didn't recognize and pummel it with my eyes closed.

Ben saw me coming, held up a hand in alarm.

"Hi! Stop!"

I skidded to a halt, eyes wide, lungs pumping. "What!? What's going on!?"

Coop rolled to his feet, began licking the person at the bottom of the pile.

It was Tory.

CHAPTER 48

I began breathing again.

Hiram had stopped his blind charge and wouldn't crush me. Thank goodness. Pushing Cooper aside, I got to my feet. Felt a huge surge of warmth.

I was no longer alone.

The Virals had found me.

Ben was beaming, unable to hide his relief. He turned quickly, wiping his glowing eyes. Shelton darted forward and crushed me with a hug.

Coop was dancing and bucking, his tail wagging so hard he had trouble keeping balance.

My boys. My heroes.

"How?" Ben asked simply.

"My wolfdog found me." Catching him, I hugged Coop tight. "I was totally lost, hiding behind this log. He appeared like a guardian angel. Where are we, anyway?"

"The woods south of Drayton Hall," Shelton said. "A mile from the river, maybe twice that from the barn where you disappeared."

So close. We barely traveled at all.

My elation quickly evaporated. Ella was still locked in that terrible cell.

I scanned the group. Noted with satisfaction that everyone was flaring.

"*Hawfield* is the kidnapper." I waved for the boys to huddle close. "The twins faked their abduction, and were working with that jerk to rip off their trust fund."

"Faked?" Blood rushed to Ben's face. "They made the whole thing up?"

"Holy crap!" Shelton reached for an earlobe. "The *cop* did it?"

"Why would they steal their own money?" Hi wondered.

"I'll explain everything later," I said. "What matters now is Ella. Hawfield took her to keep her quiet. I found the twins hiding in the barn, but they took off. Hawfield showed up, and my flare bugged out. Then he locked me up with Ella in the cell from the video."

"So you confronted the twins alone, without waiting for us?" Ben couldn't keep the anger from his voice. "After making us promise not to do anything like that?"

"We can discuss my impulsiveness another time—"

"Oh, we *will*," Ben assured me.

"—but right now, *Ella* is all that matters. That cell is somewhere in these woods. Deep underground, at the bottom of an old well. I flared and escaped, but ran into Hawfield and had to leave Ella behind."

My voice broke.

I'd left her there, alone in the dark.

Ben's hand found my shoulder. "You had no choice. But the pack is here now. We'll find Ella, and deal with that dirty cop, too. Just lead the way."

Ben's words stiffened my resolve. Reaching up, I squeezed his hand before he released it.

Shelton's eyes darted around the clearing. "Hawfield's in these woods?"

"Armed. He's taken a few shots at me already."

"Then he's toast." Ben's tone was glacial.

The boys looked my way. Cooper sat at attention, his total focus on me.

Hi gave a shaky thumbs-up. "Do your thing, Tor. Stir the drink."

I nodded. "Let's join hands. Coop in the middle."

We formed a circle around the wolfdog.

My eyes closed. I pushed all doubts away.

The flaming cords sprang to life, a fiery lattice connecting the five of us.

Centered on Coop. The nexus. Our touchstone.

The disturbance was gone. The lines seemed frozen in place, awaiting my command.

Working by instinct, I expanded the cords, then untethered my consciousness and sent it racing through the channels.

My perception flicked from person to person.

Hi. Ben. Shelton. Coop.

I'm here.

My eyes opened. I saw the boys staring at one another in wonder.

Without quite understanding how, I flashed to Hiram. Looked out from his eyes.

I saw a redheaded girl covered in grime, face pinched in concentration. She smiled.

It's working. We can trade.

I felt Shelton's anxiety as he took a peek through my eyes. *I'll never get used to this.*

Amazeballs. Hi stepped forward and poked Ben in the chest.

Ben slapped Hi's hand away. Grinned wolfishly. *Everyone ready?*

For what? Shelton sent.

Hunt.

My gaze dropped to Coop, standing in the center of our circle.

We hunt, the wolfdog sent. *As Pack.*

Coop laced the sending with the concepts of friendship, family, and trust.

Kneeling, I kissed his doggie snout. *I couldn't have said it better.*

◇　　◇　　◇

Gun drawn, Detective Hawfield stalked through the woods.

The barking had come from somewhere just up ahead.

Late-afternoon daylight angled through the trees—blinding sunbeams alternating with lengthening shadows—making it harder to see.

But he'd be damned if he was giving this chase up.

That meddling, terrible, unbelievable Brennan girl.

She was some kind of evil spirit.

How in God's name did she escape that cell?

The Francis kid had still been inside. She'd screamed for Brennan to run, obviously unable to flee herself. He'd thought about dealing with her right then and there, but decided to wait. He might still need a hostage.

Because, right then, all of Hawfield's plans were in shambles.

The twins were gone. Out of his reach.

Brennan was somewhere loose in these woods.

He was supposed to receive the ransom tonight. If the twins kept their mouths shut just a few more hours, he could still pull this off. He could *win*.

But Tory Brennan threatened everything.

That she-devil *had* to be found. And dealt with.

Hawfield checked his HK45. Seven rounds in the cartridge, plus one in the chamber. Another clip was strapped to his ankle.

More than enough for one little girl.

This time, no prison cell.

Something rustled in the brush to his left.

Hawfield froze. Brought the pistol around.

He wasn't worried. One teen, alone in the woods. He'd catch her eventually. They were miles from anywhere, and Brennan didn't know where she was to boot.

No one would hear him take care of this problem.

I just have to find her.

A twig snapped.

Hawfield spun, trying to locate the source. Game roamed these woods. He didn't want to give away his position wasting some deer.

A silver streak shot from the bushes dead ahead.

Something huge bounded to within a dozen feet of where he stood.

Hawfield found himself face-to-face with a wolf.

The beast growled, saliva dripping from his massive jowls.

Hawfield fired reflexively, but the animal had vanished into the sea of gray trunks.

"Jesus!"

A wolf! Here, in the Lowcountry.

Then he went cold, one hand dropping to the lacerations on his leg.

Was that the animal that attacked him on Morris Island? Brennan's maniac pet?

Hawfield raised his weapon, scanning for more predators. Wolves rarely hunt alone.

Silence. Stillness. As if he'd imagined the creature.

Hawfield chuckled darkly. "Go find the Brennan girl, you mongrel."

Leaves crunched to his right.

He turned.

Brennan stood in plain view, twenty feet away.

She glared. Made no move to run.

The girl's eyes had that same yellow tinge. Unnerving, but Hawfield had been in tough spots before. Some creepy teenage waif wouldn't get under his skin.

"Freeze, and I won't fire." Hawfield inched closer, looking for a clear shot.

Brennan stepped behind a trunk.

Hawfield sped forward, determined to finish this once and for all.

Snapping branches. Hawfield glanced to his left.

The wolf was charging his flank, on a direct collision course. As he watched, the beast coiled and sprang.

"Holy—"

Hawfield spun, backpedaling. A root caught his ankle and he crashed to the ground.

Crack! Crack!

Bullets ripped into a tree trunk twenty yards away.

No other sounds. The creature was gone.

Hawfield clambered to his feet. The first tinglings of fear gathered in his massive belly.

What's going on?

Movement in the corner of his eye.

Hawfield swung his weapon. Squinted through the patchwork shafts of light.

One of those boys!

Ben Blue.

For a second, the detective could only stare in astonishment. By the time he thought to shoot, Blue had darted behind a fallen log.

This was bad. Brennan's friends were in the woods, too.

I might be outnumbered.

A whistle behind him.

Hawfield pivoted.

The fat kid smiled, waggling his fingers before slipping from sight.

Hawfield's rage exploded. "Think you can toy with me, you punks?"

A hungry growl was his only warning.

Riiiip!

Searing pain tore through Hawfield as a furry gray rocket slammed into his side. Before he could blink, his attacker bounded into the bushes.

"Ayyyeeee!" Hawfield collapsed in a heap, one hand grabbing his backside.

Crack! Crack! Crack!

Slugs tore into the space where the beast had vanished.

Blood ran down Hawfield's pant leg. He felt a hot wetness pooling in his shoe.

The dog. Those boys. They found this place somehow.

Hawfield spotted the black kid on a log, ten feet ahead. He grinned, then disappeared behind a row of prickly pears.

The fat one followed close on his heels.

Ben Blue darted between the oaks to his left, sliding from his field of vision.

With cold dread, Hawfield realized the kids were closing.

Tightening the noose.

They're playing with me. And that's the same wolf from Morris Island.

Then Brennan stepped from the trees right before him.

Arms crossed, she stared down at him with glowing, inhuman yellow eyes.

"What are you?" Hawfield asked hoarsely.

A cold smile curled her lips. "Your worst nightmare."

Hawfield snarled. Arm jerking up, he fired wildly.

Crack! Crack!

Click.

Too late, Hawfield realized his mistake. His hand had barely moved for the second clip when a drop of hot liquid struck his forehead.

Hawfield looked up.

Stared directly into a pair of canine jaws.

CHAPTER 49

E asy, boy."

I stepped from behind a cluster of oaks.

Cooper's eyes flicked to me, but he didn't move away.

Hawfield's neck was a centimeter from the wolfdog's gleaming incisors.

Hold. I sent. *Nothing else.*

Coop growled, clearly in disagreement, but he eased back a few inches.

Hold.

The boys raced from the forest. Hi pulled the empty HK45 from the detective's fingers. Shelton ran to my side, unsure what to do.

Ben walked directly to Hawfield and kicked him in the stomach.

"Ben."

"Yes?" His eyes never left the detective.

"Just search him, please."

Ben ran rough hands over Hawfield, freeing the handcuffs from his belt and the extra clip strapped to the detective's ankle. He tossed the latter to Hiram.

Hi immediately walked both weapon and ammunition over to me. "Yours."

I ejected the spent clip from the HK45, slammed the new one into place, then worked the slide to chamber a round. Then I held the weapon loosely at my side, barrel pointed at the ground.

"I'm terrified of you right now," Hi said, wide-eyed. "And in love. Take me shooting with your aunt Tempe next time."

Intensely aware of Coop's proximity, Hawfield hadn't moved a muscle. He seemed almost hypnotized by the wolfdog's gaping jaws.

"Remember Coop, Detective?" Ben stroked the wolfdog's head. "You two have met once before. I don't think he likes you."

Coop growled low in his throat, causing Hawfield to recoil.

Power down, I sent to the other Virals.

Ben shot me a hard look. *He's not secure.*

We can't let him see any more, I answered. *Cuff him. I have the gun.*

"She's right." Hi turned away. Shelton quickly followed suit.

SNUP.

The power fled, but I didn't stumble.

Something had changed. With the flares. Within me.

My powers had . . . righted themselves somehow. The lines were unclogged. I can't describe it any better.

Ben cuffed Hawfield tightly, then stepped back, his irises fading to dark brown.

I clicked my tongue for Coop to stand down.

The wolfdog snarled at Hawfield one last time, then complied, retreating a few feet and dropping down on his haunches. Coop was still favoring his injured forepaw.

I stepped forward. Placed the gun barrel against Hawfield's cheek.

"Is Ella okay?" I asked softly.

"Yes." Terror filled Hawfield's eyes.

"Quickest way to her cell?"

"The stairs." Voice anxious to please. "The GPS coordinates are in my pocket."

Ben rifled Hawfield's pants, found a slip of paper, and handed it to Shelton. He began punching the numbers into his iPhone.

"Let's hurry." Rising, I looked to Ben. "Should two of us stay and watch him?"

"No splitting up," Ben said firmly. "Not again. We'll drag this sack of crap with us."

And we did.

Following Shelton's lead, we cut through the forest, pushing and prodding the detective along with us. Daylight was fading to dusk, giving the forest a sinister, spectral aspect. I couldn't wait to get out of there.

Hawfield didn't resist. Answered my questions without expression.

At the cave mouth, I told the boys to wait. Ordered Coop to sit.

Alone, I hurried down the stone steps, through the crawl, and into the tunnel. Following Hawfield's instructions, I located a hidden niche with both a key and extra lantern.

The cell was through the last opening on the left. I raced inside.

Ella was standing by the bars, having seen the light approach. Spying me, she burst into tears. "Oh thank God!" She reached a hand through the barrier. "I thought it was him again."

I met her fingers, hugging my friend as best I could. "Told you I'd come back."

Locating the lock, I inserted the key and opened the cell door. Ella stumbled out.

"Let's get the hell out of here." She was holding back sobs.

I wiped away a few tears of my own. "I couldn't agree more."

Hand in hand, we hurried from the chamber, ran the whole way back to the surface. Emerging in the failing light, I felt a sudden elation. A sense of fulfillment.